THE GIRL IN T

LOUIS

Mana Publishing

UNCORRECTED PROOF

Other psychological suspense by Louise Mangos

FIVE FATAL FLAWS

THE BEATEN TRACK

STRANGERS ON A BRIDGE

THE ART OF DECEPTION

Writing historical mystery as L.S.Mangos

THE SECRETS OF MORGARTEN

This novel is entirely a work of fiction. The names, characters and incidents portrayed in it are the work of the author's imagination. Any resemblance to actual persons, living or dead, events or exact localities is entirely coincidental.

Mana Publishing, Mana AG 2025

PROLOGUE

Speeding past the last chalets and the Wildenberg Castle in the car, the valley fell away behind them. The road ahead narrowed, and the lights of the village of Zernez soon faded into the night. As they gained altitude, the quality of the snow-clearing deteriorated. A plough had left a snow-packed ridge in the centre of the road, and each time their wheels met it, the heavy vehicle lurched in protest.

'We don't want to get stuck around any of these steep bends. I don't think I'll be able to get going again if we come to a stop, and the thought of reversing all the way back to the valley is not an option,' said the driver.

The hairpins were becoming tighter and more frequent the closer they came to the pass. Powdery snow stirred up from the speeding vehicle swirled into the beam of their headlights around the tight corners. Whenever there was a stretch of road between the hairpins, the driver accelerated to give the car momentum to carry on around the next bend. But the vehicle still slewed around the icy curves.

'If we're being followed, they're taking their time to catch up with us. I don't relish a car chase on the mountain. We're unlikely to win that race,' he said.

On the next straight section of the road, his passenger twisted around in her seat and peered through the rear window.

'They're getting closer. I can see their lights now.'

'I'm going to pull over when we get to the top. It's probably just some random tourist driving into the South Tyrol. In which case we'll let them pass us, and I won't feel so stressed with them on my tail as we head downhill.'

'No! We have to continue! I have a feeling it's the same car we saw back there in the St Moritz valley. We can't risk getting caught at this stage. We're in too deep now,' she said, eyeing the walls of snow on either side of the vehicle, locking them to their trajectory.

'I have to be very cautious on the downhill. This car isn't designed for winter driving. There'll be absolutely no point if we crash.'

The passenger looked behind again, and the stab of headlights through the rear window blinded her briefly before she turned back to face the road. She didn't have to look around now as the headlights reflected in the wing mirror on her side. The shadow of their two heads was projected against the curving interior of the vehicle's roof. The road straightened out and the gradient lessened a little. The driver's body tensed and rose as he pressed his foot on the accelerator. A sign announcing the *Buffalora Mountain Guesthouse 200m* slipped past.

'There's a big wide parking lot at the back, below the guest house's terrace. I'll pull in there,' said the driver. 'If someone is following us, we should be able to swing round and fool them by accelerating out again onto the road. If it's just another random car, they can continue ahead of us.'

'Sounds good.'

The chalet-style building ghosted past them on the right. One window was lit with the blue-white of a lightbulb, perhaps solar-powered, used as a deterrent to anyone wanting to gain entry while it was closed up during the winter months.

'Hang on, it's a tight turn.'

The driver yanked on the steering wheel, as much as one could yank on the steering wheel of such a heavy vehicle, and the car tipped forward down the slope to the parking area. The passenger tried to grab the strap above her head, but her hand swung away with the sudden change of direction. It was as though they were entering a void, a vacuum. Time slowed as the car drifted through clouds of snow whooshing up past the windows, obscuring any remaining view in the dead of night.

The silence seemed to stretch. Had the vehicle stalled? All was momentarily quiet. As they stared at each other, eyes reflecting the low lights from the instruments on the dashboard, they felt the brief weightlessness of flight before the *whump-crump* of impact. The passenger's torso was thrown forward. Her head hit the lacquered walnut dashboard, and everything went black.

1

JAMES

On Monday I spotted a young woman in the recessed archway of number 27 while setting up an exhibit for the bookstore's upcoming festival of Greek Classics. Perched on the display unit, I'd just finished hooking up a banner and was bending down to sort my Homers from my Aristotles, when it occurred to me that I might need to take my jacket on my lunch break. The forecast was for rain. I glanced out of the window, first up at the sky and then down to the street. The tops of the buses resembled a model railway from four floors up, the occasional black cab coupled between the crimson carriages along Piccadilly.

And that was when I saw her.

She was sitting cross-legged on the step of number 27 with a blue sleeping bag draped over her knees. She wore a Nordic-style bobble hat with furry ear flaps and plaited wool ties hanging to her chest. Wisps of hair poked out from the sides of the hat around her cheeks. My forehead bumped against the window as I tried to get a better view, but I couldn't see her face properly from that high up. I wondered where the homeless guy I jokingly called Oor Wullie had gone.

People hurried along the pavement, umbrellas opening like spring flowers in a time-lapse film as rain began to fall. Jacket, then.

My shop phone had beeped, and I was summonsed back to the ground floor to answer a question about the recently short-listed Man Booker novels. I quickly forgot about lunch, the weather and homeless people.

Tuesday morning was brighter, and I was re-stocking some titles in the indie publishers' section on the first floor when I glanced outside and my attention was drawn to the girl again. It was warm enough for her not to be wearing her hat. She was watching the human and vehicular traffic moving back and forth along Piccadilly. Her dark blonde hair was a little dishevelled. It blew in front of her face as she focused on something westwards towards Green Park.

As my gaze lingered on her, I thought about the time I offered Oor Wullie – don't worry, I always called him Willie to his face – some books destined for publisher returns.

'I cannae read, laddie' he'd said in his broad Glaswegian accent.

The irony of a homeless illiterate living twenty yards from Europe's biggest bookstore was not lost on me. Practical donations often involved take-away coffees or ham rolls from the café upstairs, along with newspapers from Current Affairs at the end of the day. He'd never mentioned his lack of reading skills again, but he was grateful for the papers, and I knew he would use them to insulate against the chill nights. Broadsheets in the literary sense. As it would soon be winter, I thought it might be time to buy him another twin-pack of ski socks from Rock and Snow, to accompany the puffer jacket I gave him last week that I no longer wore. Willie was always grateful for these things. He said he had to fight hard to keep the patch. West One was a prestigious postcode. Which made me curious about what had happened to him now.

A strand of hair caught on the edge of the girl's lip, and she hooked it delicately away with her finger. She was holding something between the fingers of her other hand, and for a sinking moment I thought it might be a cigarette. But then she leaned down towards the footpath and made a swirling motion with the object in her hand, and I saw she was drawing some kind of a design or picture on the stone paving in front of her. The object in her fingers must have been a piece of chalk.

My throat tightened and I hurried to finish my tasks. I pushed my trolley loaded with potential candidates for the Great American Novel like a stroller full of sleeping book babies to the other end of the floor. When I reached my destination, I slid Salinger's *Catcher in the Rye* out of the American Classics shelf with my index finger and replaced it with three copies of the newly-issued publication. I removed the old pocket-sized version, and hesitated as a customer moved in front of me.

I'd intended to put the book on the trolley – it would be sent back to the publisher and would likely go for shredding as an obsolete title – but the elderly gentleman now squinting at the shelves was blocking my way. My stomach rumbled. I didn't want to disturb the man, so I tucked Salinger's masterpiece into my back pocket. Retreating from the American Classics, I made my way to the staff room to fetch my jacket. It was five minutes until my lunch break was due to start, and I wasn't going to miss it again today.

I left the store and ran across Piccadilly, dodging the usual convoy of buses, taxis and super-cars. A torn poster on the whitewashed window of number 27 behind the girl flapped in the breeze. It announced the imminent opening of a sports clothing store. I'd lost count of how many new shops had appeared in that location over the years. The rent on Piccadilly was only sustainable for the type of money-spinning luxury goods businesses now found on the upper end of Bond Street, but every few months another regular shop gave it a go down here.

The girl looked up in alarm as I leapt from the road to the curb to avoid a puddle remaining from the previous day's rain. Her lips rounded to a perfect rosy circle as she reached out to protect the Pret cup with a few coins in it next to the piece of art she had been working on. It was the image of a mountain, chalked directly onto the paving stones, and from the direction I had come, it looked eerily like one of those three-dimensional street art images that you feel you could step into.

'Sorry, didn't mean to frighten you,' I said as I careened towards her.

Her brow furrowed.

'I was wondering what happened to Willie, the guy who used to be on this spot,' I continued.

'I think he went to hospital,' she said, a guarded tone to her voice.

'Oh! Nothing serious I hope?'

I envisioned Willie's flaking skin, his wheezing breath and his bulbous purple nose. I studied this girl's face. Her clear skin was marred only by the jaundiced remnants of what looked like an old bruise on her cheek. She was older than I initially guessed. More my age; mid-twenties, maybe.

'I don't know, but I'm sure he'll be back,' she said with a tone of hopeful determination.

Most street people were usually staunch defenders of their hard-earned homes in my experience, so I wondered whether she would relinquish the spot to Willie on his return. I pointed to her sleeping bag. 'Are you... sleeping here? Are you homeless?'

'I, um... Not yet,' she said. 'But it might come to that.'

Oh, that didn't sound good. I waited for her to elaborate, but no more information was forthcoming. I kept my curiosity under wraps, not wanting to appear rude.

'That's an amazing piece of chalk work,' I said, pointing to her art. I reached into my wallet and put a fiver into her cup. She smiled. 'May I?' I said, indicating the step next to her.

'Of course. But you won't get a good view of it from there.'

She pulled the sleeping bag away from the stone step, and I sat down a little awkwardly. And sure enough, the 3-D picture now resembled a giant messy oyster shell.

'I'm James, by the way.'

'I'm... E-Emma,' she said slowly.

James understood her wariness. She must have thought it was weird a stranger was engaging so enthusiastically with her. She wouldn't have known he'd already spotted her from across the road twice now.

'Have you known Willie long?' I asked.

'I don't... know him. I'm just aware he went to hospital. There might be something wrong with his heart; a dicky valve.'

I smiled at the old-fashioned expression my father might have used.

'They have to do an ECG or an EK something-or-other, and a load of blood tests,' she continued. 'He said he was going to try and get the doctors to keep him in as long as possible. Get a few hot meals in him.' She was more comfortable talking about Willie than herself.

I tried to recall the last time I'd spoken to him. It must have been before the weekend. He hadn't said anything about having to go into hospital.

'This might seem like a nosy question, but you don't seem like someone who's... What I mean is, why are you here?'

'Street art,' she said. 'Haven't you seen any before?'

'Of course. Sorry. It's just that it's a big change to see you here instead of the grumpy old Scotsman.'

She huffed. 'Hmm, yes, he was quite obstreperous, wasn't he? Isn't he?' She corrected herself. Her tongue rolled on the second 'r' of obstreperous, and I wondered whether she also had Scottish origins.

'Did someone hurt you?' I asked gently, studying her yellowed cheek. 'That wasn't *Willie,* surely?'

She placed her palm against the bruise. I was shocked that Willie might have assaulted her and then confused as to why she was here and not in a more artsy environment like Camden or Brick Lane. Her presence on this part of Piccadilly wasn't making any sense. She turned back and smiled, although her eyes were still wary. Her fingers feathered her cheek and she lowered her hand.

'Yes... he... No, I mean, NO! It's a long story.'

Emma looked towards the crowds milling around the ankle-tapped statue of Eros in its perpetually frozen stumble towards Lower Regent Street, biting her lip as though Willie might suddenly come marching back to claim his patch.

'Look, I'm on my way to Pret. Can I bring you a sandwich or something? A coffee?' I asked.

She frowned and smiled at the same time, one of those looks that I interpreted as *are you nuts or something?* But after a moment she said that would be lovely. I asked her what she would like.

'No preference. I'll have what you're having. I'm not a vegan or anything. No allergies. Coffee with any kind of milk.'

I mimed pulling out a notepad and writing the information down like a waiter taking an order, and she laughed. As I stood up to head to Pret, a passer-by put a coin into her cup and she thanked them. Her soft voice went with her angelic looks, and I suddenly worried she was so vulnerable out here on the street.

I had to queue for ages at Pret. I hadn't managed to beat the lunchtime rush. I returned with two smoked salmon wraps and two cappuccinos.

She was looking at her mobile when I returned to the doorway of number 27, then slipped it under her sleeping bag.

'Is this table taken?' I asked as I approached.

She patted the smooth stone ledge, and I sat down, handing over her wrap and coffee. The book in my back pocket had shifted and was digging into me. I pulled it out.

'Would you be interested in reading this? An old classic I know.'

Emma's eyes lit up. 'Oh yes, I'm sure Cauldon would feel right at home on this step,' she said. 'It's been years since I read it, but I'll give it another go.'

I smiled. She was likely to be a book person, then.

'Here you go,' I said, handing it over.

'Love me a classic,' she said. 'It'll help pass the time until it rains again and I have to start over.' She pointed to her chalk drawing. 'Thank you.'

As she took the book, her fingers brushed mine.

And that was how it started.

2

SALLY

Returning from a rare three back-to-back days off because of all the Saturdays I'd worked at the end of the summer, I saw that there was going to be a double book launch from a crime imprint in the basement of the bookstore that evening. Aside from comedy writers, crime authors tended to be the most entertaining bunch out of all the fiction genres. They were certainly the ones capable of consuming the most alcohol. So although there was inevitably more work with the volume of glasses and bottles to be portaged from the bar, crime fiction launches were usually a hoot, and made the bookstore a good profit.

But there was another reason for staying. James Marsh was scheduled to be the duty bookseller at the event. When the assistant who usually set out the chairs and banners for these events developed a sore throat during the day, I told her to go home to recuperate. And I jumped at the opportunity to put myself on the roster.

'Sally Crime!' Jamie exclaimed in delight, which caused a warm glow in my chest. I was carrying a tray of wine glasses down to the basement to line up on a table at the front of the room. 'Didn't know you were on tonight. Thought I had Jennifer.'

Jamie was the one who started calling me Sally Crime. He said I had a voice like Sally Traffic on the BBC. A pleasant radio voice. I'd take that. It was the first thing that made me fall for him. The Crime part of Jamie's nickname for me came from my reading choices – Christie, Rendell, PD James – and the fact that we first met when I was re-stocking in the Crime department. We often co-read books, and I inevitably worked out who'd done the deed several chapters before Jamie, much to his amused annoyance.

I was also the only person who could occasionally beat him in a game of Scrabble. We often met in Fifth View, the café-restaurant on the top floor after work to play, and would sometimes coordinate our lunch breaks to meet for a game in Green Park if it wasn't bad weather. I hoped all these attributes kept me in favour with him. I didn't let anyone else call me Sally Crime. And I'd never met anyone else who called him Jamie.

'Jennifer's gone home,' I said. 'Not feeling great. Probably just as well. No one wants her handing out books and wine glasses covered in invisible microbes to hundreds of guests.'

'Too right. It's the type of thing a few years ago that would have been labelled a "super-spreader" event. All those crime writers hugging each other and guffawing germs everywhere.' James laughed. 'Well, Sally Crime, we've a police procedural and a psych thriller launch this evening. You'll be up for this. Perfect for you.'

'And I guess you'll be after one of those hardbacks, dedicated and signed,' I said, raising my chin in the direction of a double stack of books with a credit card reader sitting between them on a table.

Jamie had a bit of an obsession with signed first editions. I often hoped, usually in vain, that the publishing rep would realise I'd played an important part in the marketing process as a bookseller and they'd give me one for free. No such luck tonight either. And my rent was due next week. I couldn't afford to buy two new hardbacks, even with my staff discount.

'Did you have a good break?' he asked as we watched readers and reviewers coming down the stairs to the event room. 'Do anything exciting?'

'I was only away for three days,' I said. 'I went to see my mum and brother. He's still quite poorly. Did you miss me? Nice result on Words by the way. Haven't managed over 600 myself for ages. I hope you weren't cheating.'

'Sally Crime! Cheeky! Some might think it was a total fluke, you amongst them, but my word skills have been picking up lately. Beware, or I'll start to call you Sally Scrabble. Doesn't have the same ring.'

I snorted, and the publicity person from the publisher turned around and told us to be quiet. We stood at the back of the room like naughty children as the speeches were delivered.

After the readings, there was hearty applause, and we passed round glasses of wine on trays. The bottles were all drunk before they had time to warm up in the mugginess of the basement, proving my point about crime fiction fans, and all the cupcakes with miniature marzipan books on top were quickly scoffed. The audience bought copies of the books and lined up to have them signed, James amongst them. I'd make him help me tidy up afterwards.

It was late when we finished. I rolled up the banners and dismantled the stands. Jamie helped me take the trays of dirty glasses and plates upstairs to the restaurant. He seemed in a bit of a hurry to leave, but I trailed after him.

When we left the store, it was dark. I hated these few days after the clocks went back. No more outdoor Scrabble, as the weather was always pants. I hoped Jamie would suggest somewhere for a drink or a bite to eat. As the doors swung closed behind us, he stopped on the pavement and stared across the road. I followed his gaze. Between the taxis and buses, a bright blue sleeping bag was visible on the step outside a closed-down store with its whitewashed windows. That grubby old homeless man must have been given a new sleeping bag. Was Jamie responsible? He was always doing charitable stuff like that.

Jamie turned back towards me quickly and flashed a smile, but not before I'd seen him chewing his lip. I thought he might have been taking his generosity a little far, worrying about the homeless crowd. It had endeared him to me at first. But he couldn't possibly save them all.

'Want to get some grub?' I asked, walking with him towards Piccadilly Circus.

'I have to get home,' he said. 'There's a thing I need to do.'

What the heck? He was *always* up for going out. It sounded like he was purposely trying to avoid spending time with me. Back in the beginning he told me he enjoyed my sassy humour and our mutual love of old books and word games. Had he changed his tune? Something suddenly seemed to be bothering him now that we'd left work.

I frowned and looked briefly back at the vagrant's spot across the road. I shrugged as we walked briskly in unison along Piccadilly. Crossing Leicester Square, we dodged tourists and shoppers and the occasional greasy puddle. When I didn't take the steps down to the tube as usual at Leicester Square, Jamie glanced at me, with a look wavering between surprise and irritation.

'I'm starving,' I said. 'Tempted by a burger, if I'm honest.' I nodded across St Martin's Lane in the direction of the Honest Burger place, and looked hopefully back at him. 'I don't mind going on my own, mind.'

Jamie smiled, almost looked relieved. 'I'm really sorry, Sal, on any other evening I'd join you.'

'That's okay,' I said, in a voice that betrayed my sentiment that it wasn't really okay. 'See you tomorrow,' I said, and he placed a hand on my arm, presumably trying to lessen the turndown.

He left me at the junction of Garrick Street and carried on up towards his place. He must have been hungry too; an iced cupcake earlier couldn't possibly have satisfied his hunger. I lowered my hand from our mutual waving to each other before we each went out of sight. I entered the tiny burger place and found myself a single stool at the bar table. As I ate my burger, a luxury in the circumstances, but a damned sight cheaper than a hardback book, I thought I should don my Miss Marple hat and see why James was concerning himself with that old drunken Scotsman.

3

EMMA

I couldn't remember the last time I'd been this cold. How long could I endure it in the damp, bitter climate of a London autumn? My coccyx and hips went numb almost immediately. The homeless man had left a grubby fleece blanket in the corner. I didn't want to touch it, but ended up folding it gingerly and placing it under two layers of cardboard to try and prevent the stone step leeching cold into my body.

After I'd drawn my picture on the first day – a tunnel with a train steaming out of it that I was actually quite proud of – I absented myself from the step, left an empty Pret cup beside it and went over to the book store. It was blissfully warm inside. To get the blood moving around my body and force some warmth back into my limbs, I walked all the way to the top floor. There were a load of boxes and some kind of exhibition being set up at one end, so I avoided that part of the shop and made my way down the wide stone staircase to the floor underneath. I walked the length and breadth of each floor, fascinated by the sheer number of books in the shop, but I couldn't find what I was looking for.

I reluctantly left the warmth of the book store and walked briskly along to Lillywhites on Piccadilly Circus. I bought myself a sleeping bag, something not too flash. The purchase was essential. It helped to protect my legs and body from the wind whipping down the street, even in the middle of the day.

But the following morning I'd begun to think I'd made a dreadful mistake. It was as though I was sitting on a block of ice, despite the sleeping bag. The rain had washed away my picture from the day before, so I set about drawing a simpler design, a mountain with a lake at its base which looked from a certain angle as though you could step into the water and sink. The irony of that image on a puddled street.

When James came right over and talked to me at lunchtime, I was so surprised, I hardly knew what to say to him. I could tell he didn't want me to think he was being creepy about it, but his concern about the bruise on my cheek and the way he looked at me almost made me blurt my whole sorry story right there and then.

I hadn't expected he'd be so nice. Like, really kind. The guy didn't even know me, and he was buying me lunch.

But in some ways, it was perfect. He asked me if I was sleeping there. He must have thought I was homeless, and I was happy to let him keep thinking that. It might garner more sympathy, given his generosity.

When I saw him leaving the bookstore later that evening with a work colleague, and he hesitated, looking over towards me before walking on, I figured he was concerned enough about me to come back.

And that made staying there worth it.

4

JAMES

As Sal and I left the book store, I hesitated on the pavement, wondering whether to go and get some food for Emma and leave it beside her. She hadn't wanted to admit she was sleeping on the street. She'd said it might come to that, but I hadn't thought she meant *tonight*. Pret had closed by then. I thought briefly about a McDonalds or Burger King meal, but she seemed classier than that. I'm not sure why I thought she wasn't like any of the others out there who'd appreciate warm food wherever it came from.

Was I being over-concerned? Truth be known, my motives were more likely blinded by something else. There'd been an instant attraction. I could trace the emotion all the way back to my first sighting of her through the bookstore window from across the road yesterday.

As I stood there on the pavement in the dark, Sal gave me a strange look and peered in the direction where Emma was presumably sleeping, so I turned abruptly towards Piccadilly Circus. As we walked through Leicester Square, the cinema and theatre crowds were milling around, dazed by the lights after the darkness of their various stage or screen performances. Nobody was hurrying anywhere fast, and they were doing so with disorganised purpose. The Leicester Square crowd always involved a more technical navigation on foot than the commuter crowd further east or the shopping crowd at Oxford Circus. It meant that Sal and I didn't really get a chance to talk.

She asked whether I wanted to go and get something to eat, which I would have done on any normal book launch night. We generally loved picking apart those events, chatting about the authors, the attendees, and guessing what it might be like to be a published author.

But the last thing I felt like doing right then was entering a busy restaurant after the crowded basement room at the book launch. Or perhaps it was the niggling guilt that I'd left Emma on the street to suffer the cold night ahead while I was able to go into a warm restaurant for a filling meal. The thought flashed through my mind that I would have instantly accompanied Emma if she'd been the one asking. I could tell Sal was mildly pissed off when I left her at the junction of Garrick Street.

I considered my mother's horror if I told her I was rather taken with a young woman I'd met, "but the thing is, Mum, she's homeless." Although I wasn't really sure Emma *was* permanently homeless. And my father, well, his eyes would have rolled right back into his head. Then he'd lecture me again that it was time to stop helping every stray I met. Something he'd already told me more than once.

He thought it was noble of me to volunteer to help train the baristas at Social Bite when it first opened on the Strand. But when I said I might stay to help organise a full-on turkey meal at Christmas, he drew a line. I was, after all, their only child; they expected me to celebrate with them, and putting myself in their shoes, I could see their point.

With those thoughts running through my mind, I backtracked a little and headed up Charing Cross Road to McDonalds. I ordered two Big Macs. Carrying the takeaway bag, I crossed the road by Brew Dog. Ron and Sheila were a homeless couple who'd made their nest in a supply doorway nearby that was only accessed once or twice a week. Their various bags and packs of belongings had a more permanent air than Willie and now Emma's patch on Piccadilly. They sat on a foam squab on the step, the streetlight from across the road illuminating their shoes.

Ron was brandishing a bottle containing the dregs of some cheap wine, a roll-up cigarette between two fingers of the same hand. He clutched it like a husband who wouldn't let go of the remote control, a complaint I'd often heard from Sally Crime about her flatmate. Ron and Sheila were often tipsy, but never outright drunk. There was a cosy togetherness about them that you didn't often see with other street people. I'd never seen them arguing.

'Bless you, handsome,' said Sheila as I passed them the McDonalds bag. Ron wore a tight smile, but nodded. He might have been a little put out that I'd supplied them with McDonalds' burgers rather than a wrap, or something healthier. I heard my father's voice again about the strays and imagined him commenting over my shoulder: 'Do they think you're made of baguettes?'

Back at my flat, I threw the post on the kitchen table, reached into the bread bin for the sliced loaf of wholegrain and plugged in the toastie machine before I'd even taken my jacket off. The strangely comforting smell of burning dust wafted from the heating elements in the machine and a line of old cheese crust in the hinges crackled. I reached into the fridge for the cheddar. I scraped off the whitish-looking scum on each flat surface. 'Waste not, want not,' my mother might have said in an unaccustomed effort to reduce her contemporary carbon footprint. I cut a few slivers and placed them between four slices of bread with some tomato relish, and squeezed the toastie machine lid shut.

As the cheese began to melt and sizzle, I felt a pang of guilt. I had to admit I was quite taken with Emma. My best mate Tristan said I needed to exercise more control about falling head over heels at first sight. But I hadn't met anyone new for months, and I'd almost have been willing to hurry back to Piccadilly and share my cheese toasties with Emma. But they'd be cold and soggy by the time I got there. I stood at the door to the kitchen and stared momentarily at my coat on the hook. It would have been ridiculous, surely, to go back there, wouldn't it? I promised myself I'd take something special to her the next day, if she was still there.

Not that I was wishing her gone, but her sudden appearance on the street had set me in a bit of a turmoil. I wondered how long Willie would be in hospital. Or which hospital he might be in. And whether he'd have an issue when he got back to find someone working on his patch.

5

SALLY

I finished my meal quickly, the noisy family behind me with two misbehaving children making my concentration on the book I was reading an impossible challenge. The small seating area in the burger place was suffocating, as the dampness from everyone's overcoats evaporated into the atmosphere, the aroma of wet wool mixed with over-used oil from the chip fryers. The coolness outside on the street was welcome, although a slight drizzle had started to fall.

It wasn't full-on raining, so before I headed to the tube, I decided, on the spur of the moment, to walk back along Piccadilly. I crossed the road to the opposite side from Waterstones. I wanted to know what had distracted Jamie enough to forgo a cheeseburger at Honest Burgers.

There were a few people out and about, some couples, people doing a bit of window shopping. Some shops were showing a bit of extra bling in a sickeningly early nod towards Christmas. A taxi emptied a group of Asian tourists onto the pavement and they trotted in front of me towards the revolving door of The Dilly. I had to weave through them, navigating my way round their giant wheely cases.

I walked nonchalantly towards the closed-down store with the white-washed windows, my eyes ahead, but trying to surreptitiously study the figure with the blue sleeping bag on the ledge. Whoever was there had wrapped the puffy material around them like a cocoon. The old vagrant who usually occupied this space was a big fellow and the wrapped-up body seemed quite petite. I frowned.

A bus chipped its horn as the taxi outside The Dilly pulled into its way, making me jump. The drivers leaned out of their respective windows to yell protests into the night. The figure under the sleeping bag stirred, and as I moved further along, a young woman, probably younger than me, flung the sleeping bag away from her face and vocalised something unintelligible in the direction of the arguing drivers.

Oh, Jamie. It was quite a transformation from the Scottish dude to this young blonde homeless person. She was a darn sight more attractive than the old fellow. In extending his charity to a new person on the street, I didn't think it was only his generosity that was at stake here. I'd known a few short flings of his come and go, and they all had something in common. The very same elfin look about them. This one was no different, and if she were to stick around, I was quite sure Jamie was going to fall for her. She was just his bloody type.

6

EMMA

I don't know why I hadn't had the foresight to pick up an umbrella when I bought the sleeping bag. Before the first heavy downpour this morning, the drizzle had been wafting over me on the wake of every passing vehicle, and my art was dissolving in front of my eyes. When it rained properly, the whole lot washed into the gutter.

I pressed myself against the whitewashed window of the shop behind me, trying to escape exposure to the damp, but the arched overhang was too high to offer protection, and I was beginning to question why the old homeless Scot had ever taken up residence here in the first place. I was glad I hadn't braved it out for the entire night yesterday.

I realised it was pointless me being there if it was raining. The moment I tried to use my chalks, the stuff simply crumbled between my fingers. In addition to which, no one was going to stop and admire a masterpiece of street art with the rain teaming down.

I tapped the weather app on my phone and checked the radar. Streaks of blue coming in from the northeast indicated moderate rain covering the capital for the next couple of hours at least. I noticed the phone battery icon had sunk into the red zone, and I swore. I'd forgotten to charge it to full that morning. The cold was probably making it weaken even faster.

Pushing my things into the corner of the archway as far as they would go, I tucked my box of chalks underneath to the back so they wouldn't turn into a sticky melting mess. I stood and walked across the road to Waterstones. As I came through the door, a warm pull of air lifted my hair in a wild tangle and I combed my fingers through my curls, pausing briefly in the hope that the draft would act like a hair dryer and make me look slightly less bedraggled than I felt.

The shop was busy. Several customers must have come off the street to shelter from the rain, and were half-heartedly shopping for books. They'd probably note the titles and all go home and order them from Amazon anyway. I felt sorry for the booksellers who had to deal with us fake shoppers in bad weather.

I spotted James talking to a customer at the end of the line of tills. Then I realised it wasn't a customer, or if it was, it was the same person I'd seen him leaving the shop with late last night.

The woman turned as I approached and her eyes widened imperceptibly, as though she recognised me. She was wearing a lanyard, confirming she was a shop assistant. James hadn't yet seen me. But as his colleague's eyes narrowed again, James turned from her to see what she was looking at, and his face lit up with a smile. I automatically smiled back. He seemed genuinely pleased to see me. He glanced back to his colleague, gave her a slight frown and was for a moment speechless.

'Hi, Emma,' he said to me after a pregnant pause. 'This is Sally, my work colleague. Sal, meet Emma.'

'Pleasure's all mine,' said Sally, and I was absolutely convinced she'd meant to say "Pleasure's all yours."

At that thought, I let out a derisory snort, and Sal's mouth dropped satisfyingly open. I could already see this was a person who was perhaps more than James's work colleague. He called her Sal, which meant they might be on more friendly terms, and when I'd seen them talking together before, they were comfortable in each other's company. Not lovers. But I knew I should be careful. Good friends were often the ones who protected those close to them most of all.

7

JAMES

Despite needing an urgent approval on the Greek classics display upstairs, I turned from Sal with a stab of guilt that I'd cut off our conversation, and led Emma away with my hand at her elbow. I thought Sal had been a bit rude to Emma, or at least not very welcoming.

'It isn't great weather out there for drawing,' I said to Emma. 'Let's go upstairs to the café. We'll get you warmed up and dried out.'

We took the lift to the top floor and Emma found us a table while I fetched two cappuccinos and a piece of carrot cake.

'How's it going over there?' I asked, placing the tray on the table and putting the cake in front of her with a fork and the two coffees between us.

'Wet. Cold. Not the scenario an art student should find herself in during the autumn break,' she said.

That would explain why Emma was there every day now. I felt quite relieved to know that she wasn't a typical homeless person, at least "not yet" as she'd said yesterday. Although I'd seen more and more of the homeless community were actually "normal" people until they found themselves without a roof over their heads, due to situations entirely out of their control.

'Where are you studying?' I asked.

'Goldsmiths. I'm doing an MFA, so I work the odd job between projects. But it's autumn break now, in case you were curious as to why I'm around here so much.'

'I did wonder, especially in this awful weather.'

'Things are a bit... difficult at home.' She touched her cheek, and I felt a spike of alarm. Was she in danger? An abusive parent, husband, boyfriend? I'd let her tell me in her own time, but I felt I couldn't leave it without saying something.

'If you need someone to talk to, I'm here.' Although that sounded a bit clichéd, at least it was neutral enough to give her an opportunity to offload if she needed to.

'To be honest, I didn't really think through the dynamics of this,' she said. 'I need to make some calls, but my mobile has run out of juice. I forgot my charger.' She showed me her Galaxy. 'You wouldn't happen to have a charger, would you?'

'Mine's an iPhone. Different plug,' I said with regret, 'But I can ask around. And if not, there's a place on Old Compton Street I can probably get a charger. Do you want me to ask here, see if any of the staff has a Galaxy?'

She shook her head and lifted the hem of her sweater, reaching into the pocket of her jeans. She pulled out a wallet that looked more like the folded leather money holder of a man than the over-stuffed purses of most women I knew.

'Look... I have a few quid. If you can get a charger and one of those small battery packs, I'd be ever so grateful. A generic one for this type of mobile will do. When this bloody rain stops, I'll need to get to work straight away on a new piece.'

She held out a twenty-pound note in one hand and showed me the socket of her phone with the other. She smiled, and her well-manicured fingers curled around the folded money. She tucked the phone into her pocket and rested the back of her hand on my arm. It lingered there a little longer than was perhaps absolutely necessary, and when she took it away, I experienced a shiver.

'Leave it with me. I'll see what I can do,' I said as I tucked the note into my jacket pocket, knowing that twenty quid probably wouldn't cover it.

It occurred to me that this was a lot of money for a student, homeless or otherwise, to be giving a total stranger. Then I almost laughed out loud as I thought about how often my spontaneous generosity had seen twenty pounds go in the opposite direction. But she wasn't to know that. She was nevertheless very trusting. She could have popped round the corner to Ryman's herself. But I was happy to do her this favour, as though I'd been given some kind of test.

'Thank you.' She smiled

'I'm working late again tonight,' I told her. 'We have a special evening reading. A new release on The American Civil War.'

'Maybe I'll pop in. Diversify the book-buying clientele,' she said, pointing to her curls that had gone a bit wild in the rain.

'You'd be perfectly welcome,' I said.

She must have thought she looked a mess. I thought she looked lovely.

8

SALLY

Did she pay for that book?' I whispered behind James as he walked away from the till. 'Only I didn't see her hand you any dosh or a card.'

He frowned. 'Actually, I paid through my account.'

Emma was waiting for him beyond the tills. I'd seen them come down the stairs earlier and guessed he'd bunked off to take her to Fifth View on the top floor.

'Staff rates, that's not allowed, Jamie.' My quiet comment accidentally came out as a hiss and he turned to look at me.

I'd been eyeing Emma with a little contempt. I thought I knew what her game was. She seemed to be taking advantage of Jamie's generosity.

Jamie stood in front of me to shield Emma from my look and I realised I should lighten up. What had got into me? I certainly didn't want to make an enemy of Jamie. But something about this girl in the doorway was putting me on edge.

Once she'd gone, carrying her new literary gift, I followed Jamie into the storeroom at the back of the shop and caught him searching through the books in the publisher returns pile.

'I hope you're not doing what I think you're doing. How are you going to account for those? There'll be a gap in the reports down the line.'

'She doesn't have anything to do while the weather's bad.'

'She could go home. Why does she need to be on the street when she can't earn any money from her art? And what ever happened to that old fella you used to take stuff to? I wouldn't have thought he'd take too kindly to her moving in on his turf.'

James's mouth twisted as though he hadn't considered that.

'I'm not sure home is a safe place for her at the moment.'

I raised my eyebrows, but didn't say anything else.

A few days later, Emma came into the shop, looking around hopefully. She'd been in every bloody day, for Pete's sake. I knew James was upstairs in the history section.

'Hello Sally,' she said with a bright smile. 'Is James around?'

'He's not actually,' I said. 'He's out with a publisher. I don't think he'll be back in the shop today.'

She frowned. 'Okay, no worries. I'll come another time.'

'I know what you're doing,' I blurted. 'Don't you take advantage of him. He's a good guy. I'd hate to think he's being... used.'

Emma shook her head. 'What? Of course not. I know he's a lovely man. We have a lot in common. I like him. I would never dream of *using* him.' She looked me up and down. 'It's nice that you're looking out for him, though. See you soon!'

She pivoted, her blonde curls following slightly later than her body, bouncing around her shoulders. Without looking back, she sashayed towards the store entrance. At the bottom of the steps leading to the door was a display of bestselling hardbacks, designed in neat piles in a graduation of rainbow colours. That had been my idea. I'd noticed many of the recent titles various publishers had paid a hefty price to have displayed there were all colours of the spectrum this season, which was unusual, and I'd laid them out in an arc.

Emma wandered close to the table on which the display was set. She tripped, and righted herself before she could fall over. She made it look like an accident, but I knew it wasn't. The solid table wobbled a little. Each pile of books was knocked slightly off kilter, and one of them tumbled off, hitting the floor on the top of its spine with a sickening thud. It teetered for a moment and then slapped open, the pages flurrying in the draft created from Emma's departure through the door to the street.

I waited until she was completely out of sight and went to pick up the book to replace it on its pile. It was the poison green cover of *Death of a Bookseller*. Despite my fury at the obvious sleight, that made me smile.

9

JAMES

I skived off early from work and visited Emma again while it was still daylight. She hadn't been in for a few days, or not that I knew of, and although I stopped by most lunchtimes, I wanted to see her again. I carried another of the books I'd found in the pile for returns and had set aside for her – *The Great Gatsby* this time. The weather had taken a turn for the better. It was still cold, but clear skies, and I figured she must be bored now that she didn't have to draw a new picture on the pavement every morning. She'd be getting through the books I'd given her much faster.

The well-proportioned doorman with the bushy red beard outside The Dilly raised a hand as I walked past on the way to see her. He was wearing a long wool coat to protect him from the chill breeze sweeping from the east end of Piccadilly, reminding me that autumn was on its way. The impending colder weather wouldn't be pleasant to be spending days or nights out on the street. I was tempted to rush in to the Dilly and book a table at Madhu's for that evening – a spicy curry would have been just the thing to warm Emma up in this weather. But it was ridiculous to think I'd invite her on a proper date. Wasn't it?

Instead I brought her a chicken and salad baguette from Pret, and a bottle of lime-flavoured seltzer water. I didn't know who would think it weirder that I was becoming involved with Emma; me, her, or the other homeless people on the street further along who might also have been clocking her presence. That thought triggered a memory of Willie, and I wondered who I could ask to find out if he was okay. At least if he was in hospital, he was somewhere warm and getting fed.

We now greeted each other like familiar friends. She seemed almost relieved to see me, as though there was a risk that I would stop visiting her on her own domain, and that made my heart beat a little faster.

'I thought you weren't... Nice to see you again James.'

I wondered what she'd been about to say.

'I'm not going to abandon you,' I said.

She thanked me for the sandwich and tucked in with gusto. And then I felt bad I hadn't brought her anything the first night we'd met, the night she'd spent in the doorway. And that I hadn't yet gone in to make that reservation at Madhu's. I didn't want to scare her off. Would it seem weird to ask her out on a proper date?

'Willie hasn't wandered back to the neighbourhood yet then?' I asked, knowing that if he had, then it would likely signal Emma moving on.

She shook her head, and I experienced a conflicting feeling of remorse for his possible medical treatment and relief that this was one more day when he wouldn't kick her off his patch.

10

EMMA

Over a period of several days last week James brought me a handful of books. They were all classics – *Pride and Prejudice, Wuthering Heights, The Great Gatsby*. After the enthusiasm I'd shown for the JD Salinger, perhaps he thought I was only interested in classical literature. Or maybe he was trying to improve my reading habits to match his. He wouldn't know what sat on my bookshelves at home (not much, in all honesty).

What I really would have liked to read was a rollicking psychological thriller with an unreliable narrator and lots of twists. But I was happy to go along with his suggestions. It would give us something to talk about when we were spending more time together away from this flipping doorway. I'd been going into the shop more often over the past couple of weeks, and I felt James and I were building a good bond.

After Sally's reaction to my presence in the shop, though, I knew for sure she must have had designs on James for herself at some stage. Jealousy was raising its ugly head, and as I figured she was a shrewd person, I should tread carefully.

11

SALLY

I didn't want to ask Jamie outright, perhaps embarrassing him by having to admit he fancied the girl across the street. I'd met a couple of the women he'd dated over the past few years, none of them seriously, some of whom he'd fallen for very quickly. But they'd never been street beggars. Okay, she was an artist, Jamie told me she was a student. But she could have been from the homeless community. And this seemed, well, just odd.

She was still there a couple of weeks later. Sometimes she came into the shop, other times Jamie seemed to be spending more time sitting next to her on the step across the road.

My negative feeling about this girl wasn't going away, so the following week I crossed to the northern side of Piccadilly. Keeping out of the line of sight of the girl, I went to the Dilly on my coffee break and asked the doorman if I could have a quick word. Without attracting the attention of Emma sitting in the doorway twenty yards down the road, I hurried into the lobby through the revolving door before he had the chance to refuse. He'd likely been told he should stay outside on the forecourt at all times, but perhaps didn't want to risk me causing trouble by letting me enter the hotel in the first place. I wasn't dressed like their normal clientele.

'What can I do for you?' he asked with a paternal air.

'Have you seen the new girl on the street a couple of doors down?' I asked.

He looked at me with a frown, as though considering how cautious he should be talking about her. Without even asking me who I was and why I wanted to know, he sighed. 'I don't have the heart to move them on,' he said, as though apologising either for his stance, or for the girl's presence. 'They tell me I should discourage them getting any closer. It's not a good look for the hotel. But they're everywhere now. I've heard the tourists express shock at the number of homeless on the streets, not just here.'

'Oh, no, sorry, I'm not asking you to actively move her on. I'm just trying to find out exactly when she took the place of the old Scottish bloke who was there before.'

'Willie? He'd been there for quite a few months, actually. Then when I turned up to work on Monday morning a couple of weeks ago, that girl had taken his place. I was quite relieved if I'm honest. Willie could sometimes get a little loud and belligerent, though mostly he was good humoured. This one seems to keep her head down. Doesn't appear to be a drinker. And I don't think she sleeps there. She's not always here when I turn up for my early shift. I've been thinking I could talk to her, ask her if she's okay or if she needs any help. I know there's a place she could get support near Charing Cross. But if *they* see me engaging with her, I'd likely get fired.' He glanced over his shoulder towards the reception desk. 'But her artwork is quite good, in my opinion.'

'Hmm. Monday the 17th?' I said, looking at the agenda in my phone, and after a moment calculating in his head, the doorman nodded.

Both Jamie and I had been working that day. I remembered him looking out of the window. That must have been the first time he noticed her. I also remembered feeling both guilty and jealous, because I wasn't the only one who'd been studying his profile. That square jaw with the hint of stubble, his straight nose and dark wavy hair. He'd caught the attention of an equally striking man in the shop.

Now I laughed. The irony. Stalking the stalker. The doorman gave me a look, presumably trying to work out what had amused me.

'Thanks, mate,' I told him, and turned to leave.

'Glad to be of service,' he said, following me out of the door and taking up his position again on the pavement. 'Why do you need to know?'

'Ah, it's nothing. Just wondered what happened to the old fellow.'

'Not sure,' said the doorman. 'But as I said before, I'm happy he's moved on. He wasn't great advertising for the hotel. If you're still looking for Willie, I reckon you should try near Fortnum's. He'd probably have a better class of food donations along there.

I wasn't sure anyone coming out of Fortnum & Mason's would be willing to part with their exorbitantly priced delicacies to give to a homeless person, but that wasn't my concern. I was more curious about where this girl in the doorway had come from, and apart from Emma's obvious attractive looks, how come she'd caught the attention of Jamie so damned quickly.

12

JAMES

I was on the ground floor registering some newly arrived titles into the database when I spotted Emma coming through the door, and my heart spiked with alarm. She looked like she'd been crying. Her eyes were puffy and the skin around her nose and cheeks was rosy, but not in a good way. Her eyes met mine, and I registered an emotion she'd not displayed before. She was scared.

I put the books I'd already registered onto the trolley for shelving and hurried to meet her. I took her hand, but she dismissed that and fell against my chest. I put my arms around her.

'Jesus, Emma, what's up? What's happened?'

'I can't go back there. I can't go back, James.' Her voice was muffled against my chest and I rubbed her back.

'Let's go upstairs. Grab a hot drink.'

We took the lift up to Fifth View and I ordered our usual two cappuccinos.

'You can't go back to the ledge in the doorway?' I asked.

'No... home. I can't go home... I've been living with someone. Nick. I've been trying to extricate myself from the relationship for a while. He's been very… controlling. He isn't very nice to me. It wasn't until I met you that I realised how wrong his behaviour has been.'

I reached out and put my hand over hers.

'Remember the bruise on my cheek when you met me?'

'Oh my God. That was him? *He* hit you?'

She nodded, and her eyes moistened.

'It wasn't the first time. I know I should have left the first time it happened. It was such a shock. But I didn't have anywhere to go back then. And I thought it was a one off. I was sure he wouldn't do that anymore. But he did. And now I'm terrified.'

'I know you said you might soon be homeless when we first met, but I thought you were joking. I thought you needed to find new student digs or something. I never realised… that's awful, Emma. I'm so sorry.'

'Uni starts again next week,' she said. 'I'd normally crash on the floor in my mate's flat. But she's in France…'

'Do you have family you can go to? Parents?' I asked.

'I called my mum, but I didn't tell her the whole truth,' she said. 'She would have wanted to cancel her December cruise with my auntie to see the Northern Lights and insisted I come home and stay through until Christmas. I told her Nick and I were having problems, but didn't say why. I'm pretty sure she's never really liked him, although she's been kind enough to show tolerance the couple of times they've met. I know my dad didn't like him at all. He told me the first time he met him there was "something in the lad's eye that couldn't be trusted."' She quoted with a northern accent. Yorkshire, maybe. 'It caused a bit of friction between us at first, but now I guess he was right. Shame he's not around anymore for me to tell him.'

'Oh, that's sad. I'm sorry about your dad. I guess it's a bit far to head back up north,' I said, hazarding a guess from the accent that was where her mum still lived. She'd presumably mimicked her father, although Emma didn't have a single note of northern dialect. She nodded, so I assumed I'd got that right. But if I were her mum, I'd have sent her the money for a train ticket right away, or even come down to London to pick her up myself.

'I know this might sound odd as we've only known each other a short while,' I said. 'But I have a spare room at my place. You're welcome to stay until you sort yourself out. I promise you'll be safe. If you're not sure, perhaps you could bring a girlfriend?'

Emma pressed her mouth closed, but couldn't suppress the smile that reached her eyes. I thought she was going to laugh, tell me I was either being creepy or that I was totally ridiculous; she couldn't possibly go home with a complete stranger. But I was secretly hoping we'd got beyond the stranger stage. It felt more like we'd been on a series of dates.

'That's incredibly kind of you, James,' she said to my surprise. 'Mandy is away in France until Sunday. She's out of mobile reach, couldn't afford a roaming package, so I can't ask her until lectures start again on Monday. She shares a house with a handful of students and as I said, I'm sure I could kip on her floor...'

I swallowed, waiting for her next words.

'I wouldn't be too much trouble. I already have a sleeping bag.' She waved a hand in the vague direction of Piccadilly. 'Though it will probably need fumigating before I bring it into your place. And I trust you, James. I wouldn't need a chaperone. So... is that okay?'

It felt so natural to keep my hand on the top of hers. And she didn't pull away.

'It's more than okay. I'm not dangerous or anything. And I have loads of books,' I said. 'And I guess Willie will be back soon to reclaim his patch anyway.'

She nodded, then frowned and bit her lip.

'What is it?' I asked.

'I really don't want to go back to the flat I shared with Nick. But... all my things are still there. I don't want to run into him. Part of me is thinking, what the hell? I'll just leave it all there in our flat. It's only stuff. But there's my uni work and text books. He can't get into my laptop because he doesn't know my passcode. But all my modules are on there, and my visual art stuff.'

She stretched her arms up, linked her fingers together above her head and leaned first one way and then the other, like a willow in a changing wind. It looked like a practised yoga move from the lunchtime groups I sometimes saw in Green Park. It was as though my offer of a place to stay had been an immense relief for her and she was shedding the strain of the past days.

'I can help,' I said. 'How about *I* go and get your things for you?'

She must have thought I was a bit crazy. Would she give a total stranger the key to her flat? But then again, she hadn't turned down my offer, so I knew she trusted me.

I could see something ticking behind her eyes. It sounded like she was ready to give it all up anyway, as though simply being in the place where Nick lived had tainted all her things with his spirit. And if I was the bad guy – I repeated again to her that I wasn't – who would steal all his valuables along with hers, she might have gleaned some ironic satisfaction from that.

In the end, she handed me a key.

13

EMMA

The offer came so spontaneously, it felt like a natural progression of our relationship. I'd only ever felt safe in James's company. Even if he liked me as much as I suspected, he would surely think it weird if I ran away from an abusive partner and was happy to jump straight into the arms of a benevolent stranger.

Not that we were really strangers any more. We'd definitely established a connection of some kind. If we were to build something more together, I had to take things slowly, and I imagined he was thinking the same thing. I shook my head as I thought that. It was a long shot that he would even entertain *building a relationship* with me, wasn't it?

I was thrilled I'd get to see his place, his things. I'd finally get to see what made him tick, what he was passionate about in life.

14

SALLY

It was now three weeks in a row that Jamie had taken extended coffee breaks and stretched his lunch hour every day almost to two. I didn't mind covering for him at first, thinking to keep in favour with him for future moments when he might need to cover for my own absences, especially with my younger brother Rory needing to be accompanied to all his medical tests, but it was soon apparent I was no longer in favour either.

'You still on for a Scrabble extravaganza this weekend at your place?' I asked on Thursday morning.

He'd already postponed from last weekend because he'd overlooked a scheduled trip to visit his parents. Or said he had.

'Ah, Sal, I'm sorry, I've got something on this weekend that I'd forgotten about.'

I knew he was lying when he said he'd forgotten about it. Something about the uncertainty in his voice. He'd been so much more genuine when he'd forgotten about his parents' visit. Something was up. Something new. My stomach dropped.

We'd never been lovers, Jamie and I. Almost Lovers, perhaps. I'd lost count of how many times I'd played that Fine Frenzy song.

We'd formed our own little bubble during lockdown, and he often invited me over on random afternoons to play Scrabble and share a bottle of wine – I always left the choice of booze up to him. I knew nothing about the wine, but he never chose one I didn't like. And he began to teach me a little about the nuances of certain cultivars and blends. Not that I could ever have afforded to fork out for the kind of stuff he drank. Books and wine. A great combo. Both of these things on his shelves were generally far more valuable than those you'd find in your average library or Tesco, respectively.

When the pandemic was over, I'd been secretly hoping he'd invite me up to his parents' country home. I'd never met them, and I thought that might be the next step for two people who'd become such good friends through the lockdowns. But as we always assumed we'd go back to Waterstones when the shops opened again, I made the stupid rule in my head not to get involved romantically with work colleagues. I'd seen a few girlfriends come and go in Jamie's life, and always assumed that one day we'd end up together, perhaps if one or both of us left the bookstore. But I'd never seen him quite as bowled over as he was now by this girl. Horses and stable doors came to mind. My own damned procrastination.

And then on Thursday afternoon, he didn't come back to work at all, and my disappointment turned into annoyance.

15

JAMES

As I approached the address Emma had written for me on a piece of paper, I saw a lone copper walking slowly down the street. Had Nick alerted the police about Emma? Either that she was missing or that she might try to take some of his property? I put my hand around the key in my pocket and remembered the thought I'd had about stealing Nick's things.

Did coppers still have a beat like this in the suburbs? If so, weren't they supposed to be in pairs? This was hardly a commercial area. But whatever the reason for his presence, I decided to wait until he moved away from Emma's door.

The whole operation was taking way longer than I'd hoped. More minutes were being eaten away from my late lunchbreak but I couldn't be bothered to phone them at work and tell them I wouldn't be back that afternoon. I'd already had a warning the day before about taking longer lunch hours than was strictly allowed. I could hardly justify myself by telling them about the girl I'd recently encountered. Not when she was occupying the street opposite their place of business.

On reflection, I knew the manager would be mega annoyed if I simply didn't turn up to work that afternoon. I quickly texted Sal and told her I thought I'd eaten a dodgy prawn baguette for lunch and was going straight home. She said she'd deal with it, which meant her having to break the news to my manager. I'd owe her.

Finally, the cop wandered out of sight and I approached the house. It was on a typical row of terraces with a recessed porch. There were two doors side by side. One for the upstairs flat and the other was Emma and Nick's door to their flat on the ground floor. Paint was peeling off the sill of the Georgian-style bay window. The front terrace was paved with red brick and weeds were growing up between the grouting. There was an unpleasant smell of cat wee.

I entered a dimly-lit hallway and I headed to the bedroom across from the living room. A pair of black-out curtains were almost half closed, so I opened them to let in the light. My heart pounded. Even though Emma had given me her key, I felt like I was trespassing in someone else's house, and it made me feel simultaneously sheepish and incredibly powerful.

Before she'd gone back to her street art after lunch, she'd explained exactly what she needed from her home and where I would find the items.

I looked around the flat. It was sparsely decorated. One black and white poster tacked to the wall above the sofa – an iconic foreshortened shot of the Eiffel Tower. But other than that, there were no photos on the walls or in frames on the surfaces, and no trinkets that would personalise the space. I could tell very little about Emma and Nick's relationship from this, let alone Emma's personal life.

I crossed the room to the bed, averting my eyes from the exposed bottom sheet as the duvet had been thrown back haphazardly. I pulled the large sports bag she said I'd find under the bed, and packed the things she needed into it. She'd given me a list of clothing, detailing each piece precisely. She told me where to find the books she wanted on a desk in the living-room/diner with her laptop, along with a handful of papers conveniently tucked into a sealed plastic folder in a drawer in the kitchen. Had she previously had an escape plan? It looked like she'd prepared for a quick getaway.

Using one of her tee shirts – I didn't want to touch anything of Nick's at this stage – I made sure not to leave my fingerprints on any surfaces. I'm not really sure what made me do this, it wasn't one of her instructions, but I didn't want to implicate myself if Nick reported a theft.

On my way out of the house, I was sorely tempted to leave a sign of some kind, in defiance of the wretched thing Despicable Nick had done to Emma, but I knew time was of the essence, I'd already wasted too much of it, and I'd be doing the very thing that Emma probably abhorred. Nick would soon be home from work and he was the last person I wanted to run in to. I almost pocketed the key after closing the front door in case Emma wanted to come back and get the rest of her things, but I posted it back through the letter box, as she'd instructed.

With a glance towards the sightless accusing windows of the neighbouring houses, I heaved the bag over my shoulder and walked as casually as possible back down the street towards the intersection.

As I turned to check the street was clear, my stomach lurched as I spotted a man wearing a hoody training the large lens of an SLR camera right at me. Was that Despicable Nick? I heard the whir of the shutter even from that distance. It seemed odd that the man was taking my picture, so I turned to look behind me. A maple tree stood at the end of the road, the watery sun making its leaves appear a spectacular fire-like red in the autumn light. With a huff of laughter – I'd felt momentarily like a spy, a fugitive or a thief – I realised the guy was a random nature photographer catching a moment of a seasonal display of colourful foliage.

I turned back to look at him – he'd probably be cursing my presence in his viewfinder – when a van drove down the road blocking him from my view. When the vehicle passed, the man had disappeared. My heart skipped briefly, acknowledging my not altogether honest deed of recuperating pieces of Emma's life. I shook my head and walked towards the train station with Emma's bag slung over my shoulder, trying not to display any strain under its weight, and trying not to make it obvious that I'd just broken into someone's home and taken what was not mine.

16

EMMA

Something you might be able to relate to,' said James, handing me a copy of BA Paris's *Behind Closed Doors*.

'Ooh, I've heard good things about this one,' I said, slapping my palm against the paperback.

'I dropped your bag at my place. It's waiting for you in your room. I brought the book from my library in case you find time to start a new read this afternoon. I'll come by and get you after work.'

'James, you're the best. My knight in shining armour.'

'I just want you to be safe,' he said.

'I'm not going to miss this place,' I said. 'My hands were so cold this morning that I've decided to chuck this street art thing in. It's only really a feasible option in summer, and I haven't made much money from my efforts.' I shook the Pret cup with a few measly coins in the bottom.

'See you later, Emma.' James smiled warmly.

I wondered whether he was as excited as me, like a small child being offered a tour of the sweet shop.

17

JAMES

My excitement about Emma coming to stay at my place was only slightly marred by the fact that I was supposed to be on the Saturday morning shift at the shop. It was always the busiest day of the week. I'd have to call in a few more favours, maybe with Sal, despite the short notice. There would inevitably be a book launch in the evening, and I wanted to avoid being on duty then, too. I wanted to devote my entire weekend to Emma, show her my flat, make sure she was comfortable. It might be early days, but once she'd got herself back on her feet after being with Despicable Nick, I was hoping she wouldn't want to leave, providing of course that we got along living together. I shocked myself thinking about a future with this person I'd only just met.

I thought briefly of my best mate Tristan, currently on a cricket tour, following the England team round their various test matches in Australia. It was just as well he was away. He'd be shaking my shoulder with all the warning signs, telling me about the perils of re-bound relationships. This one would be moving way too quickly for anybody who had half an interest in how my love life was currently going. But I shouldn't be thinking that far ahead. For now, I was simply offering her shelter and safety.

I arrived back at the shop in the late afternoon, even though I'd told Sal I wouldn't be back that day. Things soon sorted themselves out about the Saturday conundrum. The manager decided to forego the required one month's notice to fire me. An excessive knee-jerk reaction, in my opinion, and one I thought didn't entirely follow HR protocols.

Along with missing a whole afternoon at work without a valid reason, and all the other absences I'd sneaked in over the past few weeks, he'd figured out where some of the books had been disappearing to. I was given no opportunity to explain myself. Theft is theft, whether the books were returns for the publisher and consequently destined for the shredder or not (which always pained me to know). It was something the store "would not tolerate." I'd always suspected the manager didn't like me very much.

My instructions to leave immediately almost made me laugh. As if I was some high-flying banker working in the city who was going to be marched to the door of his office with instructions to hand over all passwords, laptops, phones and key fobs. I was rather fond of my lanyard, and placed it reluctantly on the manager's desk before fetching my things from the staff room.

Anyway, this solved one problem. It meant I was unexpectedly free for what remained of the day and the entire weekend.

It was time to move Emma into my life.

18

SALLY

'Ooh, that's a bit harsh. Do you want me to have a word with Simon?' I said, referring to the manager. 'I'm sure there's a procedure for things like this, and it doesn't sound like he's following it.' I know they'd never seen eye to eye, but sacking Jamie on the spot for the odd absence here and there didn't seem very fair. 'I'm sure he'll change his mind once that temper of his has simmered a bit. We're coming up to the beginning of Christmas. It means everyone else will have to cover the extra hours until he finds someone else. They'll all be grumpy about that. Me included. As I said, bloody harsh.'

We'd all have to rally because of Simon's impulsive decision. More flipping hours when I totally didn't want them. Especially if Jamie wasn't going to be there.

Jamie didn't even look up. He kept on filling a tote bag left over from an author event the other night with his things from the staff room.

'Why are you so bloody happy, mate?' I asked him.

'Ah, just that it makes decisions for my future easier. I hadn't planned to work at Waterstones forever, you know. It's not really my kind of place.

I've always secretly wanted to work at one of those book shops in Cecile's Court,' he said.

'Well, good luck with that,' I replied, knowing it would be near on impossible to get a job there, and was a little personally affronted that this wasn't *his kind of place*.

He was always so damned positive. Convinced he'd get another job, pronto. Not that he even needed it. Which was why he likely *would* get another job easily, because he didn't wear his desperation like the rest of us when it came to making sure there was enough money to pay the rent, put bread on the table, and in my case try to cover my brother Rory's astronomical medical expenses. Life wasn't always fair.

'I'll keep in touch, Sal, I promise,' he said.

I felt a sudden pang, remembering I'd really messed up this time. Not only had Jamie been sacked without even having been given notice, there was the girl across the street to consider. No time left for me to surreptitiously plan any kind of slow seduction over a game of Scrabble. Consummating our wordy relationship was very likely now out of the question. I felt like I'd missed the boat I'd been holding two tickets to the captain's suite for.

I remembered his text message from earlier. Making excuses. Dodgy prawn baguette, my arse.

19

EMMA

Towards the end of the afternoon, he bounded over the road with his usual positive enthusiasm and sat on the step beside me. I suppressed a smug little smile. He was a little earlier than normal; he must have been impatient to show me his flat.

'Are you ready?' he asked, beaming like a kid at Christmas.

'Of course! Have you finished work?' I asked, as I began gathering my few things together, placing them into the backpack I brought with me every day.

He cleared his throat. 'Yes... definitively.' I thought I heard him say. Unsure what he meant by that, I glanced at him, but he didn't say anything else. I stuffed my sleeping bag into its impossibly small sleeve with a drawstring.

Then I stood up, and we made our way towards Piccadilly Circus, leaving my latest art work behind me forever. We chatted about what our favourite three-course meals might be. With the memory of the penetrating cold of the past days, mine involved various flavours of soups, curries and steaming apple pie. His choices were a bit more Gordon Ramsay – pillars of unusual seafood, perfectly seared steaks and complicated sauces. I had the feeling I was going to be spoiled over the next few days. Against my better judgement, part of me was looking forward to spending some more time with this man. He was actually good company.

20

JAMES

As we walked away from 27 Piccadilly together, I had a brief thought about Willie and how he might be faring. I didn't want to press the point with Emma; I'd already banged on about it a fair amount. I'd probably pass him next week, back on his home patch, on my way to pitching a job application at another bookstore.

I soon forgot about him in the excitement that Emma was coming to stay. I'd been trying to work out suitable living arrangements since I got back from Tesco the previous evening. In truth, I'd have been happy for Emma to share my king-sized double in the master bedroom from the outset, but we hadn't even kissed, and I was overcome with nervousness late the previous evening, as I had no idea whether she was beginning to feel the same way I did. Until I could prove whether the romantic tension I thought I'd detected was genuine, Emma needed to be treated respectfully as a new acquaintance. I was supposed to be making her feel safe. She might only consider me a saviour, nothing more.

So, I'd made up the bed in the guest room, placing a brand-new goose down pillow with a freshly laundered slip at the head board. This simple thing could make the difference between wanting to get away after a couple of nights' refuge at my place and the beginning of a wonderful relationship.

I glanced at Emma as we headed east towards Piccadilly Circus. Her blue sleeping bag, packed into its tight little sleeve with some of the material bursting from the top, was slung from its string over her shoulder next to her backpack. She gave me a grin.

'Now for my next adventure!' she said as she grabbed my hand. I was surprised, and for a moment thought she was going to lean in for a kiss, but as I braced to receive her lips on mine, her head veered away as she turned to look at the crowds around the statue in the middle of the circus.

'I'll be happy to get out of these clothes,' she called over her shoulder.

A couple of heads turned at her comment. She sounded so delighted to be away from the street where she'd spent the past weeks, and although her comment made me blush, her humour made me smile.

She paused by the entrance to the tube and I tried to imagine what was going through her mind. I'd told her nothing about where I lived. Did she think I lived in city digs? A Victorian basement? A canal houseboat? A Thameside penthouse? Or a leafy suburb much like the one she used to live in with Despicable Nick? She looked at me with what I ascertained was curiosity, her next journey as yet unknown.

'Where to James?' she asked with a fearless, monarchical accent, as though I was her movie chauffeur.

I offered to take her backpack, and she agreed, shuffling it off her shoulders. I hauled it onto my back. I felt the weight of her books in there. As we set off again, she reached once more for my hand. Our palms met like familiar pieces of a puzzle, and I hoped the warmth I was now feeling inside wouldn't cause mine to sweat.

'Time to show you *my* castle mi'lady,' I said, with a spring in my step, and we walked in the direction of Leicester Square.

We passed Eros to our left, and I raised my head to see the bow clasped in his left hand directly facing us. Anteros. The God of requited love, avenger of unrequited love.

It was the first time I'd noticed that he'd already released his arrow.

Continuing on through Leicester Square and crossing Charing Cross Road, I was tempted to see whether Sheekeys could squeeze us in for an early dinner. They were usually booked up months in advance, but I knew the Maître'D. He would be getting his tables ready and might work his usual magic to find us one for an early sitting. Emma deserved a celebratory meal for her escape and freedom. Their shellfish bisque was the finest I'd ever tasted, barring a little seafront gem of an Osteria in Positano on the Amalfi coast.

I said none of this to Emma, and walked past the turning to St Martin's Court, putting the idea to the back of my mind without mentioning my connection. The restaurant was expensive. Somehow, I thought Emma might be the type of person who, rather than appreciating such generosity, might frown upon the fact that I had the means to eat there in the first place. She'd just spent many days trying to earn a paltry living on the street. I didn't think a meal at a five-star restaurant would deliver the right message.

As we continued onto Monmouth Street, Emma's pace slowed briefly in front of a couple of clothes stores before catching up to walk beside me again. I tried to think of a way I could offer to increase the number of items I'd placed in her bag from her wardrobe without appearing to act like a creepy sugar daddy, or worse, that I might be critical of her current fashion choices.

We walked across Seven Dials, pausing at the obelisk in the centre to let a road cleaning truck navigate the narrow road around the curved dais. I stopped next to the Moroccan Restaurant to fish my keys out of my tote bag. Mounting the steps, I kicked away a crumpled page of newspaper. This corner seemed to be a perpetual rubbish trap. I'd never worked out whether this was due to careless litterers or the unfortunate cornering of the swirling winds that often blew up Shorts Gardens. A little of both, perhaps. It belied the neatness of the courtyard behind the iron gate at the top.

I stopped at the mailbox to pick up the mail; my quarterly subscription of *The Book Collector*, and some utility bills. I unlocked the gate and ushered Emma through to the neatly paved courtyard with well-tended planters looked after by the housing association we were all part of.

'James! You're a dark horse! This is your neighbourhood?' Emma was clearly impressed.

'It is,' I said, the ubiquitous guilt of my privilege wavering on the edge of the affirmation that I could at least offer her a comfortable place to stay.

'How can you afford to live here on a bookshop assistant's salary?' she asked.

I bit my lip, wondering how she'd react when she saw inside my flat. It wasn't your usual student bedsit. She might not completely believe my answer.

'Diligent saving and careful budgeting,' I said.

She'd been part of two quite different worlds today, starting out as a homeless person on a West End street having escaped an abusive relationship and ending in the well-tended garden behind the gate of Seven Dials Court. A stones-throw away along Monmouth Street was one of the most expensive hotels in London. Writers and creatives with deep pockets often stayed at the Covent Garden Hotel. I'd been known to dine there myself from time to time, especially when my parents came to visit, as they often booked a suite there rather than staying at my place, which ultimately was their place, until the money in the trust was completely mine.

After gently instructing Emma to leave her shoes at the entrance to my place, a habit I inflicted on all my visitors since my time living in the Swiss Alps, I showed her the guest room upstairs in the duplex and put her pack on the chaise long at the end of the bed next to her bag of things I'd taken from her flat. She took off her coat, placed it over the back of the chair by the dressing table-come-desk, twirled in a remarkably delicate pirouette, and threw herself backwards onto the bed in a starfish pose.

'God, James. It's like I've just walked into the five-star hotel of my dreams. This is gorgeous, especially after the discomfort of that doorway on Piccadilly.'

I felt like a contemporary Henry Higgins in *My Fair Lady*.

'Fancy a cuppa?' I asked, to stop myself from jumping onto the Egyptian cotton duvet next to her.

'Thank goodness for you,' she said with a smile. 'Builders, please. A splash of milk. No sugar.'

'Feel free to use the space in the wardrobe,' I said as I slid the mirrored panel open to show her the mainly empty shelves and some hangers.

'There are a few sports things of mine in here, but plenty of space for your clothes.'

'I need a shower. I already feel guilty I just threw myself on that pristine bed cover. Then I think I'll throw these clothes away. Thank you, James.'

I retreated downstairs and crossed the airy space of my open kitchen-diner-living room. The windows cast elongated squares of framed sunlight across the solid oak floorboards to the windows on the far side facing Monmouth Street. I felt I'd picked the best of the flats here on the end of the terrace above the businesses below with windows on two sides.

I heard the faint sound of the wardrobe door sliding upstairs and the zip of Emma's bag opening. I reached into the fridge and pulled out some Manchego cheese and serrano ham I'd purchased from Pick & Cheese, along with a fresh ciabatta from the bakery in the food hall.

The shower in Emma's ensuite bathroom began running and I tried not to envision her taking off the clothes she'd mentioned she couldn't wait to shed earlier. I'd bought some herbal hair and body shampoo, a new toothbrush and toothpaste in preparation. They were things she hadn't asked me to take from her flat. Marta, my cleaner, had placed a set of fluffy new towels on the heating rail. Emma's humming of a tune I couldn't quite put my finger on floated down the stairwell, and my heart lifted at this simple sound of contentedness.

I put the food on the dining room table with small dishes of herb butter, Himalayan salt crystals and virgin olive oil, along with two wine glasses and the bottle of vintage Château d'Armailhac my old man had shoved at me when he'd dropped me off at the station last Sunday evening.

Was that only five days ago? It seemed more like a year since then. Over a matter of days, I'd invited the girl of my dreams to come and live with me, stolen books, semi-trespassed on someone's property, and lost my job. Something told me I should be prepared for a bumpy ride.

21

EMMA

'You know you can stay as long as you like,' said James.

'Don't you need the room for guests or family?' I asked. He was being so nice. I could hardly believe this was true.

'My parents sometimes come. But it's unlikely they'll need it any time soon. They anyway prefer to stay at the hotel down the road. It seems to have become their home from home in London. They probably feel like they're cramping my lifestyle here. The only other person who stays every now and then is my best mate Tristan after a late night out. But he won't mind sleeping on the couch if the need arises. Honestly, make yourself at home.'

I put down my wine glass, hopped up from my chair and went around the table to plant a kiss firmly on his cheek.

As I stood up and backed away, he reached out to grab my arm, seemingly an instinctive reaction on his part, then let his hand slip down to my wrist and release it as I returned to my seat. His lips pressed together with something unspoken. It felt like he wanted to tell me he really liked me, but was trying not to come on too strong. I was supposed to be getting over the trauma of an abusive boyfriend. The last thing he probably thought he should be doing was to fawn all over me. But I felt the attraction fizzle, and I thought I should leave a casually optimistic door open, without him feeling like he was frightening me off. I smiled at him as I returned to my seat, hoping to convey that I knew precisely the intensity of his feelings for me.

I concentrated on the food, wrapping a thin slice of prosciutto around a stick of cheese and eating it like a sandwich. I'd consumed way too much bread over the past weeks. It was time to change my carbo-rich diet.

'This place is heaven after the hustle and bustle of the dirty streets of the West End,' I said, looking around at James's tastily decorated flat. 'I often thought I'd never be warm again. And I think I have a lot of sleep to catch up on. I've had some anxiety ridden nights. Your guest bed is mega comfy.'

'As I said before, it's yours for as long as you need it. Will you let me do something while you're here, though?' asked Jamie.

'That depends,' I said with a teasing smile, encouraging him to continue.

'I saw you gazing at the shops as we came up Monmouth Street. Would you let me buy you a couple of outfits? I know I left a lot of things behind in your flat. But rather than going back for them, I'd like to replace them.'

'I can't let you do that,' I said. 'You've already been so good to me.'

But I knew he could tell from my unconvincing tone that I would be swayed.

After we'd finished eating, he gave me a quick tour of the rest of the flat. I drew my finger along the spines of the books on the shelves spanning an entire wall of his living room. When I reached the end, I turned towards a glass-fronted cabinet of books and raised my eyebrows.

'Special editions,' he explained. 'The cabinet is facing away from the window to protect the books from strong daylight, although the glass is specially-tempered to keep out any damaging rays.'

I crouched down to check each shelf, holding my hair back from my face to get a better look.

'That's some collection,' I said.

'Yep, I love my books,' he said as I stared at each of them. 'I'll show you where you can do laundry,' he continued after a moment.

I nodded. That sleeping bag particularly required a wash, not that I'd be needing it in my plush new bedroom. We mounted the stairs and he led me to an extra shower room next to his ensuite which housed the washer and dryer.

'James! You have four bathrooms, including the loo downstairs. Living the life.'

'Yes, well, my office over there was intended to be a family room I guess. It's certainly a luxury today to have so many wet rooms in a central London flat. It's not as though I'll be putting a strain on the city's waste water system though, given I can still only use one bathroom at a time. I have more bathrooms than my parents' rambling Suffolk home.'

'More books here!' I said, pointing at the piles of them in his office, much more messily arranged than the neat shelves in the living room.

'You can help yourself to anything to read. If you can't find anything that grabs your fancy downstairs, feel free to rummage here. Although I'd appreciate you putting the ones you take from here back where you found them. It looks haphazard, but there's a system. Research.'

I nodded.

'And this is my room.' I glanced at him, his cheeks colouring. His confidence was at odds with his embarrassment when he said *my room*. He opened the door and walked in before me, pushing a stray pair of discarded socks under the end of the bed with his foot. I looked around, my gaze trying not to pause on his rumpled duvet.

'Lovely,' I murmured, and bit my lip. It was as though I was a potential buyer and he was a real estate agent showing me a property.

The awkward moment about each of us being aware that we were in James's sleeping space soon passed and we returned downstairs. He showed me how to set the alarm if I intended to go out and made me repeat the code for the door back to him. He explained the iPad controls for the blinds, the lighting, the music system and the TV.

The following morning, we went out to discover a bit more of the neighbourhood, although all I wanted to do all weekend was flop on his giant sofa.

'Here's the deli where I bought all that stuff for dinner last night,' he said. 'There are a few Tesco Metros within walking distance. I don't really need more than I can get here or at those mini-marts, but I occasionally go to Big Tesco up near Finsbury Park. I cook from time to time, but I tend to go for the easy stuff, living on my own. Seems a shame to invest so much time in preparing something that'll be shovelled down in a minute with no compliments to the chef.'

I didn't believe that for one moment, thinking he was being modest about his home cooking skills, especially after he'd described his favourite meals earlier. He probably did most of his food shopping at Fortnum & Mason but didn't want to admit it.

'Do you like Italian food?' he asked. 'I can cook that, simple ingredients. But maybe not tonight. Max's is a great restaurant down Monmouth Street. Would you like to go there for dinner?'

He was rambling. Trying to impress me, and then seemed to be embarrassed that he might be impressing me too much, or inundating me with suggestions I was unable to choose from. I didn't know many posh restaurants in London, but I'd heard that Max's Brasserie was the signature restaurant in The Covent Garden Hotel.

Basically, along with those antique-looking books in his cabinet in the living room, all these things told me that James Marsh was truly loaded.

22

JAMES

I'll be back around five tonight. I have a few hours overtime owing,' I lied. That had been my excuse on Friday when I told her I'd been granted the day off to help her settle in. 'Meanwhile, make yourself at home.'

I could have spent all morning watching Emma eat the fresh flaky croissants I'd bought from the local bakery. She sat opposite me, delicately rubbing her thumb and forefinger together on her right hand after she slipped the last morsel into her mouth. The crumbs fell to her plate. She lifted her napkin to her mouth to wipe away another flake stuck to her lip. The flat was filled with the aroma of warm buttery croissants and rich arabica coffee. I didn't feel like leaving home for the company of books, which was a rare lack of enthusiasm, but knew I should start the search for a new job immediately.

I'd almost told Emma last Thursday that Waterstones had let me go. But I wanted her to think things were normal, and that I was heading out to work. If I told her I was now unemployed, not only might the potential for a relationship be put in jeopardy – who wanted to hang around with a jobless book geek? – she might feel guilty that she was part of the reason I'd lost my job.

'Have a wonderful day at work, darling,' she said jokingly, and kissed my cheek before I could express surprise. Her still damp hair smelled of fresh shampoo.

When I left Seven Dials, I'd intended to wander down to Cecil's Court to scout the bookshops for a new job. None of them would be open just yet, so I considered stopping at a café to wait. But as I headed south along St Martin's Lane, I hesitated. This would be a good opportunity to see whether Willie was back on his patch.

When I reached Piccadilly, I didn't want to walk past the vast windowed shop front of Waterstones and risk being seen by Sally Crime or any of my other former co-workers. Sal would probably rush out and give me a piece of her mind for leaving her in a work mess at the weekend. Instead, I crossed to the north side.

I weaved my way through tourist crowds already milling at this time of the morning. How could I occupy my days until Emma went back to university without her worrying that she might have been the cause of me losing my job? This sudden abundance of free time was a gift I should take advantage of. With my membership at the British Library, and a long-simmering ambition to write a novel, I had plenty of options to be away from home during weekdays.

When I arrived at Willie's patch, I stopped abruptly and uttered a surprised 'Oh!' The previously closed shop was now a bustle of activity. The whitewash on the windows had gone, the posters had been torn down, and bright rows of puffer jackets and thick polar fleeces hung on display racks inside the door. It had transformed dramatically over the weekend. The newest business had finally opened. It made sense that this prestigious address wouldn't remain empty for long. The last place a homeless person would find solace was in front of these floor to ceiling windows. The raised step within the archways of Number 27 bore no occupants.

I ventured inside the shop.

'Can I speak to the manager?' I asked the woman at the checkout desk.

She was emptying boxes onto the counter, registering new stock into the computer. A frown flickered across her brow, as though already expecting a complaint about an article of returned clothing.

'That's me,' she said warily.

'When did you open?' I asked. 'Congratulations on the new venture, by the way.'

'Thank you.' She seemed relieved that I didn't appear to have an article of clothing to return. 'This morning,' she continued, answering my first question. 'It's all been a bit of a whirl to be honest. We wanted to speed up the process to take advantage of the pre-Christmas consumer surge.'

'This is going to sound like a strange question, but were you involved with the set-up of the store, cleaning the windows, getting the storefront ready?'

'Of course,' she said, her eyes narrowing in curiosity.

'I work over there,' I said, pointing to Waterstones. Using that phrase in the past tense might not elicit the same enthusiasm to answer my questions. 'There was a homeless person who used to occupy the front step of your shop. He was usually tucked into the corner of the arch over there. Do you know anything about his re-location?' The shop manager's mouth crumpled into a more negative expression. 'I used to bring him a hot drink and a sarnie from time to time,' I added. 'Just curious, really.'

'There was someone there when we first took over the lease,' she said. 'We did tell him he should be aware that the business was opening imminently. You might recall the windows were whitewashed while we were setting up. Then when some stock arrived last week, there was a girl who said she'd be gone for sure very soon. When we opened, I was relieved to be honest that no one was there. I hope your people have found somewhere safe.' She said this last with a hint of sarcasm, and I figured any more questions weren't going to get the mystery solved. I thanked her, and left.

I looked at Google maps and studied the hospitals within a three-mile radius. Emma had been quite evasive when I asked whether she'd heard news of Willie. She'd said he'd been admitted to hospital, but would he even still be there? Perhaps she felt guilty that she hadn't paid more attention to his absence.

I had nothing better to do at this point, so thought a bit of walking would do me good. Clockwise on the map there was Barts, Guys – maybe a bit far – St Thomas' and UCH. I was lucky enough to never have needed any hospitals, but had no idea where I should start. The easiest solution would have been to phone each of them, but I had a whole day to kill, and not a lot to fill it with. In truth I would have been happy to snuggle up on the sofa with Emma and a good book, even the same good book she was reading. There was something Dickensian and cheesily romantic about reading aloud to each other. But I felt I needed to keep up the semblance of being fully employed if I wanted her approval. I left my job search for another day and turned eastwards.

It took me almost an hour to get to Barts with distractions along the way – more book shops in Soho. At the inpatients' reception I explained that I'd been keeping an eye on a homeless person called Willie or William and that he'd been admitted to an unknown hospital a few weeks ago. When they asked what his last name was, or his last known address, I hadn't a clue and the receptionist shook her head and frowned. He was easy to describe, but if this person hadn't been on duty when he'd been admitted, recognition wouldn't be forthcoming. No luck there. I did the same thing at Guys, where the receptionist at least asked the colleague behind her in the office whether that rang any bells. He would be hard to miss on admittance, but no one could remember a belligerent homeless person with a broad Glaswegian accent. At UCH, my question even elicited a disgusted look from the staff, and I knew my search would be in vain.

Looking for a man whose surname I didn't know, and trying to find out whether he was admitted for an operation in a department I was at a loss to guess at, my investigation came to an abrupt halt.

Where the heck was Willie? I imagined Emma in her kindness might be disappointed to know I hadn't found him. I had really wanted to trace him, if only to thank him. If it hadn't been for him, I might never have met Emma.

23

JAMES

My feet were hurting by early afternoon, so I headed back to the flat. I would tell Emma I'd taken the afternoon off – a white lie – to help her further settle in. I wanted to make it hard for her to leave. As I turned into Shorts Gardens, I spotted Marta, my cleaning lady, coming towards me up the road carrying a heavy bag. It looked like it contained freshly laundered towels and bed linen. She hadn't seen me, and jumped when I said hello. I offered to take the bag from her and she smiled gratefully.

'She here yet?' she asked as I unlocked the gate. 'You take day off to help her move in?'

I nodded with a smile. I didn't want to tell Marta that I'd lost my job either. She might worry about where the funds would be coming from to pay her cleaning fees, despite knowing more about my family situation than Emma did.

'Ah, you have that shine in your eye, Mr James. I think this girl make you very happy.'

'It'll be good to introduce you to her, so she won't be surprised when you come in. I forgot to mention you to her earlier. I hardly know what day of the week it is at the moment.' I grinned like a fool when Marta nudged me with her elbow. 'I'm afraid there'll be a bit more to clean now that the second bedroom and ensuite are being used. But let me know how many extra hours I owe you at the end of the month. It's no problem.'

'Monday afternoons are all yours,' said Marta. 'I don't pick up Beatriz from school until 5:30 because she has guitar lessons. I think we manage.'

I marvelled at how her English had improved over the years she'd been cleaning my place. When she first started, we'd conversed in Italian, the language we could both master with a modicum of understanding.

'Let's go and meet Emma, shall we?' I said.

When Marta and I entered the flat together, Emma had been texting on her phone on the living room sofa, and she immediately put it into the front pocket of her sweatshirt.

'You're early!' she said, smiling sweetly, her eyes sliding from me to Marta.

It was a smile that didn't altogether reach her eyes, and a hot pulse went through me as I interpreted this as her not wanting to share me with anybody, even my cleaning lady. Marta, on the other hand, had a curious expression on her face as she put her bags on the floor and held out her hand.

'Took the afternoon off,' I said. 'This is Marta. I don't like to call her a cleaning lady as that sounds a little demeaning. She's my housekeeper.' I smiled fondly at Marta. 'Twice a week. Mondays and Thursdays. I forgot to mention her earlier.'

Emma hesitated a fraction of a second before taking the proffered hand.

'I'm Emma. Emma Smith. James's new house guest.'

In my enthusiasm to host Emma, I realised it was the first time I'd heard her utter her surname. And here I was determined to eventually persuade her to share my life forever.

I was glad to be able to introduce Emma to Marta. If the latter had walked in and surprised Emma, I couldn't imagine what the reaction would have been. I'd warned Marta, but had completely forgotten to tell Emma.

'I'll try and keep out of your way,' said Marta. 'I brought some *pasteis de nata*. I'll put them on the counter. You can eat them later. But don't wait too long. I know you, you'll put them in the fridge. And the pastry will go soggy. No frigo.' She used the Italian rather than the Portuguese.

Marta placed a Tuppaware container on the kitchen counter, took the lid off and covered the container with a paper kitchen towel. Emma tipped her head to one side, curiosity either for the familiarity Marta seemed to have in my space, or for what might be in the container.

'Marta makes the best custard tarts in the entire city of London,' I said.

'Aw. You too kind, James. Portuguese speciality,' Marta said, for Emma's benefit.

'Do you fancy having a look at those shops now, Emma?' I asked. 'We can leave Marta in peace to do her thing.'

Emma looked around as though searching for a corner that might need a good dust. Marta didn't have a tough job of it; I was certainly not a slob, awarding my living space, except for my office, the same treatment as my books.

'Um. I'll just pop up and tidy my room. I left a few things lying about,' said Emma.

'I leave your room if you like,' said Marta. 'It been closed for two weeks anyway. Will be clean as a pipe.'

'Whistle,' I said kindly.

Marta smiled at me and then looked at Emma who had paused, her hand on the bannister.

'Okay. I'll fetch my jacket and I'll be right with you,' said Emma.

As she rushed up the stairs, I eyed her jacket slung over the back of one of the dining chairs but didn't say anything. As I heard her bathroom door closing in the ensuite, I breathed out. She only wanted to go to the bathroom. How sweet. Too shy to say.

Marta fussed around the kitchen, putting things away and preparing for her usual jobs. I could tell she would prefer we weren't there. I was usually at work when she arrived to clean my flat.

I took Emma's jacket from the back of the chair, and leaned against the wall at the bottom of the stairs to wait for her. As Marta clattered about in the kitchen, I heard the water run in the sink in the bathroom upstairs, and over the combined noise of both women's tasks, thought I heard Emma speaking on her phone in a hushed, urgent tone. Who could she be speaking to? It was none of my business, of course, I knew nothing about her personal life apart from Despicable Nick, her parents – or mum – up north and her student colleagues who were due to come back to uni this week after an extended half term. I hoped she wasn't trying to find out whether her friend was already home – Mandy was it? I hoped the box-spring mattress, Egyptian cotton sheets and the piles of fluffy towels in her own personal bathroom would take preference over a lumpy sofa in a student flat.

She came out of her bedroom and our eyes locked as she came to the top of the stairs. Her gaze slid down to her jacket in my hand.

'Ah, there it is, thanks!' she said, with a bright smile. 'Sorry; loo.' She pointed back over her shoulder to justify her absence and came down the stairs.

'Grazie, Marta,' I called as we left the flat. 'See you soon!'

It was sometimes several weeks until I saw Marta again. But now I was, temporarily at least, without a job, I might be seeing her more often. It might be hard to hide the fact that I was now unemployed. I should keep my routine of seemingly going to work during the week to make my life appear perfectly normal even though I could survive on the stipend from my trust, and with Christmas approaching, I knew my parents would be bestowing the usual charitable bonus on me.

I crossed the courtyard to go down to the street and caught Emma looking back through the kitchen window, following Marta's movements.

'Marta's partner is the head chef at Casa do Frango, not far from where you were on Piccadilly, and they have a gorgeous little girl called Beatriz.' I felt compelled to supply this information, despite realising Emma may not know every classy restaurant in the West End after only a couple of weeks. It was almost as though she'd been spying on Marta whose shadow I could see brandishing some cloth around the stainless steel surround of my oven. I wanted to allay any worry that Marta might be competition for my affections on a higher scale.

Could it be Emma was actually jealous of our banter? Or was it something else?

'Okay, mademoiselle, let's shop.' I held out my arm, and Emma put her hand in the crook of my elbow as we synchronised our footsteps towards Covent Garden.

24

EMMA

We visited a couple of high street stores, some of which already had Christmas decorations in their window display – Victoria's Secret had a row of Love-Actually-inspired mannequins dressed in ruby red lacy camisoles edged with narrow strips of – hopefully – fake ermine and matching red and white Santa hats. The *Wet Wet Wet* cover song that had discovered a successful re-birth when the film had first come out was playing through the loudspeakers outside the shop. I glared at the display, finding it too glittery and kitsch, and chose not to go in.

In the shops we did enter, I could tell James felt awkward being amongst so many teenage girls, even though I could claim he was accompanying me as my boyfriend. Correction, Boy *Friend*. None of the other shoppers had male partners with them. James chose to wait by the door, close to the check-out, in case I found some articles of clothing I wanted to buy. But after some minutes I approached him with a frown.

'Let's go,' I said, 'That's my second aborted attempt at trying something on. Another shop with a gazillion girls waiting in line for the changing cabins. I can't keep you waiting all afternoon. Look at the queues for the tills! Where do they all get their money from?'

I almost added 'sugar daddies' to the end of that sentence, but the creepy irony of that remark would probably not have gone down well for either of us.

James suggested we go and find a café in Covent Garden where we could decide what to do next. The adjacent street was quieter, and something caught my eye in a shop window. We were in the middle of a row of some fine designer names, and I couldn't imagine what the price labels might be on some of these clothes. I turned to James, caught him looking with his eyebrows raised and shook my head.

'No, really, go ahead,' he said. 'You've seen something you like.'

'I couldn't. These prices will be off the scale!'

'I have to treat to you *something* this afternoon,' he said. 'A promise is a promise. I'll feel like a failure if we return home without a new outfit.'

'Okay, I probably won't *buy* it, but... let me have a look. No harm in trying it on.'

James held the door open as I entered the shop. I expected a snooty welcome from the staff, perhaps to look us up and down à la *Pretty Woman*, dressed as we were in our casual clothes. But the shrewd shop assistant's eyes slid from my face to the expensive-looking watch on James's wrist and she slithered seamlessly into sales mode. She was very observant and probably working on commission. She must have seen the film. I didn't want to prematurely disappoint her with the fact that although James was a handsome guy, I didn't think he was in the Edward Lewis league.

Nevertheless, he was shown to a plush comfy couch and offered some orange pekoe tea while the shop assistant whisked me away to the rails further back in the shop. I tried several things on and did some mix and matching in the cubicle with the shop assistant running around finding me the right colours and sizes. Half a teapot later, I skipped towards James.

'I know I said I wouldn't, but James, isn't this adorable?'

I was wearing an oversized-collar-and-cuff vintage-style shirt that I'd left untucked. It was tailored perfectly to my waist, and on the shop assistant's advice, I'd paired it with some wide soft-linen beige trousers.

James seemed shocked into silence. He stared at me, a small smile playing at his mouth. I knew I looked good in this outfit. I sashayed over to where he was sitting, bent down, put my hands either side of his face and kissed him, my lips slightly open. He closed his eyes, the contact of our mouths making him lean towards me. I stood up, hardly believing what I had just done, but when I saw him smile, I put my hand to my heart.

While he gathered himself, perhaps trying to work out what had just happened, I turned to the assistant and said I'd take the entire outfit, shoes and all. After James had paid, we left the shop with me swinging the carrier bag in one hand and holding James's arm with the other. The little smile on James's face lasted all the way back to his flat.

On the way, we popped into Zara, where I picked up a couple of long-sleeved V-necked cotton tops and a comfy pair of sweatpants at a considerably lower price. I wanted to prove I wasn't going to milk him for his offer of visiting every designer shop in the West End.

James said we should go out that evening. He wanted to woo me at Max's, the gourmet restaurant down the road from his place in the posh hotel.

'They're probably fully booked,' he said as he keyed in their number on his phone. 'At times like this, I'm happy to take advantage of a little nepotism. I think they keep a table free for people like my parents all the time.'

He'd mentioned before that his parents preferred to stay at the hotel rather than in his flat, although there was plenty of room. After seeing his fabulous flat, buying me clothes, and reserving a table at an expensive restaurant, he hadn't really talked much about his wealth. I wanted to ask, but thought it might sound crass if I did. It was imperative he didn't think I was some gold digger hoping to get her hands on his fortune.

We changed for dinner in our respective bedrooms, an anticipatory fizz crackling. James poured us a gin and tonic as his Café del Mar playlist wafted gently out of the integrated sound system throughout the flat. I applied a touch of mascara, some colour on my lips, and remembered kissing him in the clothes store that afternoon. Was it too soon for this? I didn't want to come on too strong, but I was sure he was game for it. I'd let the evening take its course. I knew he was attracted to me.

I hardly tasted the food at dinner, hoping I was reading all the signs right. The waiter picked up the vibe at our table and paid me extra attention, asking me, rather than James, if everything was to my taste. I was hoping to skip desert. Going from a shitty diet on the street to the richness of this menu was doing me in. But I couldn't resist Max's signature dessert – a perfectly baked *moelleux au chocolat* with home-made Cornish clotted ice cream. It was an exquisite, sensual culinary experience and James' eyes shone with the anticipation of what might come.

There was a chilly breeze blowing down the street as we left the restaurant. I clutched my coat at the collar with one hand and leaned into James, tucking my arm through the crook of his elbow. I didn't want this electric feeling to chill off in the breeze.

When we hurried into the flat, we tore our coats off in the hallway as the drop in temperature outside had made the underfloor heating kick in. But there was another heat I hoped James was experiencing. This hadn't been my plan, to start something so quickly, if at all, but the atmosphere was perfect.

'Are you tired?' he asked me tentatively.

'Are you kidding me?' I said as I slid my hand round the back of his neck and pulled him towards me for a deep kiss, making my intentions plainly obvious.

There was a brief hesitation as we silently considered whether to go to his room or mine at the top of the stairs. Our mouths trying to keep in contact, we stumbled past the entrance to my bedroom towards his, and the only trajectory left for us was to James's bed. As our clothes were strewn about the floor, I mentally declared that the evening couldn't have ended any better.

25

JAMES

The following morning, I left Emma reading in my bed with a fresh cappuccino and a slice of marmalade toast beside her. As hard as it was to leave her beautiful tousled hair and soft smooth skin between the sheets of my bed, it was time for me to absent myself for the day. As I showered and dressed, I hadn't wanted to break the magic by talking about where we might go in our relationship from here. There'd be plenty of time to discuss it later. Things had escalated extraordinarily quickly, but there'd been no awkwardness this morning, and I was hopeful this wasn't a one-night fling. We'd made each other feel good. *Really* good.

I took my laptop and made my way to the British library. The place was buzzing again after the eerily empty halls right after the pandemic, and I worried I wouldn't find a carrel. After I'd checked my backpack into my locker with my phone and put my laptop, notebook and pencils into a clear plastic bag, I took the escalator up to the second floor, knowing I would be completely distracted in Rare Books, so found a carrel in the corner of Manuscripts. I settled in for the day, jotting down ideas in my notebook, transposing others into a draft document on my laptop, and allowed a bubble of excitement to grow about finally writing the novel I'd been thinking about for the past several years. I paused only for a quick salad at lunch in the cafeteria downstairs, and was happy to return to the silence of the reading room, the only sound the occasional cough and sneeze, and the pleasant tick-tickety-tick of laptops making up a quiet concerto of creative urgency.

At the end of the afternoon, I made my way back to the flat in Seven Dials. Time to woo Emma a little bit more.

When I arrived home, she was lying on the sofa in the living room reading a signed copy of a Mick Herron novel.

'That's a good one,' I said. 'Delinquent spies and wry humour.'

'I see you have some classics in the cabinet,' she said, pointing to my collection.

'Most of them are first editions. All signed by the authors,' I said.

'Wow!' she exclaimed. 'Can I see *Great Expectations*? Charles Dickens. He's mega famous!'

I frowned a little at this unexpected crassness. *Mega* famous.

'Can you imagine?' she continued. 'He held that in his hands, used his pen to sign, probably blew the ink dry with a puff of his breath. There'd be a little of his DNA mixed with the spirit of the work he'd produced.'

I raised my eyebrows, changing my mind. So, a lover of books, too. We really would make the perfect couple.

'The glass of the cabinet looks delicate, but it's really quite strong,' I said.

'Are you worried about thieves? This place is tied up like Fort Knox,' she said.

'Not really. Sometimes being in a place like this right in the middle of the city, with so many people and a regular police presence in the area, ensures for a secure environment. Anyway, this isn't about fear of theft. The cabinet is made from a specially tempered glass that stops any damaging UV A and B rays entering the space. Even indirect light can damage these historic tomes. It's also humidity controlled. I want to keep them in as good a condition as possible. But I don't want to hide them in a safe. That would be a great shame.'

I didn't want to tell her how much that copy of *Great Expectations* had cost at auction. It would make me sound like such a snob, even if it was my father who had given me the book on my 18th birthday. I wasn't supposed to know its worth, but I'd later read about the sale in a Sotheby's publication and guessed it was my father's acquisition.

When Emma excused herself to visit the bathroom, I reached under the bookshelf near the TV to take out the key to the cabinet.

Before opening it, I smoothed a white cotton cloth onto the dining room table and took two pairs of clean cotton gloves from the drawer next to the cabinet. When Emma returned, I gave a pair to her, and when I'd unlocked and opened the door, slipped my hands into my own pair. Then I lifted the book out of its stand and laid it on the cloth on the table.

I showed Emma how to lift it in the crook of her hand, open the cover without bending the spine and to turn the pages without rubbing them or blowing them to split the pages. I wouldn't allow her to read the entire book anyway. I only wanted the book to remain outside the cabinet long enough for her to take a quick look. The most precious of those pages was the title page with Dickens' signature. Assuming she was afraid to do any damage, she asked me to open the book to his signature, and I knew she was giving the priceless piece the respect it deserved.

'That's so amazing,' she said. 'Are all these first editions? And are they all signed by the authors?'

'All of them,' I said, feeling a little sheepish. I'd be the only person my age in the entire city with such an extensive collection.

'That one doesn't look too healthy, the Somerset Maugham. Probably wouldn't touch it, looks like it might fall apart at even my delicate finger-tips.'

She pronounced Maugham's surname 'Mor-gum.' It was the first time I'd heard something that might have indicated she was covering some northern roots. I narrowed my eyes at her briefly then decided not to correct her. I didn't need to be showing her up. *Of Human Bondage* was indeed the most damaged of the editions in the cabinet, and anyone who wasn't interested in books might question what it was doing there in the first place. Despite its tiny yellow-brown pages crammed with a minuscule font and challenging line-spacing, some of which had disintegrated from the original coptic binding, the book was probably the most valuable in my collection, as it had been personally dedicated and given to Gerald, Maugham's secret lover, in the days when they'd been terrified of being discovered homosexuals. At that stage everyone was still talking about Oscar Wilde's trial, and fear of discovery was rife.

'I won't taint your treasures any more than necessary,' she said, taking off her cotton gloves as I put the Dickens back in the cabinet. 'Which one is your very favourite?'

'The Maugham,' I said, and that was the truth, not because I wanted her to know how to pronounce his name properly.

She raised her eyebrows imperceptibly.

'I know, the ugly duckling. But I love the story behind the dedication.'

'I think that font might be too challenging for me, even though I have good eyesight,' she said, flopping onto the sofa and picking up Herron's novel where she'd left it tented on a cushion. 'I'm enjoying this, though.'

'I do have book marks,' I said, locking the cabinet and handing her a leather bookmark. 'Even trade paperbacks deserve a little respect.' I hadn't wanted to admonish her for mistreating a novel of commercial fiction, but if our relationship was going anywhere, she would have to learn.

I pocketed the key, and would return it to its hiding place later.

26

JAMES

My mother called on my mobile late on Wednesday afternoon as I was on my way back from the British Library. I'd spent the day in Manuscripts, choosing a carrel in the same corner that was likely to become my fixed workplace for the duration of plotting and hopefully continuing to embark on the first draft of my novel.

Now that I was keen on the idea, I was less enthusiastic about finding a new job. I planned to talk to Stanley who was in charge of my trust, tell him I needed a new computer or something. He was always willing to sign off an extra grand or so when it was needed. I'd work around my father at Christmas.

Employment at the bookshop had been more of a hobby. The dream job would have been in one of those antique bookshops in Cecil Court. But I had enough unread books at home for the moment to keep my book obsession tamed.

I wasn't going to tell anyone I was writing a novel. For the moment, that included Emma, who would wonder where I found time to write when I was supposed to be at work every day. I knew too many authors who'd made the mistake in their early days of telling their friends and family. *Finished your bestseller yet?* and *Where can I buy it?* were questions that made any potential author quake in their boots before an agent had even taken a sniff at their manuscript.

So by the time I'd packed up and hopped on a bus taking me down Tottenham Court Road, it was the equivalent of the end of the working day.

'Not walking from work today, darling?' My mother could clearly hear I was in a form of public transport, the high-pitched whine of the vehicle a new addition to alert pedestrians, ensuring that with the development of electric vehicles, the London streets would still remain noisy, albeit less polluted. 'Is it because it's raining there? We've had such a lovely day up here. Your father has been clearing the lawns with his new sit-on leaf collector. I'm shocked at how quickly autumn has come on. It'll soon be Christmas.'

'Ah, yes, Mum, I wanted to talk about that.'

'Oh do tell me you're still coming to the chalet for more than just a few days, James. Have you confirmed the days off with the bookstore? I know you said you couldn't come during the whole of the busy shopping period, but surely you can come at least the day before Christmas Eve.'

'Yes, I think I can manage that. In fact, I may be able to wangle a couple of extra days off and come over earlier... but listen, I wanted to give you and Dad a head's up about something else.'

'A "heads-up" about what, James? That's such a horrible American expression.'

'I have a new girlfriend.'

'Oh, darling! Why didn't you say?'

He had an answer for that, but didn't voice it.

'I'd like you and Dad to meet her.'

'Of course! Why don't you bring her up to us for Sunday lunch this weekend? Your father's not so keen to come down to London at the moment. His leg is causing him a bit of bother. It gives way every now and then, and you know how averse he is to using his walking stick.'

Sunday lunch had become my bi-weekly obligation to touch base with my roots. I didn't dread it like some of my peers, who often avoided even speaking to their own parents. Mine might sometimes have been a little overbearing, but they meant well and there was genuine affection between us. Sometimes I even stayed the Saturday night before, especially if any of my old mates were around and a meet-up had been planned at the village pub.

I'd normally be horrified at the thought of taking a girlfriend to the family home where I grew up for their first meeting. However, time was of the essence if I wanted to win their affections for Emma before organising the Christmas trip. I intended to ask her if she wanted to come with us. I was sure she would love St Moritz. Who wouldn't? To some this might be happening awfully quickly, but I knew she'd have a good chunk of time off from uni at Christmas, and she'd already told me her mum was going on some Norwegian cruise to see the Northern Lights.

But I knew I couldn't just turn up to Switzerland and spring her on my parents. I'd never invited a girlfriend to our traditional alpine Christmas. Tristan was the only other person who held that honour, and that hadn't turned out too well in the run of things.

If I was going to hatch a plan, I wanted to give every part of it a chance to succeed.

27

EMMA

As we approached the outskirts of Suffolk on the train, I tried to remain confident about meeting James' parents. He was an only child, and I knew how much more precious parents were about their offspring when there was only one.

'Are you nervous?' James asked as we gazed at the countryside flashing by.

'Not really,' I said. 'If they produced a cool guy like you, they must be okay. Are you? Nervous, I mean?' I was unsure I would have been at all relaxed if he was the one going to meet *my* parents.

'No. They're going to love you.'

I smiled. He was so confident.

'Sunday lunch at the Marsh's Mansion usually involves a traditional roast,' he said. '

'"Marsh's Mansion,"' I said with a laugh.

'My nickname for the place. It's really just a rambling cottage.'

'I can't wait. Love me a Sunday roast,' I said, although there hadn't been many of those in my youth.

'The housekeeper has weekends off. We'll all be roped into a task in the kitchen. Part of the tradition since I was a kid.'

Just a rambling cottage turned out to be a gorgeous two-story thatched building that had enough windows and wings to warrant the word *mansion.* It sat amongst a couple of acres of beautifully tended gardens. The vision was straight from a chocolate box, although many of the summer blooms had now faded and various shades of gold tinged the surrounding trees.

'This week we have a fine cut of roast beef with mini homemade Yorkshire puddings, gravy, a creamy horseradish sauce, roast potatoes and two veg, the last from the garden,' declared Mrs Marsh after we'd been greeted at the door. 'With the lateness of the season, this week it will be curly kale fried lightly in the wok with pancetta – that can be James's task, and an oven-baked cauliflower cheese. You can help me with that, Emma. Frank will be in charge of the roast potatoes and carving the joint, as usual.' The amount of food spread over the kitchen counters ready for preparation looked enough to feed a family of eight. There was certainly enough to win over any waif of a girlfriend being introduced to their partner's parents for the first time.

James' parents seemed to be delighted he'd brought his new girlfriend home, and I could tell his mother wanted to ask a hundred more questions about me than might normally seem polite. She kept surreptitiously glancing at me, and I knew she was gauging my suitability for her only son. Judging by the expression on her face and the crows' feet lines accentuated by a rise in her sharp cheekbones, I thought that, so far, she approved.

'Where are your people from?' she asked at one point, and I smiled at the expression *your people* which could have been taken as a class insult. But the way Mrs Marsh said it so gently simply meant your *folk*, your *parents.* I chose to believe there was nothing derogatory at all in her statement. Nothing that made her sound like aristocracy looking down on a common being.

'My Dad was originally from Northumberland,' I said. 'He met my mum when he moved down to London for work – he was a computer programmer for IBM. I grew up in a village near Hertford. They moved back when I started uni. My Dad passed away a couple of years ago and Mum stayed up there.'

I winced inside, thinking this explanation sounded a little rehearsed. I wanted to share only the most essential information. I didn't really want to talk about my parents or my upbringing. James had never really been curious. He'd only coaxed limited information from me so far, and probably assumed that with my recent domestic situation, I wasn't ready to share all the gritty details.

'James tells me you're studying at Goldsmiths,' said Mrs Marsh. 'Such a fabulous university. I adore that sculpture on the roof of the main building. What's your subject?'

'I'm doing an MFA. I have a couple of ideas on the go. I haven't decided which will be my final project yet.'

I spent most of these supposed study hours in the spare room in James's flat, where I still kept my clothes in the wardrobe. It was still really *my* room, and we had this strange ritual of using our separate ensuite bathrooms before hitting the sack in James's room later, unless our frivolity started in his massive rain shower. I wanted him to think I wouldn't be so completely wooed immediately, that I was keeping one foot in the door for a sense of independence. I'd learned through experience this should keep James on his toes. I didn't want to appear too easy.

'You can move your stuff in here if you like,' he'd said, looking around his room after we'd been sleeping together for a week or so.

'Oh, it's okay,' I'd said. 'I can't be bothered to move everything now. It's all hanging and folded in the cupboards next door. And I'm fine doing my zoom lectures in there when I don't have to be in the studio at uni. Not disturbing you.'

It's not like I was taking anyone's space there. The elusive Tristan hadn't yet requested an overnighter, and I wanted James to be aware that under normal circumstances, he should recognise that our relationship was moving at breakneck speed.

When we'd finished lunch, James and his mum cleared the plates from the table and left his dad to chat to me. After Mrs Marsh's comment about "my people," I received only a mild interrogation from his father who had a gentle demeanour and seemed a little less draconian. He asked mostly about my studies and my art, and I asked him about the house and gardens. After a moment of small-talk, I excused myself to visit the bathroom.

As I was returning down the hallway to the dining room, I passed the kitchen and paused to watch as Mrs Marsh donned her oven gloves and removed a divine-smelling crumble – that I later learned was plum – from the oven. Purple juice had overflowed and burned the edge of the Pyrex dish. Despite my full stomach, the dessert smelled delicious. They had their backs to me and I paused by the door when I heard Mrs Marsh say: 'She's lovely.'

'Emma's had a hard time in her previous relationship,' said James. 'Her boyfriend wasn't very nice to her. He was quite violent actually. She moved out suddenly and didn't have anywhere to live. I told her she could stay in the spare room at Seven Dials.'

'So, you haven't known each other very long,' she said, stirring something in a small saucepan on the hob. 'But I can tell the romance is blossoming.'

James turned and I pulled back out of sight.

'The thing is, we're properly living together,' said James.

I imagined Mrs Marsh's cheeks rosy, from a little embarrassment and the heat of the oven.

'I would have said don't rush into things, that there's plenty of time to continue to get to know each other,' she said. 'But it looks like that advice would be redundant. Not that your father and I are any example to go by. I assumed everything was a bit different today. Everyone was throwing caution to the wind in the eighties. Apples never fall, and all that.' I heard the humour in Mrs Marsh's voice and imagined her giving James an admonishing, but affectionate, look.

I took a breath and walked into the kitchen.

'Can I help with anything?' I asked jovially.

James picked up a jug and poured steaming water that I presumed had been warming it down the sink, then handed it to his mum who tipped a silky-smooth sauce into it from her pan. Ah, custard. The traditional English ingredients continued.

'Here, you can take these,' said James, handing me a cloth around four stacked bowls from the warming rack above the stove. He put on the oven gloves and took the plum crumble into the dining room and Mrs Marsh followed, holding the custard jug ceremoniously in front of her.

Now that his parents knew the seriousness of our relationship, James seemed to relax even more. I knew he was glad he had "found" me. Everything was moving fast, according to his mother, but everything was falling together perfectly at the same time. As sweet as plum crumble and custard.

Next week he was going to tell his parents there would be one more guest for their traditional alpine Christmas. Everything was working out perfectly.

28

SALLY

In the lead up to the festive season, central London was full of joyful, noisy banter. On a Saturday in mid-December, a group of us decided to participate in the annual SantaCon parade. Instead of dressing in traditional Santa uniforms, we all decided to wear different Christmas suits. Even though it would exclude us from the official Father Christmas parade, it was fun to mosey along with the crowd, everybody becoming more unsteady on their feet as the event turned into more of a challenging pub crawl than an actual parade.

Stuart, Kate and Neil, my mates from Clapham, wore three-piece suits with different festive designs that made them look like well-wrapped Christmas parcels. I went dressed as a reindeer. Watching the parade was an absolute hoot. We must have nicked at least a dozen mince pies from the volunteers who'd brought them along for the Santas, and we laughed so hard at some of the costumes.

As the crowd moved through the West End, we found ourselves swept up Shaftesbury Avenue and veering off towards Seven Dials. I was aware we were in Jamie's neighbourhood. Strings of LED snowflakes were strung between the houses on Montgomery Street and the Crown on the corner. The pub was overflowing, patrons spilling onto the circular road around the obelisk. I couldn't see Jamie's flat windows from there, but it reminded me that it was now several weeks since he'd been fired from Waterstones. I'd left him a couple of messages on his mobile and was a bit pissed off that he hadn't returned my calls. He was still playing Words-With-Friends with me, one or two plays first thing in the morning, probably, like me, while he was sipping his first coffee or having his first ablution. But I never really liked that gaming app, as it was a different board layout from physical Scrabble, and I was missing our occasional in-person games.

I'd been to his place a few times to play, more frequently during the pandemic when we declared ourselves officially in each other's bubble. Since then, not so often, but after the appearance of the Girl in the Doorway in his life, not at all.

'Oh my God, hi!' said Jamie as I rolled a little drunkenly out of the Crown with the gang.

He'd come up Mercer Street with his new girlfriend, loaded with bags. They'd probably been Christmas shopping in Covent Garden together. Jamie was carrying a cardboard box containing some baked delight from Neil's Yard, and I tried not imagine their plans for a post lie-in breakfast the following morning.

'Are you with SantaCon? It's nuts out there. Hey, I like the costume, Sally Crime! Or should I say Madame Rudolf.' He pointed at my antlers and pulled gently on the red ball covering my nose. His companion was staring at my plunging brown and cream sweater which I'd topped with a neck scarf blinking with a string of LED stars to stop my boobs feeling too frozen.

I narrowed my eyes at the girl. This person had implicated herself in Jamie's life so completely over the past weeks, to the extent that he couldn't even reply to my texts. I felt a surge of unhealthy anger, especially as I could have done with his support, moral or otherwise, for what was going on in my family.

He seemed genuinely happy to see me though, so a desire to make some sarky comment was quashed by his obvious affection. I was sure he would have hugged me if he'd been on his own, but a glance at the girl at his side made us both realise that this somehow didn't seem appropriate.

'Great to see you!' I said. 'You remember these guys. Kate, Stu, Nolly. They were all with us in the Glassblower that time.' I felt compelled to bring a previous encounter to his girlfriend's attention, wanting her to know we'd had a history before he met her.

Stuart was wearing a bright red three-piece Christmas suit covered in miniature reindeer, and I remembered he'd been a bit of a sarcastic knob the night we'd been in the Glassblower. I hoped Jamie wouldn't retort with some clever comment that might make me look bad.

'Jamie, darling, how *are* you?' I asked, putting on an accent that sounded a little like a character in Ab Fab, and slinging my arm across his shoulder. I was far drunker than I realised. When a blob of beer froth from the bottle of Dos Equis I was clutching dribbled down Jamie's lapel, the girl at his side frowned.

'*Jamie*,' she stressed, obviously never having called him that. 'Does Sally know our good news?' Was that jealousy I detected in her tone? I couldn't work out how this made me feel. Jealousy, although not an attractive emotion, was nevertheless one that perhaps confirmed she didn't want to share him with anyone, even a female friend. This might not bode well for Jamie in the long run, and I hoped desperately he recognised that. I felt so petty and juvenile as this slipped through my mind. But it gave me a huge amount of satisfaction.

'Of course, forgive me. Sally, our good news is that we are now officially an item. Boyfriend and girlfriend. But you know that already. I told you at work a couple of weeks ago, right Sal?'

I raised my eyebrows, and as my beer-addled eyes locked onto Jamie's, I could feel a whole lot of psychic projection going on. What was he was trying to convey? I hadn't seen him for a couple of months.

'Jamie, what the—' As I was about to ask what the hell he was talking about, Stuart bumped into me in his drunkenness, and I didn't finish my sentence. My mind was clear enough to register that James had taken a deep breath of relief. I frowned.

'Come on, Sallywally, let's head to Leicester Square,' Kate slurred loudly. 'Last stop on the parade.'

As I swung back from pushing Stuart away with my hip, I caught another look from Jamie, eyes wide over the top of her hair, shaking his head almost imperceptibly. I felt his plea of silence and said no more. I wanted to ask a ton of questions. He was keeping some kind of secret. If he had he told her he was still working at Waterstones, then why?

As the SantaCon group moved off down Monmouth Street, Stu, Kate, Neil and I were swept along with them, and I looked back a couple of times over my shoulder towards Jamie.

'Merry Christmas!' I heard him call after us, before taking that wretched girl's hand and climbing the steps to his gate.

29

EMMA

'Aren't you going to miss your mum at Christmas?' James asked, our gloved palms meeting each other as we came out of *Carols for Christmas by Candlelight* at St Martin in the Fields. I'd been quietly surprised by James singing the descant to *Adeste Fideles*, impressed that he not only had a great voice, but that he knew the Latin version. But then he'd probably learned it at the private school he'd attended.

I wasn't sure whether the general public's singing was encouraged by the choir master, but judging by his skill at holding the tune, I was sure James would have fit right in on the other side of the conductor's baton. People even turned to look for the owner of the voice in the pews.

'Knowing she's content on her cruise is enough to keep me happy,' I said, pulling him close. 'I'm more envious about her seeing the Northern Lights than anything. It's not the first time we haven't spent Christmas together.'

I bit my lip, knowing James was dying to ask with whom I'd spent however many Christmasses in the past.

Jamie had broached the subject of me spending Christmas with them in Switzerland over the phone with his parents that afternoon. Stage one had been introducing me to them at Sunday lunch a couple of weeks back. They seemed delighted that I'd be accompanying him at Christmas, especially as it meant he'd be staying longer than just a couple of days, which I gathered had been the arrangement before he'd met me.

'I hope you don't mind us going on the train instead of flying,' I said.

'Of course not! I actually prefer train travel, though I usually fly to Switzerland. Paris gets in the way of a smooth journey.'

'Paris!' I exclaimed.

'Let's make it a stopover. I haven't been for ages,' he said. 'Anyway, with the speed of Eurostar and the TGV, it'll probably only take the same time to Zürich, what with waiting at busy airports and delays due to air traffic control. We'll have to get you over that fear of flying though, if we ever decide to go further afield to an exotic destination for a holiday.'

'You really don't think your parents mind?' I asked, ignoring the fact that he had implied our relationship would last into a future where more holidays would be on the cards. 'If I thought they were worried about me, I'd be happy to meet them again before we go.'

'No need. You charmed the socks off them,' he said, beaming. 'It's such a traditional family time for us. I always promise to spend Christmas with them, even if we don't see each other often at other times of the year. Will you get to see your mum at all over the holidays?'

'She's going to send me the money for a train ticket in the new year. I'll go and visit her during the study phase right before my art history exam. Not so many distractions for a bit of cramming.' I nudged him and laughed, my breath vapouring around my head on the chill night air. Did he already feel like a lovesick puppy in anticipation of a few days apart?

'I'll make it up to you with a proper white Christmas,' he said, 'Although that's not strictly guaranteed.'

'I'm so excited,' I said. 'Snow or no snow. It will be wonderful to visit the Alps. Thanks so much for inviting me.'

I tucked my arm around his waist and pulled him towards me.

'Do you want me to organise a ski instructor for you in St Moritz?' he asked. 'I'm a patient teacher, but I know some people don't like their partners or members of their family telling them what to do. Learning to ski is a bit like learning to drive.'

'I went on a school ski trip once,' I said. 'What are those mountains in Scotland called? The Corngrams or something? Not very nice weather, but I do remember learning a bit of skiing. Hopefully it's like riding a bike; you never really forget the basics.'

Jamie frowned before continuing.

'Well, if you do decide you'd like some official guidance, let me know. The ski school gets pretty booked up at Christmas. It's the busiest couple of weeks of the season, but I don't want to stress you out. There'll inevitably be queues for the lifts and crowds on the slopes. The resorts at lower altitude usually don't have decent snow around Christmas, so many locals head up to St Moritz where the weather is colder.'

'That's okay. We can just hope there'll be snow.'

'Even if they don't have much, they keep the pistes open with the help of snow canons,' he continued. 'There's guaranteed snow, even though it might be man-made. The only way there'd be none at all is if there's a heatwave. Climate change has affected a lot of other resorts, but the Graubünden is the eastern-most canton in Switzerland, and is the ice box of the country.'

I bit my lip. He was beginning to sound like a travel brochure. It would be nice, though, to have a snowfall right before Christmas to transform the town into a scene worthy of a Christmas card. I guessed he felt compelled to impress me with his knowledge and excuses, stressing that we had no influence over Mother Nature.

'Honestly, I trust your teaching ability, James. I've never been to the Alps. Is it really as beautiful as all the posters and cards say it is?'

'It's glorious,' he said. 'Since Dad bought the chalet when I was a kid, we've been going there every year for Christmas, except once during the pandemic. Much like Mum's Sunday roast, we have a traditional English Christmas lunch every year on the 25th. The locals all celebrate on Christmas Eve, the 24th. Mum even calls the *Metzger* – the butcher – in the village several weeks beforehand to make sure he's logged our turkey order. You'll still get your fair share of cheese fondues and alpine dishes. I wouldn't want you to miss out on the full Alpine experience.'

'And don't forget the shed-load of Christmas chocolate.' I winked and laughed. 'But look, the ski teacher thing, I don't want to hold you back. You must know loads of people who are far more expert than me to go skiing with. Especially as you only get to do it a couple of weeks in the season.'

'It would be nowhere near as fun to ski without you. It'll be my pleasure to spend every snow-filled day with you.'

I almost laughed out loud. That sounded a bit cutesy, even for James.

'But don't you have people you meet up with every year?' I asked.

'Not many of the old crew come out for Christmas any more – the guys of my generation with their own kids tend to go to their in-laws in the UK – spending it with the mother's family seems to be the norm.' he nudged me, perhaps letting me know I was far from the norm. Or that he thought we might one day spend Christmas with my family. I swallowed, while he continued: 'They travel out at half-term in February or March with their families when the slopes are less crowded. There's also a better chance of fresh snow and better availability of ski school places for their kids.'

'How many people do you know out there with properties? Sounds like it's quite the community.'

'My parents have acquaintances there who go way back. I'm not sure their wealth has been earned from entirely honest means or whether they even declare all their taxes in the UK, but that's a different conversation and one we'll turn a blind eye to.'

'They'll get their just deserts. Karma, and all that,' I said, and when James raised his eyebrows, I cleared my throat. 'Will we meet any of them?'

'Oh, I assure you these people are nothing exciting to write home about. The endless rounds of Christmas cocktails have become a little tiresome over the years. My parents' friends will remind me how small I was the last time they saw me. They don't seem to remember any of the twenty intervening years when I was busy growing up with their own sons and daughters. I seem to be the only one who consistently accompanies my parents year after year. But although some of these gatherings have become a bit boring, it pleases my parents no end that I still go with them. And it'll be great to have you there with me. We can always make our excuses to leave early. So yes, you'll get to meet some of them. And I shall enjoy ripping them to shreds afterwards with you. My parents are sometimes a little blinded by tradition.'

He smiled and patted my knee, and I swallowed at the prospect of wealthy traditions.

30

JAMES

'You're living at James's place then?' Tristan couldn't keep the hint of incredulity out of his voice, and I knew what was running through his mind.

I'd had a tendency over the years to enter rather too quickly into 'serious' relationships. Emma and I had surely beaten the record with this one. Since becoming a responsible adult, Tristan was always going on about taking things slowly.

'For the moment, anyway,' said Emma.

I'd managed to squeeze in a double dinner date with Tristan and his girlfriend Savanna between his return from Australia and our imminent departure for the Alps. I'd wanted to introduce them to Emma, as my new girlfriend.

When Emma excused herself to go to the ladies, Tristan turned to me.

'Blimey, James, you're rushing into this thing pretty damned quickly.'

'Don't make me remind you about Christmas and our subsequent skiing trip five years ago. Jaegermeister bombs.'

It was all I needed to say. Tristan grimaced and then laughed, remembering the chalet girl in St Moritz he'd declared to have immediately fallen in love with.

Savanna, an American he'd met through his job in the city, shook her head in confusion and put her hand on my arm. 'She seems… secretive, somehow,' she said. 'Be careful, James. I mean, you hardly know her, right?'

I raised my eyebrows. It would likely take a few weeks for the old *rushing into things* comments to cease. 'I don't think she's being secretive. I'm not sure what you mean.'

'Hmm. I hope she's not a gold digger. It would turn anyone once they see the inside of your place.'

I frowned. 'I don't know how that would have been possible. She didn't know where I lived until I offered her a place to stay. I don't think so, Savanna, but thank you for your concern.'

'You know, I always thought you'd end up with that Scrabble-playing girl you worked with at the book shop,' she said.

'Sally Crime,' said Tristan, laughing. 'Me too, actually. She's a laugh and a half.'

'We're just good friends,' I said.

My thoughts had turned to Sal a couple of times recently; I hadn't texted her in a while. And Savanna's comment heated my cheeks with a wave of guilt. But Sal hadn't texted me either, and she was usually the one to nudge me to say she was waiting for me to retaliate with a fight-back word game. I remembered running into her outside the Crown near my place with her troop of SantaCon pals and I could tell she'd been a bit pissed off that I hadn't called her.

When Emma re-joined us at the table, Sal wasn't mentioned any more, but I promised myself I'd peruse the book shops in Cecil Court for a Christmas present for her. It was mean of me to ignore her just because I had a new girlfriend, but the vibes between Sal and Emma told me they were never going to be best friends.

'Jamie told me where you guys met,' said Tristan, smiling at Emma. 'You might not want to talk about it, but I'm so curious. What was it like, living rough on the street?'

'Tris,' I said. 'This isn't the Spanish Inquisition!'

'It's okay, it's history now,' said Emma, turning to Tristan. 'It's not like I was sleeping out. I was doing some street art – 3D chalk drawings – to try and earn some pocket money during my autumn break. I knew it wasn't going to be forever, obviously.' She looked at me and placed her hand on my thigh.

'You mean you were sure you were going to get swept off your feet by a handsome bookseller?' Tristan asked jokingly.

'Naturally,' she said, laughing.

'Where would you have gone if James hadn't offered you a place to stay?' asked Tristan. I flashed him a look. We were entering sensitive territory now. I didn't want her to have to recall the terror of her partner's abuse and the worry of not knowing where to go.

'I'm not sure. Hadn't really thought about it at that stage. I would've probably gone to stay with my mum for a while. I can do most of my courses online, since the pandemic. Not everyone attends lectures, even now, although my studio work would have been tricky. But James offered before I had to consider that.'

'Where does your mum live?' asked Tristan.

'Up North. Yorkshire. Middle of nowhere. Not sure I'd want to be up there. I could also have looked into student digs, although there aren't many rooms going in the middle of the semester.'

I was sure Emma had said her mother lived in Northumberland, but I must have been mistaken, and didn't want to call her out on a geographical error – she'd probably said Northumbria. I knew a couple of stalwarts who lived in the northeast who still called it that, even though they most definitely lived in Yorkshire.

31

JAMES

We took advantage of our journey through Paris for a night's stopover on our way to Switzerland and checked into a charming boutique hotel in the *Quartier Latin*. After a delicious meal at the *Tour d'Argent* which I'd reserved at the same time I'd booked our train tickets a couple of weeks ago, we walked hand-in-hand along the left bank of the Seine. I'd taken out some Euros from the ATM when we'd arrived at the Gare de Nord, but my supply of notes for the homeless had run out by the time we passed the *Musée d'Orsay*.

Emma shivered and I pulled her close to me.

'Let's head back as soon as we've seen the tower,' I said, and she nodded.

The earlier cold drizzle had stopped, and a light mist lay over the city, creating soft globes of gold around the street lamps.

'The City of Light is living up to its name,' I said, as we reached a curve in the Seine and stopped to stare at the lights frantically sparkling along the vertical length of the Eiffel Tower.

'Also, the City of Love,' said Emma, putting her arms around the back of my neck and pulling me towards her for a long kiss.

'Hmm. That was certainly illuminating,' I said, as we pulled away from each other to gaze at the Christmas lights along the river.

'Did you know it's called the City of Lights because Paris was the first city in Europe to illuminate its streets with gas in the nineteenth century?' she said.

'I did not,' I lied. 'Did you know it's called the City of Love because of this?' I pulled her in for another kiss and felt a joyful lightness in my chest. Emma had asked to take the train to Switzerland because of her fear of flying, and although I would have preferred to take the plane to get to Zürich faster, I was now pleased we'd had a chance to overnight in Paris.

We returned along the river on the right bank, past the Tuileries Gardens and the vast buildings of the Louvre. As we crossed the bridge to the island where the Notre Dame stood in all her shining new glory, having recently shed the scaffolding from its years of restoration, I felt the tiny feathery chill of a snowflake on my cheek. Emma held out her hands and her tongue simultaneously. She looked so happy, so excited, so beautiful. I wanted nothing to burst this bubble.

'Next stop, Switzerland,' I said, after we'd made love that night in our Parisian room. We'd left the curtains open. Our window faced the Île de la Cité with a partial view of Notre Dame. One would be forgiven for thinking that the building had never suffered the effects of a devastating fire a few years before. With Emma in my arms, I looked forward to our own bright new future.

Mum and Dad had already flown in to Zürich and taken the train to St Moritz a few days before to open up the chalet and prepare for Christmas. Snow was forecast not only in the mountains, but also at lower altitude, and although the roads would have been well cleared, neither of them were as confident as they used to be about driving in wintry conditions, even on the lanes in Suffolk. Dad now left his Swiss car permanently at the chalet and unless I was to be their chauffeur, they preferred to travel on the efficient train system.

When we changed from the French TGV to Swiss Rail in Zürich, we could already feel that the temperature had dropped. Before we boarded our connection for the east of Switzerland, we visited the Christmas market under the cavernous roof of the Zürich *Hauptbahnhof*. Clusters of wooden pop-up chalets surrounded the traditional Christmas tree at the centre with thousands of chocolate Lindor balls hanging from its branches. The stalls offered a variety of sweets, cookies and traditional crafted gifts.

I knew Emma didn't have much money, so I purchased a *Stollen* cake and some *Güetzli* – Christmas biscuits – to give to my mother as a gift when we arrived in St Moritz. I bought Emma a soft cashmere scarf to keep the wind from chilling her neck. We drank a cup of warming *Glühwein* – mulled wine – before hurrying to the platform for our onward connection.

The train took us along the southern shores of Lake Zürich, whitecaps visible on the anthracite surface of the water, even from the elevated position of the railway. The mountains in the distance were shrouded in snow clouds. Perhaps not the sun-glittered slopes of my ski dreams, but this was better than the slanting rain of recent years around Christmastime. I hardly wanted to utter the words "climate change" to someone who'd just experienced the coldest days of her life on the London streets. As though on cue, Emma shuddered and I put my arm around her shoulder.

'Looks freezing out there,' she said, tucking her body into my side.

Flakes resembled missiles of snow as they sped past the window of the moving train, restricting the view of the mountains ahead.

'It's getting heavier the further east we travel,' I said. 'My wish to give you a white Christmas might be coming true.'

The train to St Moritz took a little longer than usual, having to slow down as the blizzard kept swirling outside. We weren't the only ones heading to the mountains for the Christmas week. The carriage was crowded, and the buzz of excited conversation added to the festive atmosphere. Emma was glued to the views of the mountains. She seemed mesmerised by the steepness of the craggy summits as we entered the canton of Graubünden.

At one point Emma's phone beeped. She took it out of her jacket and looked briefly at the screen before turning it off and putting it back in her pocket. I wanted to ask who it was. Did I have the right to do that? We were, after all, in a committed relationship. But I didn't want to appear nosy, or worse, insecure.

'Bit foggy here,' I said instead. As the train climbed, we were enshrouded by low cloud and my spirits fell a little. 'Shame. It's a beautiful lunar-type landscape up here. Snow can sometimes drift so deep – despite the protective fences – the valley sometimes gets cut off.'

Almost as bad as rain at Christmas was the threat of fog, which to be fair was quite rare at this altitude. But I hoped the poor visibility meant the clouds were rising, getting ready to dump more snow on the alps.

Once we arrived, I hailed a taxi outside the station. On snow-packed roads, we drove up above the lake, which had only just started to freeze, past the famous red tower of the Badrutt's Palace Hotel. The road curved past the iconic Chesa Futura with its sensuous flowing design and shingled exterior. We turned on to the Via Tinus where there were a line of chalets with views down to the village and the mountains on the other side of the valley. Dad had hired some electricians to put a string of LED lights up along the pitched roof of the chalet some years ago, and many of the neighbours in our cluster of chalets had followed suit. With the weather still socked in, we arrived just as the lights were turned on, making for a romantic welcome.

I paid the taxi driver and keyed the code into the heavy oak front door to let us in.

'We're here!' I yelled, as we tumbled into the warmth of our Swiss chalet.

32

EMMA

The chalet has the same gadgets as you have at your flat,' I said, as James placed our luggage in our room.

I picked up the remote and pointed it at the computer display on the wall by the door to turn on the lights in the walk-in wardrobe, in preparation for unpacking our bags.

'I suggested they install the same equipment as me, as I knew I was inevitably going to be the one who had to come over here to show them how to use it. Dad's mastery of the German language and the electrician's knowledge of English were as equally confusing to each other. At one point, Dad called me to say he'd locked himself and my mother in and couldn't work out how to open any of the doors.'

We were in a room on the top floor that I guessed was James's usual room, although there weren't many personalised objects to confirm this. The exposed larch beams were aged to a pleasing burnished warmth. The brushed oak-planked floor was warm underfoot, combining traditional chalet architecture with modern luxuries.

'Where's the button that delivers our cocktails and turns down our bed,' I said, sidling up to James with my hand on his chest and pulling his face to mine.

James took the remote from me and dimmed the lights, kissing me.

'I wonder whether we could be excused for twenty minutes while they wait for us downstairs,' he said huskily.

'Darlings!' his mother called with impeccable timing from the bottom of the stairs. 'Before you unpack, come and have a hot chocolate by the fire. Frank has just made some frothy milk with his new coffee machine. An opportunity not to be missed!'

'Do you think she has a hidden camera up here? That was uncanny!' I laughed.

'We'll pick this up later,' James said, kissing me one more time. 'Be right down!' he called through the gap in the door.

'You don't feel weird about doing it in the same house as your parents?'

'To be honest, it would be a first, but no, their room is far enough away from ours, and it's somehow not the same as if we were at home in the UK. The Suffolk place is a creaky old house and you can hear every little squeak. This one's a solid Swiss wooden chalet. Well insulated,' he said with a wink.

'Come on, James,' I said, pulling him by his arm. 'Let's not keep your mum and dad waiting. I get the feeling they're very excited to have you here.'

James helped his mother bring through a tray of hot chocolates and a plate of the sliced *Stollen* cake I had proudly presented to her earlier. We sat by the fire, the flames of which ducked every now and as the wind whipped down the chimney with an occasional gentle moan.

'It's proper snowing outside now, James, look!' I said, pointing out of the window.

The light outside had turned a deep royal blue against the blanket of snow now covering the balcony and the sloping garden in front of the chalet, with the twinkling lights of town below barely visible through the blizzard. James's excitement was contagious. He was loving this, showing me his little piece of paradise in the Alps.

'It's a long time since we've had heavy snowfall like this before Christmas,' said his mum.

'Forecast is for 30 centimetres,' said his dad. 'I presume you young ones will be out on the slopes tomorrow. Have you sorted rental equipment for Emma?'

'I called ahead with her measurements,' said James. 'Hopefully they won't be too busy in the morning. I'd go down there now, but I don't feel like leaving the house,' he said, reaching for another slice of cake.

'Off you go and unpack, then,' said Frank Marsh. 'By the time you come back down it'll be cocktail hour. Nothing like a round of *Glühwein* for your first night here.'

James' cheeks dimpled with a suppressed smile and a twinkle in his eye. I knew exactly what he was thinking, and hoped we'd still have time to unpack before his father called us down for Happy Hour.

33

JAMES

Ski passes and rental equipment for Emma sorted, we made our way to the lift station where there were thankfully not too many people queuing. Many of the die-hard skiers had caught the early lifts to the upper slopes to make the first tracks in the best of the powder snow.

We took the mountain funicular to Corviglia where I knew of a particularly wide, easy blue slope for Emma to practise her beginner turns. She did a stellar job of reconnecting with her childhood ski abilities and made an excellent student. By lunchtime she had quickly progressed from a beginner's snow plough to some closed, almost parallel turns, and seemed to have no fear of the slope.

'You're a natural. I wasn't expecting such amazing progress,' I said as we took the lift back to the top. 'A model student.'

'That's because I have such a fabulous teacher,' she said, grinning.

After a few runs, her style improving at each descent, we took a break for something to drink at *La Marmite* at the Corviglia ski station.

'First day, I'm a bit knackered to be honest,' she said after we'd done a few more runs. 'I wouldn't mind going back to the chalet and trying out that hot tub on the terrace. But can we come back here tomorrow? I really like this slope for practising.'

'Of course! It's a good gradient, and not too short.'

'I can make my way home if you like, and you can ski on, do a few fast runs on the harder slopes. I feel like I'm holding you up from something way more exciting.'

'I'm happy to come back with you,' I said, although her offer was very tempting. We didn't often experience conditions like this.

After a soak in the hot tub at home, Emma helped me make a traditional Swiss *Älplermagronen* – a rich macaroni cheese – and the four of us stayed in for a quiet evening. There were plenty of Christmas parties coming up.

'You've kept this recipe quiet,' Emma said. 'This is delicious, I would have insisted on this every night at home in your flat if I'd known.'

'*Our* flat,' I said quietly, giving her an affectionate nudge.

'James has never been known for his culinary expertise,' said my mother. 'This, though, is a recipe we can always rely on him for. I see a lot of elbow pasta in your future, young lady.'

'Which is what I have been trying to avoid over the past months. So many lunchtime sandwiches,' I said, patting my stomach. Apart from a lot of walking around the city, and today's skiing, I hadn't been doing much sport recently.

I was delighted, however, that Emma seemed to be endearing herself to my parents.

On the second day, the sun still shone out of a cerulean blue sky. This was the stuff of ski posters and winter dreams. We could hardly have been blessed with better conditions. We graduated to a slightly more challenging and longer *piste* with a chairlift to take us back to the top, which Emma declared was like skiing from your living room couch.

We stopped mid-morning at a *Ski-Hütte*, and as I was lining up to collect our cappuccinos from the outside drinks counter, I recognised someone I knew wearing the red and black uniform of the ski school, talking to a couple of skiers at the entrance to the terrace. His ski helmet hung on its strap in the crook of his elbow. I might not have noticed him had he been wearing it with his goggles on. As the two skiers turned away from him and collected their skis from the racks next to the restaurant, I called out to him.

'Hey, Klaus!'

He hesitated. Had he heard me? I was torn whether to abandon the coffees or try and chase him down with tray in hand. But luckily he turned and saw me across the terrace. I carried the tray, trying not to spill the drinks as I clomped over the rough wooden flooring covered in rubber mats with my ski boots. I put the tray down on the end of a table, excusing a random couple sitting there, and grabbed Klaus in a bear hug.

He grinned back. 'Hey James. Long time.'

'It must be five years since I've seen you! How's life? Still at the ski school I see.'

'*Ja*, well, it pays the bills,' he said. 'Only taking on private clients now though, so I can pick and choose my days. I only just started for the season. This is the first big snow, and the first tourist invasion.'

'I'm with someone,' I said, pointing my chin vaguely in the direction of where Emma was sitting on the terrace. 'Can you join us?'

Klaus's eyes narrowed slightly. 'I... yeah, sure. But I won't get anything,' he said, nodding towards the drinks counter. 'I don't have much time. How long are you here?'

'Just for a week over Christmas. We should at least swap numbers. Mate, you're looking great. Haven't changed a bit! There must be a way we can meet up over the next few days or so?'

Klaus nodded. I picked up the tray and he followed me to the table. Emma looked up as we approached and her eyes widened almost imperceptibly. Klaus did have that effect on a lot of people. He was tall and broad-shouldered with dark blond hair, always a little sun-bleached, enhancing his ruggedly handsome looks. I experienced a dart of concern that Emma might find him instantly more attractive than me, but I needn't have worried. She placed her hand on my thigh and gave it a squeeze as I sat next to her. Klaus sat opposite us.

'Emma, this is Klaus, an old friend,' I said.

'Nice to meet you, Emma.' He held out his hand and Emma pulled off her ski mitten to shake his.

'Likewise.' She hesitated. 'How do you know each other?'

'We skied together as kids,' I said. 'Christmas holidays and half term with a gang of kids over from the UK. Sometimes we'd get into to a bit of trouble. Fun trouble.'

'When he says we used to get into trouble together, he really means he used to get *me* into trouble,' said Klaus. 'Making me skip school in March as our holidays never coincided with the English break. Used up all my school joker days with this guy, and then they persuaded me to skip classes for the rest of the time.'

'Your English has really improved,' I said. 'You must have had some good instruction from those English ski bunnies.'

Klaus's eyes met Emma's and they smiled at each other. And just for a moment my world tilted.

'If you were such ski buddies all that time ago, you must find a time to go out together,' Emma said turning to me, and what I thought was a spark between them was snuffed out when she kissed me on my cheek and grabbed my hand. 'I don't need to go out skiing every single day, and I don't want you to miss out on a hardcore ski.'

I had resigned myself to the job of ski teacher for the week, but now she was offering to let me have a day on the black runs, the prospect was exciting.

'Well, that would be great... if Klaus is free?' I said, turning to him.

'There's another dump of snow announced for the day after tomorrow. Why don't we touch base on Christmas Eve? I'm free then. Most of my potential clients will be celebrating Swiss Christmas with their families. There could be some great powder.'

'That works fine for me,' said Emma. 'Your mum asked if I'd like to go to the Glatschin Christmas market that day. I think it would be a good opportunity for us to... bond.'

I raised my eyebrows and gave her a smile. This was music to my ears.

'Awesome,' said Klaus. 'Let's swap numbers. We'll try and get on the first lift. Station opens at 8:00, but they'll be queuing for the train from 7.30. Send me a text to confirm in the morning, in case avalanche danger is too high.'

'Look forward to it! See you the day after tomorrow.'

34

JAMES

As predicted, the weather closed in again on the afternoon before Christmas Eve. Emma and I had taken the train down from Corviglia just as the first flakes began to fall and spent the rest of the afternoon by the fire in the chalet roasting chestnuts and listening to Christmas songs on Spotify.

The neighbours in the chalet next to ours came in for a raclette dinner in the evening. Andrea was originally from the Engadine Valley. She was married to a retired watch maker and their permanent home was in Schaffhausen in the north of Switzerland. They'd come for Christmas with their two adult daughters who both worked in Zürich. Emma seemed to be getting on well with them by all accounts. They were roughly the same age as us.

When the guests had gone after dinner, I helped my mother clear the table and load the dishwasher in the kitchen.

'Thanks so much for offering to take Emma to the Glatschin market tomorrow,' I said as I popped a leftover raclette potato into my mouth before rinsing a glob of stubborn melted cheese off a plate.

'I didn't offer. She asked me. Well, sort of.' She looked up at the wooden beam directly above the sink with a frown, as though trying to work out who had actually asked who.

'Andrea from next door asked me, oh I don't know, the day before yesterday, I think. Ron and Deirdre down the lane are arriving tomorrow and you know how Ron hates that kind of thing. The three of us texted each other and arranged to go. I think Emma overheard and asked if she could come too. And you'd organised to ski with... Klaus was it? How is that boy? I don't think we've seen him for at least ten years. Isn't he the one you gave all your Christmas presents to one year?'

I bit my lip and nodded. I'd forgotten about that. When we were kids, and allowed to ski on our own as long as we stuck together, a group of us met Klaus on the slopes one Christmas. He'd won a weekend ski pass at a local lottery event and was skiing by himself. His friends hadn't wanted to go; locals would usually wait until the quiet month of January with optimal snow to hit the slopes. Klaus showed us all the best places to ski, where the best snow conditions could be found, and the lifts with the fewest queues. After the two days on his pass were up, he said he couldn't afford to ski anymore, so we paid for the rest of his week and took him under our wing, shouting him après-ski hot chocolates. We met up almost every Christmas after that, clubbing together to buy his ski pass and ply him with beers instead of hot chocolates by the time we reached our teens. Helmets and goggles were a great way of hiding the identity of an under-age après-ski drinker.

I'd often caught him looking enviously at those who advertised their wealth on holiday. The glitzy skiers who came to St Moritz because that's where the money was. He'd told me his dad was a concierge at the Carlton and never had any time off as he had to work extra hours to feed the family, and his mum was the daughter of a farmer who hated the snow. I figured he'd escaped the mountain when he'd left school as we didn't see him again once we were adults. So I was surprised he'd returned to become a ski teacher, but I was happy to have the opportunity to ski with him again.

'Well, thanks anyway Mum, for looking after Emma. The snow should be fantastic tomorrow on the slopes.'

'I'm sure you'll be fed up with *Weihnachtsgüetzli* and *Glühwein* before the holiday is over,' she said, referring to the biscuits and mulled wine ubiquitous at all Christmas markets. 'You go off and have a good ski with your friend. It's lovely that you're still in contact.'

Klaus and I met as promised at the Corviglia funicular station and were amongst the first to board the train. We clutched take-away coffees in one hand with our skis and sticks tucked under the other arm, and a buttery *Gipfeli* – croissant – stuffed in each of our mouths.

Without needing to ask each other, when we reached Corviglia we headed to the cable car that would take us to Piz Nair at over three thousand metres. The sun was shining again, although the wind had picked up. The cable car lurched from time to time in the gusts. Spindles of ice crystals winked in the air against a sky so deep a blue we felt like we were on the edge of the stratosphere.

'Come,' said Klaus as we exited the lift station, and I turned to follow him.

A seed of concern niggled when I saw the yellow and black tape pulled across the top of one of our favourite runs snapping in the wind.

'It'll be okay if we keep away from the cornice,' said Klaus. 'Are you wearing a Recco?'

I nodded, pointing to the tag on my sleeve showing I had a detector in my jacket.

'Okay. Let's go!'

'Wait, Klaus...' But it was too late. He'd gone.

I pushed off and dropped into line beside him, the feather-light powder cushioning our turns as we bounced in synch down the slope. When we reached the bottom of the first gulley, we turned to admire our identical serpentine tracks.

'That was... amazing!' I said, breathing hard. Any fear of an avalanche had been replaced by the adrenaline high of that first satisfying descent.

'Let's get back up there. Got to do that again. Before it gets skied out.'

I was less nervous about ducking under the avalanche danger tape the second time round. This time Klaus moved over to the left hand side of the gulley, and again I dropped in beside him to mirror his turns.

About half way down, I realised he was no longer beside me. I was almost at the bottom of the runout, in the most dangerous spot on the mountain should the snow slip. I skied to where I thought I'd be safe and turned to look back. Klaus was more than half way back up the slope. He'd stopped on an almost vertical ridge at the side of the gulley. He seemed to be waiting for me to acknowledge his descent.

I tore off my glove with my teeth and pulled my phone out of my pocket, pressed the video icon and waved my stick above my head. Klaus teetered on the ridge, stamping the snow down so he could make himself a platform from which to launch himself down the slope.

'Come on, come on,' I whispered, aware I was standing in a vulnerable area.

I looked away from the image on my phone to the top of the gulley. A crack appeared and a slab of snow moved, slowly at first then gathering momentum. The soft *whump* of the detaching snow reached my ears seconds later. I wanted to shouted up to Klaus, but my glove was still shoved in my mouth. As I hurriedly turned my skis downhill, I saw Klaus out of the corner of my eye skiing the safest line down from the ridge. I stuffed my phone back into my pocket, even as I was turning, and with my glove still in my mouth, urged my skis to pick up momentum so I could traverse to the side of the gulley.

I couldn't see the cloud of powder behind me, but felt the pressure of air at my back as the avalanche gained on me, and I prayed I could make it to safety. But like a wave closing out on an unsuspecting surfer, it caught me. I was briefly surprised at the feeling akin to a bully pushing me in the small of my back. And then I was tumbling.

Both my skis clicked off and one arm wrenched as my ski pole caught in the drift. Time slowed down and yet everything happened in the blink of an eye. I was aware that a powder avalanche was the most dangerous of all. Anyone caught in one might not suffer great injury, but the greatest mortal danger was the inhalation of fine powder snow crystals.

I was saved, ironically, by the glove still clamped in my mouth. It covered my face and meant snow wasn't forced up my nose and into my lungs. I had a miniscule pocket of air between my face and the glove that prevented me from effectively drowning.

Once the slip had settled, I was aware of a deep hue of blue light above me, relieved that I must not have been buried very far underneath. My goggles had torn off in the fall and my eyes were stinging from freezing snow crystals. The first thought was that I hoped the goggles were still attached to the back of my helmet. That was followed up rapidly with the hope that I hadn't broken any bones.

'*Scheisse!*' Klaus's voice was muffled somewhere above me.

I reached up with my arms, the burden lessening as snow slid off the sleeves of my ski jacket. The brightness of the sun blinded me temporarily.

'Hey, James. That was close,' said Klaus, leaning over me. 'Come on, we don't want to lose you just yet, *Kumpel*.'

I reached out to grab his hand and he pulled me up.

'Sorry, mate, I didn't manage to get a photo,' I croaked.

He laughed. 'Let's try and find your skis. Just a small slip. The perils of fresh powder.'

I looked around. That small slip had come from the top of the gulley near where he'd been standing on the ridge. The snow had fanned out into a delta. Not such a small slip, and one that could still have suffocated me. I spotted the tip of one of my carving skis sticking out of the snow about five metres above me. I put my glove back on, my hand red raw with the cold. Both ski poles were still attached to my wrists by their straps, but one was bent at an angle. I used them both to pull myself up the slope towards my ski, and used the one that wasn't bent to probe the snow around me for the other ski.

'Here is it!' called Klaus, digging with his gloved hands and then pulling out my other ski a few metres away.

He didn't seem at all concerned that he'd led me into an avalanche. I stopped myself from saying anything. I was an adult and could have used my better judgement not to follow him in the first place. It also reminded me that not every season had been fun and games on the ski slopes in our wild past.

'You ready for another run?' he asked as I placed my skis perpendicular to the slope and tapped the snow from my boots before clicking into the bindings.

'I don't think so, Klaus. That shook me up a bit.'

'Are you okay? Nothing broken. Bones, I mean,' he said, eyeing my pole.

'I'm okay. My pride is a little bruised. If I'd been paying more attention, I could probably have skied out of the trajectory of the slip onto the ridge, like you.'

'You need a *Kaffee Lutz* at the *Alpehütte*, then. Come on.' He slapped my shoulder and skied down to the bottom of the slope. I followed slowly behind him.

35

JAMES

After a coffee at the *Alpehütte*, diluted with a large measure of local *Schnapps*, I told Klaus he should take advantage of his day off to continue skiing, but that I was feeling a little fragile and would call it a day.

'If you're sure you're okay,' he said. 'Let's catch up at Bobby's Bar sometime this week, maybe after Christmas Day.'

We shook hands and he skied off. Unsure which parts of my body were causing the random aching in my bones, I ordered myself a bowl of Graubünden *Gerstensuppe* – barley soup with thin shreds of smoke-dried beef in a thick broth. I checked my phone. The video function was still running. It was just as well I'd had time to shove it into my pocket or it would certainly have been lost under the snow. I turned off the camera and checked my messages. Nothing from Emma. I wondered if I could get back to the chalet in time to go with her to the Christmas market.

I texted: *Have you left yet? Thinking of coming back early. Klaus wore me out.* I pressed send with a winking smiley face. She wasn't online so I didn't want to panic her or have her pass a worrying message onto my mother about me getting caught in an avalanche.

When I arrived back in town on the funicular, the pain was focused on my hip and I really wanted to take off my ski boots. I left my skis at the funicular station and carried my poles to the ski shop to swap them for a new pair. I called in at the pharmacy next door for some pain killers. Now I was back amongst the hustle and bustle of the town getting ready for Christmas, it seemed surreal that a few hours before, I'd been caught under the snow and that things could have gone very wrong for me.

I picked up my skis and walked the short distance up to the chalet. When I arrived, Dad was in the car port chopping kindling for the fire.

'I'd offer to do that for you, but I had a little fall on the slopes and I'm aching all over.'

'Oh dear. Not too broken I hope. The girls have gone to the market already. Why don't you have a soak in the jacuzzi with the jets running? I can manage this, not to worry.'

I put my skis in the boot room and climbed the stairs to our room. After a hot shower I felt a little better. I lay on the bed to consider where I was now hurting most. I felt like I'd been thrown from a horse, a delayed sensation I'd known all too well in my childhood with a particularly grumpy pony, leading to my determination never to ride again.

But getting caught in an avalanche was another matter, especially now I was out of my invincible teens. The thought of what could have happened had probably shaken me more than I realised. When it came to a tumble on a pair of skis, I knew I would be getting back on that horse, probably by the next day. Teetering on the edge of an uncertain black run, however, was a more dangerous prospect.

To try and take my mind off the recurring thoughts of suffocating in an avalanche, I glanced to Emma's side of the bed, looking forward to when she would be home and we could have a snuggle.

One of her bags was lying on the floor next to the bed and through the open flap I spotted a book in there. Never one to miss an opportunity to find out what someone was reading, I slipped the book out. Highsmith's *The Talented Mr Ripley*. It looked like an old copy; it had been well-thumbed. Perhaps she'd bought this at a charity shop or a second-hand book market.

I flipped open the book and noticed a dedication on the title page.

To Eva,
Happy studying.
Love always,
C.

I smiled as I recalled often strolling along the Thames and stopping at the Southbank Book Market. I'd sometimes pick up a gem that the booksellers had overlooked. One of my favourite pastimes was looking at personal book dedications and imagining the lives of both the giver and receiver. In this case I imagined a tall dark beauty, her lover, Callum or Caleb, had given her this book as a reminder that although people might not always be what they seem, he would be true to her for eternity. The thing is, though, this Eva hadn't kept the book, and now it was Emma's.

I tucked the book back into her bag and reached for my phone. The battery was almost out, so I plugged it into the charger on my bedside table. Someone had made a new move on the Words-With-Friends app. That would take my mind off the events of the afternoon. I opened the app to see a new game request from JMarple. Sal. I felt a flood of warmth, and a compulsion to talk to her. The avalanche thing was still playing on my emotions. She'd played a seven-letter start word. Jammy cow. What kind of insane luck was that? We hadn't played for weeks, or rather, *I* hadn't played for weeks, and I must have timed out on several games she'd started, judging by the number of icons with her avatar listed below this latest game.

I dwelled briefly on her seven letter word, trying to work out how I might be able to make up at least half the score with the shitty choice of letters I'd been given, picked a half-decent scoring word and hit the play button. As soon as I'd done that, the solid speech bubble appeared in the top right-hand corner of the screen. Sal had sent a comment on the chat function of the game. It had been ages since I'd connected with her, and with a stab of guilt, I touched the bubble.

Jamie, check your messages. I've been trying to get in touch. Sal x

With an equal amount of obedience and curiosity, I checked my messages. Nothing from Sal. Wondering which of the myriad channels she might have messaged me on, I tapped my contacts list. I couldn't find Sal. What the heck? I entered my settings, tapped on storage, and there, in the recycle bin, was Sal's contact card. She'd been muted on phone and

SMS. I unmuted her, restored her details and then tapped on WhatsApp. A string of unread messages appeared, her magnifying glass avatar with a giant eye staring at me accusingly from the top left corner.

I need to talk to you.

Have to ask you something, can't text.

Don't want to message this issue in case it's misinterpreted.

Something's not right. Can we talk?

I'm being serious, it's about your books. Call me.

And finally,

James, please call me. It's really important.

All these messages had been sent over the past three days. Should I call her while she was still at work?

I looked at my watch, wondering how long Emma would be with my mother. Was this about Emma? Was Sal so jealous she'd said something, and now Emma had retaliated by hiding her contact details on my phone? Or was it Emma who was the jealous one?

As the UK was an hour behind, I thought I should wait an hour or so until Sal had finished work, be on her way home and free to talk.

I scrolled through my emails and other messages. Nothing out of the ordinary. Then I pressed play on the video I'd started taking before stuffing the phone in my pocket on the ski slope right before the avalanche.

The blue sky was so innocent, the snow so perfectly glittery and smooth. Klaus stood high on the ridge descending from the top of the gulley. A cornice I hadn't noticed before had developed overnight, caused by the wind blowing across the top of the gulley. Klaus was precariously balanced on the edge. I zoomed in on him as he began stamping on the snow with his skis. I remembered thinking he was creating a platform from which he could launch himself into the powder gully, but on second thoughts it looked as though he was deliberately trying to dislodge the snow on the cornice. Was this some kind of joke and he thought to frighten me? We'd sometimes dared each other as kids, but had never done anything to each other that was life-threatening. My head felt cold. Should I show this to Klaus, ask him what the hell he'd been doing up there?

Then my WhatsApp beeped and a message from Sal appeared.

Thank Christ, there you are. Can you call?

I hit the call button.

36

SALLY

I picked up within a split second of seeing Jamie's icon on the screen.

'Hey, how's it going?' he asked. I couldn't work out whether he sounded happy or irritated to hear my voice.

'James, you might think I'm overreacting and don't get the wrong idea, but I'm not sure about your new girlfriend, Emma.'

'Woah.' I almost felt his eyebrows raise. It was the first time in forever that I'd called him James.

'Sal, look, I feel really bad I haven't talked to you in ages, but don't you think—'

'This isn't about me being jealous. I know it sounds weird, and don't get the wrong message about me hanging around, but I saw her one day a couple of weeks ago outside your place—'

'Wait, what were you doing near my place?' Irritation crept into his voice. I guessed it did sound weird, especially as we'd also seen each other during SantaCon not far from his home in Seven Dials. I hoped he wouldn't think I'd been following him.

'I was on my way to see you, was going to drop off a sweatshirt you'd left at my flat ages ago. Anyway, that's not the point. I saw her with a guy. They were discussing something... intimately.'

'Jeez. Intimately. How intimately, Sal? It could have been anyone she knows from uni. It's not uncommon to bump into people, being so close to Covent Garden. She's allowed to have friends. There must be a ton of people she knows that I haven't met yet; mates she's studying with, shared flats with. I know our relationship took a serious turn very quickly, but that was due to her living circumstances. We're a good fit, Sal. You just have to get to know her.'

'It was their body language, I guess,' I said. 'When I saw her with him, I wondered whether the two of you had broken up, but I didn't want to text you about it, in case it wasn't true. But that's not why I texted you *this* time. There's something else...'

I heard the swish of fabric, perhaps sheets or a duvet. Was he in bed? With her? But he wouldn't have been replying so openly about my concerns if he was. He wouldn't want anything to ruin his perfect romantic bubble. I hadn't talked to him in weeks, and yet I felt compelled to deliver an entire train smash.

'Wait, can we go back to the Emma thing?' he asked. 'What was your gut feeling about her and *this guy*? How old was he? What did he look like?'

'I didn't get a good look at him. He was wearing a beanie and he had his back to me. But he looked pretty fit, broad shoulders. Athletic. Look, I wish I hadn't mentioned it. Because the second thing is more important.'

He sighed, as though he was waiting for a toddler to admit to some minor misdemeanour. His brain was undoubtedly computing who this man could have been.

'James, listen! Fenella at Sotheby's has alerted me to a rare Dickens. The sellers have requested catalogue registration for the next auction.'

My friend Fenella often kept me informed of interesting items coming up for auction, and I would pass the information on to James. I had another friend at Bonham's who did the same.

'I don't think I can afford to bid on anything new,' said Jamie, sounding a little confused. 'And I certainly wouldn't be able to afford to pay top dollar to get it off the books before it goes up.'

'I agree this might be beyond your trust fund salary,' I said. 'But what would you say if I told you it might be your own book?'

'What?—'

'*Great Expectations*. Signed first edition, first impression. Bound in royal blue crushed levant morocco. Gilt bands, ruling and turn ins. Gilt spredges. Jamie, who else has that edition?'

'Not anyone I know, apart from me, of course. For the full value, though, it would need the provenance. Dad holds that. If it *is* mine, and I'm pretty sure it's not, the seller won't be able to get much more than a few grand for it.'

'A few grand's not to be sniffed at, Big Bad Bookman. I just thought you should check it out. Do you have a webcam in your flat? Is there any way you can check The Tardis?' It was me who'd named his book cabinet the Tardis, as the piece of furniture did everything to protect those tomes except actually read them out loud. And what lay inside the cabinet was much bigger than anyone could ever have imagined upon first look at the books.

'No. And I'm not back until after new year. I could ask Marta. She's the only other person with access. But she wasn't due to come in until after we get back. I expect she's gone to Portugal for Christmas to see her family. Does Fenella's team have the physical book?'

'No, so I guess we shouldn't dig too deeply until you know for sure,' I said. 'If someone is alerted to the fact it might be stolen, they'll pull it, probably disappear, perhaps try New York or go on the black market. Anyway, listen dude, why have you been ignoring me? Little miss street lady get a bit jealous? Sorry, that came out wrong. But you have been neglecting your Words lately, mister.'

I heard the echo of distant laughter on Jamie's end and some thumping.

'What's that noise?' I asked.

'The women have all just come back from the Christmas market. They're stamping snow off their boots. Bags, hats, scarves and coats are undoubtedly being flung all over the place. I'm up in my bedroom with the door open. I fear my father's quiet afternoon reading has also come to an abrupt end. Look, Sal, I have to go. I promise I'll keep in touch, but there's nothing I can really do about this until I get back to London.'

'But what if your place has been broken into and you don't even know about it?'

'I'll call my neighbour, Mrs Appleby. If anyone in the complex has seen something suspicious, they'll have called the police. The main gate is secure, don't forget. I'm sure Mrs A will at least be able to tell me if the front door and kitchen window look like they've been tampered with.'

'Jamie, I—'

'I have to go, Sal,' he said, and I assumed they were Emma's footfalls I could hear on the stairs.

37

EMMA

'Hello gorgeous,' I said as I entered the room. I glanced at James's mobile as he placed it on his bedside table. 'How's my ski champion?'

I closed the bedroom door and leapt onto the bed. James held his arms up in a defensive gesture, as though trying to protect himself. I sat astride him gently and kissed him deeply, genuinely glad to see him.

'I had a great morning, until a bit of a tumble in the powder,' he said.

'Oh, no! What happened? That doesn't sound like the daredevil, expert skier I thought you were.'

I lifted his tee-shirt and ran my finger down his chest and he sighed with pleasure.

'A mini avalanche, actually, but it's okay. I had a fright, but I'm here now, and don't really want to talk about it. We were being irresponsible. We should never have skied where we did.'

'Ah, the age-old testosterone challenge. What is it about sporty men and their egos? Does anything need kissing better?' I asked coquettishly. 'I'll be gentle with you.'

I tugged at the waistband of his sweatpants and he didn't protest. He wasn't hurting enough to ask me to stop the playfulness and what he must have known I had in mind.

I felt a kind of abandon, riding him, my head raised and eyes closed. Was I falling for this guy? The setting was perfect for a Christmas romance, except maybe the fact that his parents were never too far away.

I curled my body into his afterwards, and stroked his chest until it grew dark outside.

'I guess we'll soon be expected at your neighbours' for Christmas Eve cocktails,' I said.

James groaned. 'Are you sure you want to go? I think we could get out of it, especially as I'm not feeling physically great.'

'Oh, come on, James! I need some gossip fuel for later. We don't need to go for long, right?'

I helped James's mother in the kitchen prepare a few things for the traditional Christmas meal we would be enjoying the following day, while James got slowly ready upstairs. I think he must have been in more pain than he wanted to admit. He was mucking about on his phone again, and I tried to encourage him to join us downstairs. We were getting on famously, but I didn't really want to be left alone in his mum's company after having spent the entire day with her. It was with relief that I finally heard him coming down the stairs.

'All set for this evening, James darling?' his mother asked as he entered the kitchen. 'Could you fetch the *Nüsslitort* from the pantry. I thought I should take something extra to theirs, along with the bottle of wine your father has chosen. I don't know where Andrea finds the time to prepare for drinks after she's spent the afternoon at the market.'

'I think they probably have help, Mum. They don't strike me as a family who caters their own parties. Their chalet is the largest one on this side of the valley. How was the Glatschin market, by the way? The usual Swiss Christmas tat?'

'Oh it was lovely, and the girls all had a little skate. Emma's rather a splendid skater, you know,' she said, beaming at me. 'Very elegant.'

I bit my lip.

'That's probably where she gets her skiing ability from – good balance,' said James, putting his arm around my waist. 'Why didn't you mention you could skate?'

'There are many things we still don't know about each other, James. Ours will be a voyage of discovery,' I said quietly to him, but telling myself that not only was our relationship still so new, it was fuelled by a lot of sex in the moments when he was likely trying to find out more of my history.

'Andrea and Deirdre found Emma utterly delightful,' said his mother, touching my arm. 'And they're all looking forward to seeing both of you tonight.'

We gathered our coats, hats and boots, and walked next door to Chalet Edelweiss. The village spread out below us twinkled in its festive cloak of fairy lights, overlooked by the surrounding snow-clad mountains, glowing an eerie blue in the moonlight. The neighbours' chalet was festooned with Christmas lights along the gable of the roof and round all the windows. Lights had also been strewn amongst the sculptured evergreen shrubs capped with snow in the front garden.

'It's gorgeous!' I said. 'Let's take a selfie in front of the house.'

'I'll take the photo,' said Frank Marsh.

A moment of confusion passed over James's face.

'And on the way home, we'll do one in front of yours,' I said, looping my arm through the crook of his elbow. He was no doubt thinking I should have wanted a photo of us in front of *their* chalet.

'Oh, you have such a beautiful home,' I gushed to Andrea as we entered their hallway and removed the gear we had only moments ago put on.

There were quite a few guests already. They were gathered around a roaring log fire set into a floating iron dish suspended from the ceiling of the great lounge through which the chimney disappeared. More fairy lights twinkled and traditional Swiss music floated discreetly to us over the crackling of the logs. The aroma of cinnamon and clove-infused *Glühwein* mingled with the smell of wood smoke and a hint of baking pastry wafted through from the direction of the kitchen.

We chatted with groups of guests, and I tried to make James feel at ease, having almost forced him to come. I put on my party charm, and did the rounds, having a word or two with some of the people James hadn't yet been caught up in conversations with.

'Andrea's daughter Petra is going to show me around the house,' I told James after we'd been briefly separated. 'She wants to show me their collection of Morano glass sculptures. Will you be okay without me for a few minutes?'

'Of course!' he said, and I knew he was glad I was fitting in so well with his family's acquaintances.

Petra and I climbed the heavy oak staircase to the upper floor of the building.

'*Gott*, all I really want to do is get away from this lot and have a smoke. Will you join me, *Emma*?'

I did a double take. Petra had drawn out my name in a theatrical way, almost as though she was going to call me something else. But when I turned to look at her, she was smiling mischievously and pointing towards a door that must have been her bedroom. She brushed past me and walked briskly past the row of colourful glass objects without a second glance, and beckoned me into her room.

I sat on her bed while she rolled a joint at her desk, telling me how much she hated these parties and couldn't wait to get back to Zürich where life was so much more exciting.

'James tells me your dad works in watches,' I said, before drawing a toke and holding in the smoke, but not for too long. I wanted to stay alert.

'*Ja*, IWC,' said Petra. 'Our family has been involved for three generations. It's where the money came from for this place...' Between sucking on the rapidly diminishing joint and holding in the smoke, Petra spoke of some of the advantages she'd experienced as a young woman growing up in Schaffhausen and going to a private school across the border in Germany. The skinny joint was soon finished, and I was glad Petra had smoked most of it. I wasn't used to the effects of cannabis.

'*Lueg*, we should go back downstairs. But let me show you Papa's wild collection of watches on the way.'

She led me out of her room and further down the corridor, opening the door to the master bedroom.

When we came down again a few minutes later, I found James and leaned into him, feeling a little light-headed, and felt a cool sheen as I put my hand to my forehead.

'Do you know that Petra's dad has a bunch of watches sitting in this little box that rocks them like a little baby?' I told him in a whisper.

'A machine for his self-wind watches,' he said. 'Yes, I've seen that. Petra's father is a retired partner of IWC in Schaffhausen.'

'It's nuts, James, she told me how much those things are worth. What did she call them? Grand complications. Amazing.'

As he turned to kiss me, I was aware that he might taste the smoke on my lips and drew away.

'Are you high?' he whispered in my ear.

I pressed my lips together. 'Petra persuaded me to smoke a joint in her room. But it's gone straight to my head, and I don't feel too great.'

'Come over here, let's take a seat.'

'Would you mind awfully if I headed back to our chalet?' I said.

'I'll come with you. Let me get our things. There are enough people here now that we won't be missed. I did want to introduce you to Lawrence and his wife over there, though. He was part of our skiing gang all those years ago with Tristan.' He bit his lip, though, and I wondered whether he'd also had enough of socialising with the filthy rich.

'Honestly, James, I just need to lie down for a bit. Maybe if I feel better I'll come back. But I don't want to scupper your Christmas Eve so early. You should stay.'

'But—'

'Really, James, stop it, I'll be fine on my own. It's a few metres down the road. It'll probably take me less time to get there than finding my way to the bathroom in this humungous place.'

'If you're sure. I won't be long. Today's skiing has taken its toll.'

He probably wanted nothing more than to go back with me. He'd already said how much his body was aching with fatigue. But I knew his parents would be disappointed if he disappeared so early, and I didn't want to be the source of that disappointment. James gave me the key code to the door of the chalet, even though I remembered it from the first day, and more importantly, the code for disarming the alarm.

'I'll be back in half an hour or so,' he said, kissing the side of my head.

'I'll probably be in bed by the time you get home,' I said. 'And by then, I should be feeling much better and will be perfectly happy for you to disturb me.'

I grabbed his crotch in a gesture that was quite unusual for me and not terribly becoming. The weed had affected me more than I realised. I giggled and turned to make sure no one had seen. We made a quiet exit to the hallway where James fetched my coat and kissed me before sending me out into the night for the short walk home.

38

JAMES

The following day my body felt like it had been hit by a sledgehammer. Emma left me in bed in the morning with a mug of tea and an ibuprofen to arrange the presents under the tree downstairs and help my parents prepare the Christmas lunch. She'd been asleep when we arrived home. My parents had insisted that I check on her and report back to them before we all went to bed. It warmed me to think they were concerned about Emma. She had certainly endeared herself to them in the short time they'd known her.

I made a quick Words move with Sal, knowing I would never be able to catch her massive score in this game. I reflected on the fact that Sal had somehow been muted on my phone. That had been Emma's doing, surely? The tension I'd felt between the two of them when we'd met before Christmas was an intensely jealous reaction. It should have been alarming that she would do something like this, but in reality, it emphasised the strength of Emma's feelings for me, and I felt a rush of affection for her.

Traditionally I would have gone skiing on Christmas morning. At the party the night before, Lawrence had tried to persuade me we should go.

His partner had said she'd be happy to ski the blue runs with Emma. But not only wasn't I feeling up to it, the prospect of skiing with Lawrence, who was probably still manic on his snowboard, even if we had all grown older and hopefully wiser, didn't appeal. He'd been reckless in the past, causing one particularly nasty accident on the slopes of our youth, and that was a memory that didn't sit well with me. Besides which, I knew the pistes would be crowded. I was happy to spend the morning at home and Emma said she'd stay with me.

Hearing the three of them – my parents and Emma – downstairs, laughing and joking, I was soon drawn out of bed. The smell of freshly brewed coffee was a good incentive and after a shower I felt much better. Emma and I walked down to the Hanselmann's *Bäkerei* to pick up fresh *Gipfeli* – croissants – for breakfast.

In the village, everyone was heading for the ski lifts, the traditional Swiss Christmas having already been celebrated at home by most families on the 24th. Instead, we enjoyed our traditional English Christmas lunch at home, spending some time in the afternoon in the hot tub on the terrace gazing at the surrounding Alps and playing games of cards and Rummikub later by the fire.

It was the one compromise I'd made when telling myself that Emma was the perfect partner for me. She wasn't into Scrabble or word games. I vowed to keep my wordy relationship with Sal a private affair, especially after the electric tension I'd felt between the two when we'd met during SantaCon. It almost felt like cheating on Emma when I thought of it, but wasn't sure how deep her jealousy ran. She was obviously a dab hand at rummy, though, and managed to win most rounds.

Mum declared the turkey of excellent quality, a French import by the local butcher who sourced only the best free-range meat.

'I don't know whether they have turkey farms in Switzerland,' Mum said.

'When I was mountain biking a couple of years ago I saw a wild turkey on the trail,' I said.

'Turkeys? Here?' said Dad. 'I thought they only had wild turkeys in the States.'

'I was surprised too,' I said. 'It was lower altitude, the other end of the valley, below Pontresina. The thing ran at my bike, hissing angrily. Tried to peck my wheels and then my bike shoes. I actually worried it was going to burst a tyre.'

'They're probably protected,' said Dad. 'I wonder if anyone hunts them? You never told me about that!'

'It was a summer trip out here. I don't think you were even here. Slipped my mind.'

I remembered the threatening bird, and that shouting at the thing didn't make any difference. It blocked the trail, tail feathers fanned, ready for a skirmish like an avian prize fighter. I had to wait until its temper cooled and it disappeared back into the forest.'

'Wonder what they do in winter?' mused my mother.

'They're not indigenous,' said Emma. 'Turkeys come from the Americas. They were introduced at some stage. Some of them escaped and found that the forests in the foothills of the Alps were the perfect place to live.'

I stared at Emma, then eyed the roasting dish on the table. With only four of us this year, Mum had ordered a smaller bird than usual. About the size of that wild one I'd seen. But there was a strange thing going on inside me. I thought this was the first time Emma had been to Switzerland. How would she know such a detail? I blinked at her.

'It's lovely to have a traditional English Christmas lunch,' she said hurriedly. 'You've made me feel right at home, and I'm very grateful.'

At the mention of the word 'home,' I wondered what Christmas would have been like for Emma if she'd spent it with her mum. Up north. Wherever.

'Your mum's probably feasting on reindeer steak right now.'

Emma frowned and looked at me as though I'd just spoken Chinese.

'The Northern Lights cruise,' I said. 'I assume the ship will be way up in Scandinavia somewhere.

'Of course!' she said, a flicker of something, guilt maybe, crossing her face as though she'd forgotten where her mum was. 'Yes, probably.'

'Have you heard from her, dear?' asked my mother. 'Please wish her happy Christmas from us.'

Emma smiled sweetly.

After a bread-and-butter pudding made with the leftover croissants from that morning and some traditional Italian *panetone* brought by the neighbours to our drinks party, we settled round the fire for more card games and charades. We snacked our way through the leftover cheese and Christmas cake. My mother's eyes widened as Emma placed a sliver of *Alpkäse* on a slice of cake and ate them together.

'Doesn't everyone combine the two?' She smiled. 'Cheese and fruit-cake. It's a winner.'

Before we turned in, I sent a message to Klaus to wish him *Frohe Festtäge* with his family, reminding him that we would only be around for the next two days for a ski or a beer. I tried to put the avalanche incident out of my mind, but intended to ask him about it if we ran into each other again.

For the remaining two days of our holiday, I skied with Emma. One afternoon after we came down from the slopes, we took my parents on a horsedrawn sleigh ride in the valley. On the last day, Emma declared she was ready to graduate from the blue slopes to a red one.

She skied slowly but competently, and I remarked how, for an adult, she'd picked up the sport remarkably quickly. She'd told me she wasn't very sporty, so the skating and the skiing were a surprise to me. No sooner had I uttered those words, though, she had a wobbly moment down one particularly steep section of the piste, and seemed to freeze with fear. I had to guide her down by tucking her skis behind mine and she held me around the waist as we skied together to a gentler section of the run.

Finally, it was time to go back to London. In an unexpected alteration of plans, my parents decided to change their flights home. Dad's dodgy leg was causing him some discomfort and he wanted to consult his doctor. I was relieved we were taking the train back rather than flying with them. Emma had probably had enough of them by then. Even though my parents had been extraordinarily liberal and non-invasive during our stay, a tedious wait at the airport was never a jolly occasion to socialise at the best of times.

Now I knew they were leaving the following day, I was sad to leave the romance of the chalet and the resort. Instead, I looked forward to nesting up in our flat back in Covent Garden until Emma went back to uni. She had exams approaching; I assumed she'd need to knuckle down and do some cramming and work on her projects at the uni studio. And I needed to either look for another job or immerse myself in my novel-writing.

That last thought sent a little stab of guilt running through me. I hadn't been completely honest with Emma, my friends, or my parents about that.

We left early in the morning, and took the TGV from Zürich to Paris, then the Eurostar back to London in one day. Emma immersed herself in a book. It wasn't the Highsmith I'd seen in her bag, but a Peter Swanson psych thriller she'd taken from my shelves at home. I played a few word games on my phone. Before pulling my own book out, I checked my What's App. I hadn't heard back from Klaus and I noticed my message had gone unread. Perhaps he felt guilty or embarrassed about the day we'd skied on the black run? Perhaps he realised his actions had started the avalanche, and that it could have gone really badly.

39

EMMA

We arrived at St Pancras Station late in the evening on the 28th December.

'Twixtmas,' I joked as I snuggled against James in the back of our taxi. 'Thank you for a wonderful holiday. I'm already missing the atmosphere.'

'It's nice to be back on our own. It must have been a bit daunting for you to be under the eagle eyes of my parents for so many days in a row. As the saying goes, it's three days before fish, friends and family start going off. You surpassed that by at least double.'

'So, have I earned my chocolate medal?' I asked.

'Of course!' he said.

As the taxi dropped us next to the obelisk on Seven Dials and we hauled our cases up the steps to the courtyard in front of the flat, a light drizzle began to fall. James hurried to get us and our luggage into the dry before the rain intensified.

'Welcome back to the dreary London winter,' he grumbled.

He punched the keycode on the pad, and leaned into the door, then drew back, a look of confusion on his face. He pushed again. The door suddenly swung inward with a grinding metal sound, and he half fell into the hallway of the flat. He turned to inspect the latch.

'I think it was unlocked!' he said.

'What?' I said, swallowing.

'It looks like the mechanism could have been jimmied with some kind of tool. The door seems to have been held closed by the edge of the forced latch.' He stood for a moment, perplexed, then he visibly paled and his eyes widened. 'Oh no! Oh God!' he said, as he turned and entered the flat.

'James! What's the matter? What's happened?' I asked, following him.

'The Tardis. I think I might have been robbed.' His voice sounded reedy as he rushed along the corridor towards the living room.

'How can you tell without looking?' I asked.

'There's only one reason the door mechanism would be broken like that, and it obviously wasn't to put out a fire,' he shouted back at me over his shoulder.

Leaving our cases in the hallway, I followed him into the living room. The cabinet in the corner by the bookcases seemed at first untouched, and James stopped and took a deep breath. Then as we approached, we saw the opposite glass side of the cabinet had been completely smashed, and the entire pane of glass lay in a splintered pile on the rug. There was a humming coming from the cabinet.

'What's that noise?' I asked.

'The air purifier in the base of the cabinet. The system now has the Sisyphean task of de-ionising, dehumidifying and circulating the air in the entire flat.' His voice was strained and his brow furrowed as his hand combed through his dark hair.

'The Dickens. The Maugham! Oh!'

'They're missing?'

'And a handful of other signed first editions including the Highsmith and the Forrester. Stolen. Shit. Shit. Shit.' He pulled out his mobile phone and keyed in 999.

'Oh God, James! I'm so sorry,' I said, retreating to stand by the stairs.

'Maybe it's best not to touch anything,' he said. 'I have to see if anything else has been taken, whether anything is damaged. We should disturb as little as possible. We'll need to wait until the police get here.'

'Do you think I can use the loo?' I asked.

He opened the small cloakroom off the hallway and looked inside, perhaps expecting a thief to jump out.

'Use this one, and then maybe wait in the kitchen. I'm sure you can sit at the bar. It doesn't look like anything has been disturbed in there.'

He took off his jacket and hung it on the hook by the front door, then ran up the stairs two at a time as I went into the bathroom. I heard him stamping about upstairs, imagined him scanning my room, then rushing into each of the others to check.

As I came out of the bathroom and James came back downstairs, the intercom chimed. The door security video showed two uniformed cops standing in front of the fisheye glass, and James buzzed them into the courtyard downstairs.

'I wonder how an intruder got past the gate?' he said, almost to himself. 'They must have waited for a resident to leave, or perhaps they came in the dead of night and found a way to climb over the wall on Shortland Gardens and over the iron spikes. I must talk to Mrs Appleby, the neighbour.'

After James confirmed to the two uniformed cops that the focus of the burglary was his very expensive book collection, they gave brief, chopped descriptions into their radios, I heard the phrases 'SOCO', 'Sarge' and 'Valuable assets' uttered by one them.

'We've just come back from holiday. It's possible the robbery took place a number of days ago,' James told them. 'I had an alert that a rare edition had appeared on a pre-auction notice at Sotheby's. At the time it didn't make sense so I dismissed it, but it was probably one of mine.'

I stared at James.

'Stay put, don't touch anything and you should make a list of anyone who knew about the cabinet,' said the cop. 'A detective will be along to take a statement and that will likely be the first thing he asks,' said the cop in charge. 'Obviously you can take a seat while we wait for them to arrive. Can I get you anything. A glass of water? Tea?'

It felt odd to be confined to the sofa while the cops moved freely about James's flat. They weren't wearing latex gloves or anything, and I thought it strange that they would be distributing their DNA when our prints would be all over the place anyway.

As though reading my mind, the cop said 'Just want to make sure you don't touch anything that might obliterate an intruder's prints. We have our methods.'

'Is the detective an expert in antique books or artwork? It'll need someone knowledgeable in the industry. Making these things disappear is… complicated.'

'I'm not sure, Sir, but they'll be able to access the best experts.'

James sat back on the sofa, and pressed the heels of his palms against his eyes.

'What a bloody shame,' he said. 'It was such a perfect Christmas holiday.'

I put my hand on his thigh, conveying concern. 'God, James. This is awful.'

He closed his eyes and leaned his head against the back of the sofa, taking a deep breath. As he opened them again, something caught his attention and I followed the direction of his gaze. It was the glint of an object underneath the armchair opposite. I jumped up and reached for it.

'No, wait!' James shouted, but too late.

I opened my fist and showed him the key I suspected was to his cabinet he called The Tardis.

'You shouldn't have done that! Weren't you listening to the policeman?' he asked in exasperation.

'Shit! Sorry! Of course. Fingerprints and all that.'

'You know what this is?' he asked.

'The key to the cabinet?'

When he'd first opened the cabinet to show me the books, I'd only been living with him for a few days. He'd felt compelled to keep the location of the key hidden from me back then. But I knew where it was.

'I remember the shape of it from the day you showed me the books. I'm sorry, I only realized after I picked it up. I thought it was a piece of jewellery or something.'

'If someone knew where the key was hidden, why did they smash the cabinet glass to get to the books?' he asked thoughtfully.

He pulled out his phone and searched his contacts for a number, then put it on speaker and placed it on the coffee table in front of us.

'George Merrison, my insurance agent,' he said as the ring tone connected.

George Merrison must also have been a friend. I was surprised an insurance agent would answer a call at that time of night. James explained what had happened.

'Bloody hell, James, that's a lot of your assets gone in one fell swoop.'

'You've seen the set-up, said you were okay with it,' said James.

'I do remember telling you to get cameras mounted, even fake ones. Were your alarms engaged?'

'I thought I'd set them before we left, but I must have forgotten. The neighbour checked the entrance, but must have only made a half-hearted effort to try the door. It was open, then manipulated somehow to keep the door on the latch so it wouldn't look suspicious from the outside. I just thought I should let you know. The police are here. They're sending in a detective. I'll call you again tomorrow.'

George conveyed his sympathy and James ended the call as the second cop came through from the kitchen with steaming mugs of tea.

'I almost want to make a quip about why they're not taking an inventory of the crockery and cutlery in my kitchen cupboards and drawers,' he whispered to me. 'It feels oddly invasive having a stranger make tea in my home.'

James was bereft. It was as though he'd lost a pet or something. It was clear that those books meant an awful lot to him.

40

JAMES

The detective looked like the last place he wanted to be was in the living room of my Covent Garden flat. He handed me his card. DS Steven Hannah. Homicide. Despite my distress, I let out a cynical snort.

'Let's hope the fate of my books involves them still being alive at the end of this.'

He shot me a look. 'I've been called in exceptionally for this. Short staffed in this borough, and quite unusually, no suspicious fatalities this week in my own,' he paused. 'Yet,' he added, as though I might be next on his list if I made anymore smart comments.

'Sorry. Of course,' I said meekly, as I handed over a list of the missing books with scanned copies of their original provenance, excepting that of the Dickens.

I'd had the presence of mind to scan and save them on my computer when I'd taken possession of each of the books, whether purchased or donated as a gift. Thank goodness for Sal in that respect, always on at me to ensure I had a track of all my book assets. I hoped this interview wouldn't take long, that DS Hannah would get onto chasing down my books and I could call Sal with the bad news and ask for her advice.

'So, you were away from when until when, exactly?' asked the DS.

'December 21st to the 28th, today. The place could have been burgled at any time. Unfortunately, although I was sure I'd set the alarm, I must have forgotten when we left. Both the police and the neighbourhood would have been alerted immediately if it had been activated.' I paused, and glanced at Emma. 'A friend of mine said she thought she'd seen one of my books on an upcoming pre-inclusion notice for a Sotheby's catalogue. That's the first place you should investigate. The auctioneers. It means the books aren't moving quickly in the normal way they would on the black market.'

Emma gasped beside me, and I looked at her with a frown. Did she know I'd talked to Sal?

'After I received that information, I called my neighbour, Mrs Appleby, at number 11,' I continued. 'Asked her to check the place. She said there didn't seem to be evidence of a break-in. I guess you'll be questioning her too. The door had somehow caught against the broken latch, so it took quite a shove before I realised it was open. She probably hadn't realised it'd been somehow forced, and even if she'd pushed against it, she obviously wasn't strong enough to shift it.'

One of the Scene of Crime Officers was examining the lock mechanism on the front door and a chill breeze blew through to the living room. Emma shivered and I passed her a fleecy throw from the back of the sofa.

'This is the key to the cabinet. I found it under the armchair over there,' I said, handing the key to the DS, who frowned.

'A primary source of prints. Didn't my men tell you not to touch anything?' He sounded as irritated as I felt.

'It was a snap reaction, we didn't think.' My affection for Emma eclipsed the frustration I felt, but as soon as I'd made the excuse for her, I wanted to take it back. 'I don't understand, though, why they would have smashed the glass side of the cabinet if they had access to it with the key. Which was hidden, actually,' I said.

'Where?'

I showed him the small magnetised block under one of the lower book shelves by the TV. DS Hannah scribbled frantically in his notepad before crouching down to inspect the door of the cabinet.

'It looks like the lock is open. I'll get a SOCO to check this.'

I glanced at Emma whose gaze was unfocused, looking at the space under the armchair where she'd picked up the key.

'Also, the intruders must have either waited for someone to access the courtyard or climbed over the wall from Shortland Gardens to get past the outside gate which is on a different keypad system. I don't know whether there is a functioning CCTV, but aren't there cameras everywhere these days? Big Brother and all that.'

'If every camera mounted in the metropolitan area was actually functioning, we'd probably be able to catch ten times the number of perpetrators we currently do. But thank you, all cameras will be checked. This is a busy area. Does anyone else have the keycode to your flat?' the DS asked.

'Apart from my parents, who travelled before us to the Alps and were with us the whole time over Christmas, only my housekeeper, Marta has the current access code. I've changed it since I had friends to stay last summer. I automatically do that about once every six months.'

'I'll need to contact your housekeeper as well, if you could give me her number—'

'I've never trusted that little minx,' Emma suddenly said.

I was surprised at her spiteful tone. If I'd at first suspected she'd been resentful of Marta's ease in my company at the beginning, this had now gone several levels beyond jealousy. First Sal, now Marta. I gaped at her.

'A couple of times I had a strange feeling about her,' she continued. 'She spent a lot of time with her feather duster and microfibre cloths around that damned cabinet. I also thought she was taking advantage of James's generosity,' she said, looking at the DS.

I frowned. I tried to suppress the thought 'pot' and 'kettle.' This was a side of Emma I never imagined she had.

'Marta has been very good to me,' I said, more to Emma than the DS. 'She's been my housekeeper since I moved into this place. I know her and her family quite well. I trust her implicitly. She's never asked me for any favours. But I really don't think—'

'We will have to question everyone who has access to your flat, Mr Marsh, even if they are unlikely suspects. Sometimes there are connections.'

I thought of Marta and her delightful little daughter Beatriz, and her talented chef husband Joao who'd been asked to become a partner in the highly successful Portuguese bakery where he worked. Marta had asked me my opinion on share agreements, company liabilities and tax issues after Joao's job offer. I hadn't been able to help with all the business issues, but after having seen the effects of the 2020 pandemic, I urged them to err on the side of caution when investing in the ever volatile catering industry.

'How long have the two of you been together, if you don't mind my asking?' said DS Hannah, and I was at first confused he might be referring to Marta and me. Then I realised he was talking about my relationship with Emma.

'Emma moved in mid-October,' I said.

'And to clarify, the two of you were in...' The DS referred to his notebook. '...St Moritz, Switzerland, was it?' he asked with a slightly condescending tone.

'Yes, so surely we are eliminated from the list of suspects?' said Emma.

'I hardly think we'd be stealing from our own property,' I said, to both Emma and the policeman.

'You'd be surprised, Mr Marsh. It's the first place an antiques insurance assessor tends to look.'

His glance slid towards the door of the cabinet and I raised my eyebrows. My heart sank as I imagined him striking a line through the case with his team later uttering the words *inside job*.

'I'm not in any financial trouble, if that's what you're implying.' I lowered my voice. 'I have access to a family trust fund. I'm lucky enough likely to never be in a state of poverty.'

I bit my lip, and looked over to Emma, expecting perhaps surprise. But she was scratching the side of her head with a distracted look on her face.

'I'm convinced Marta had something to do with this,' she said, as though she hadn't just heard about my independent wealth. 'She was looking so fishy the last time I saw her. You were at work, James. And I had this feeling...'

'You have a family trust, and yet you are still gainfully employed?' said the policeman, ignoring Emma, but writing *Marta, housekeeper* on his notepad. 'What do you do? A bit of the antique book trade yourself?'

'I wish. No, I... Actually, I used to be employed at a branch of a high street book shop chain, but stopped working there a couple of months ago.'

As I was processing the fact that Emma hadn't shown unbridled delight at learning of my family fortune, reassuring me she was no gold digger, it was now Emma's turn to look at me agape.

And I suspected something was about to unravel.

41

EMMA

It was late when the police team left, but they returned early the next morning.

'We haven't been able to locate your housekeeper,' the DS said to James after a further look around the flat. 'Or her husband. They apparently went back to Portugal for the Christmas holidays. Her husband isn't due back into work again until January 6th.'

'That sounds suspicious, doesn't it?' I asked.

'No! This couldn't have anything to do with Marta. I know her too well for this,' said James firmly. 'Early January is when school starts again for Beatriz. She wasn't due to come to me until after that, but we hadn't fixed a specific date. I'll try her myself if you like. She'll see it's my caller ID and might be more likely to answer. But I suspect she has a different phone when she's in Portugal, to avoid roaming charges. We talked about it once. I don't know that number.'

James pulled out his mobile and tried what must have been Marta's UK number. We all heard it go straight to voicemail. He left a message for her in Italian.

'You speak Portuguese?' asked DS Hannah.

'Italian. It's our common language.'

I gave James a curious look but didn't say anything. As far as I remembered, Marta spoke perfectly acceptable English. I wondered what he'd said to her in Italian.

'Well, I'll get back to the Met and get onto this. The SOCOs should be finished here shortly. If you think of anything else, please call me, however insignificant you think it might be.' The DS handed James his card.

The SOCOs left with various fibres tweazered into tiny ziplock bags and a gazillion photos of the inside of the flat, along with the DS who took with him an attitude that told us he'd much rather be investigating a murder. James went to the kitchen, threw his cold tea down the sink and made a double espresso.

'Why didn't you tell me you'd stopped working?' I asked, frowning.

'I didn't want to put you off coming to stay with me,' he said, placing his hand on my arm. 'I should have been honest with you from the start. I thought you might not want to move in with someone unemployed. I know we hadn't yet... established the seriousness of our relationship at that point, but I've never hidden my feelings for you.'

'Did you resign?'

'No, actually, I lost my job.'

'Was that my fault?' I asked, trying to sound sympathetic, but my mind racing. 'You spent a lot of time with me those first days when I suppose you should have been working.'

'Of course not, it was an accumulation of things, actually.' He sounded relieved that he'd finally got that little deception off his chest.

'What've you been doing since I moved in, then? You've been gone almost all day every day.' My voice had a ring of exasperation to it. My heart was beating hard, and I tried to rein in a rising nervousness.

'If you must know, my secret project, which I've told absolutely *no one* about, is to write a novel. I spent most of those days at the British Library.'

'Oh, wow, James. Why would you keep that from anyone, especially me? That's something you should be proud of.'

'It's a long story, but once you let the cat out of the bag that you're writing a novel, it's hard to deal with the perpetual commentary from friends and family. Yes, I should have told you, but I feel more motivated to write when I know that *nobody* has any expectations of word counts, chapter completions, submissions processes and publication pitches. I have too many friends who have become disillusioned writers. I know what goes on in the psyche of an aspiring author.'

'I would have supported you all the way, James. I mean I *do* support you all the way.'

As the coffee machine grunted the last drop of Arabica foam into his cup, I put my arms around him.

After a moment's hesitation, he hugged me back. Was he still irritated that I might have accidentally tampered with an important piece of evidence? The cops hadn't been so careful either. I wanted to point out that any organised thieves would surely have been wearing gloves, not only to avoid leaving fingerprints but also to protect the precious booty they were stealing. But I had the feeling my hugs and comments of sympathy were more likely to get him through his angst. And I didn't want to draw any more attention to the actual theft.

'I still can't get my head around this. I think I need to take a walk. The sight of the ravaged Tardis sitting there like that is upsetting me.'

'Sound like a good plan, James. I'll hold the fort here; I have a load of studying to do. And I'll be here when you get back for some old-fashioned comforting.'

He smiled, kissed me, and gathered some warm gear to face the changeable London weather before heading out of the door.

42

JAMES

I was glad to get out of the flat, as though putting distance between me and my home could alleviate the feeling of having been violated.

Instead of calling Sal to arrange a meeting, I thought I'd surprise her by calling in at the shop to see if she could make time for a quick coffee. I also wanted to test the ground as to whether I was still persona non grata there.

It was a clear day, relatively mild for the end of the year. The city was gearing up for the new year celebrations. The lights in Leicester Square and Piccadilly Circus seemed even brighter than usual. The Christmas angels in Regent Street swayed in a chilly breeze. They were turned off during the day now in an attempt to economise on the city's power, but the bulbs still twinkled in the dull winter light.

The post-Christmas sales had brought out hordes of shoppers and the sequence of traffic lights and crowds crossing Regent Street meant I found myself on the north side of Piccadilly. Instead of waiting for the next green pedestrian light, I stayed on the same side with the intention of popping across to Waterstones once I reached the point along the avenue where there was a central island and I could dodge the traffic.

As I walked past the Dilly, the doorman stepped into the middle of the pavement and held up a white-gloved hand, startling me.

'Jimmy!' he called, his usual smile replaced by an expression I couldn't at first fathom.

Willie was the only person who'd ever called me that, and as my heartrate calmed, I was confused the doorman would use the same nickname. Then it dawned on me he would have often heard Willie greet me from his patch in his raucously loud voice in the days I'd stopped by. The doorman must have assumed Jimmy was my given name.

'The police are looking for you,' he said.

I put my hand to my chest. Had news of the theft reached West One? I thought back to the days I was visiting Emma in the doorway of number 27. Had Waterstones reported the theft of their books? I'd offered to pay for them. Told them to deduct any expenses from my final salary. It was a bit mean of them if they'd taken matters further, especially as I hadn't worked there for several weeks. They would have been able to obtain my address from HR. Surely the police would have come to my residence first?

'It's about that homeless man that used to be resident at number 27,' said the doorman nodding in the direction of the archway along the pavement. 'When they asked if he'd had dealings with anyone, I told them about your occasional chats with the old fella.'

Willie? *Dealings with anyone* sounded alarmingly illegal, and I frowned.

'Do you know where Willie moved to?' I asked, pointing with my chin at the clothes shop that still seemed to be doing good trade. 'He was supposed to be back here in November after his hospital visit, but the new business must have forced him to find somewhere else.'

The guilt returned that I'd never persevered with checking up on Willie after Emma had moved in. But I couldn't think how I could possibly have tried any more to look for him, having visited most of the hospitals.

'The police wouldn't say what had happened, but when I told them about you, that I hadn't seen you for a while, they went over to your work,' said the doorman, nodding at Waterstones. 'Then came back to tell me they couldn't find you, that perhaps I'd been mistaken and you didn't work there. They gave me this card in case I came up with any information about where you might be.' He reached into a decorative pocket on the front of his winter uniform coat.

Should I feel flattered that the doorman remembered who I was after all this time? It was probably one of the necessary qualifications for a doorman, to remember everyone they saw so they could say 'Welcome back to the Dilly, Sir,' when the occasion required it.

I imagined the police wandering into Waterstones and asking if they had an employee called Jimmy. With the turnover of staff recently, it was likely no one made the connection, and they obviously hadn't happened upon Sal in the shop; she would have sussed it out straight away.

The doorman handed me the business card with a small ball of fluff clinging to one corner that told me it had been sitting in his pocket for a while. I frowned at the logo and the name John Reynolds, Detective Sargent, Metropolitan Police.

'When was this?' I asked the doorman.

'Before Christmas, mid-November maybe. It's chance I still had the card in my pocket here,' he said.

So this was long before the theft. Wouldn't be related then. I huffed a laugh. Willie seemed even less likely to have stolen my books than Marta. However, my recent encounter with the law was hardly a positive one, and curious to know how I could help them with Willie, I felt I should contact this DS Reynolds as soon as possible as a kind of good deed. Banking my chances.

'I know you wouldn't have done anything bad to the old fella,' continued the doorman. 'I told them that; told them you brought him stuff – food and drink and sometimes clothes. I know you're a kind soul. I'm sorry if it looks like I dumped you in it, but they were most insistent.'

'Is the Met close by?' I asked. I hadn't a clue where the police station might be. I knew where Scotland Yard used to be, but that was only because I recognised it on British police TV programmes from my youth when they used the iconic steel cubes as a backdrop to their various dramas.

'The headquarters are down by the river, on the Embankment,' said the doorman. 'There were two plain clothes and a uniform.'

The doorman hadn't realised he'd just added to my angst by offering that information. It sounded like a lot of artillery to be sending out for a missing homeless person. And why were they looking for Willie anyway? My curiosity was doubly piqued.

Before I talked to Sal, I needed to clear up what was going on with Willie. I could have called DS Reynolds on my mobile. I had his card in my hand. But I didn't want to go home yet, and still felt the need to clear my head. I crossed Piccadilly to Lower Regent Street and made my way to The Embankment on foot. It was probably better to present myself rather than have them seek me out again. If anybody at my ex-employer had told them I'd been fired, that probably wouldn't have looked too good either. I hadn't told DS Hannah when he'd questioned me at home.

43

JAMES

At the Met, I explained my presence and showed the business card to the woman on the front desk, which looked like the reception for a classy hotel. After a complicated back and forth of explanations and the use of the phone on her desk which left me none the wiser, I was asked to wait in the glass atrium to the side of the main entrance. Across the polished dark granite floor from my uncomfortable tube chair, the water of the Thames swirled sluggishly past.

After half an hour I asked the woman how much longer I might be expected to wait. I assumed I'd done nothing wrong and was only there to clarify something the officers had been wanting to ask me about a homeless man on Piccadilly.

'DS Reynolds is out on a case at the moment. He knows you're here, though. He'll be back shortly. Please be patient.'

An insipidly weak tea and a visit to the men's loo later, a man in a suit approached me with a lanyard clicking against the shiny out-dated metal buttons of his suit jacket. If the policeman had been wearing Ray Bans, I might have thought I'd entered the reception of FBI headquarters. This impression was soon banished when the man's jacket flapped open to reveal a creased shirt and an unfashionably wide tie that didn't quite reach midway down his paunch.

'DS John Reynolds,' he said, holding out a hand, which seemed uncharacteristic to me and yet hopeful. If I was a suspect for anything, the cop was hardly going to offer his hand to shake. 'And you must be our elusive Jimmy. Sorry to have kept you. You've been on our list of people to question for quite some time, but as you must have surmised, we've been unable to find you. You're Jimmy...?'

'Marsh. And it's James, actually. James Marsh.'

The DS's brow creased briefly, and I could see virtual bells ringing behind his eyes. 'Come on up. We just want to ask a couple of questions. It's good you've shown up. Two birds, stone and all that. It would make our lives a tad easier if we could sort this out.'

'Sort what out?' I asked, hoping that by a miracle, I would pass by a shelf in the corridor and see my pile of antique books there, waiting to be collected.

'Let's go to my office,' said Reynolds as we exited the lift and walked along a grey tiled corridor.

'Mr Marsh!' DS Hannah chirped with surprise as he walked towards us with a few files and papers in his hands. He stood to one side, and DS Reynolds looked from DS Hannah to me with a frown. 'This is a coincidence,' continued Hannah. 'What are you doing here? What's he doing here, John?'

'I'm as confused as you are,' I said. 'I think I might be the Jimmy your colleague DS Reynolds here has been looking for. Jimmy being James, obviously.'

'The McTavish case, Steve,' said Reynolds to Hannah as he opened a door to an office with a view across the river.

'Please, take a seat,' he said to me. 'I'd like to ask you some questions about William McTavish who we understand you were acquainted with.'

I snorted.

'You're kidding me,' I said.

'I'm sorry?' DS Reynolds said, frowning.

'McTavish. His last name is McTavish? I mean, this feels like a bit of a parody.' I was about to ask what Willie had been up to, prepared to pay bail or whatever it was one was supposed to do to avoid jail, despite "jail" perhaps being a better option than the step outside number 27, when I realised DS Reynolds had used the past tense. My jaw dropped, not quite far enough for my mouth to open, but DS Reynolds clocked that I'd understood. '*Were acquainted...* You mean?—'

'The body of a man was found in Green Park a few weeks ago. We understand from the homeless community that it may be William McTavish, and that you might have been one of the last people to see him. We've had no one else come forward, can't trace any family. He's been deceased for some time, the body is, well... not in a very good state. We were hoping you might be able to enlighten us as to his situation when he was alive.'

'When was he found?' I asked. 'I can't believe he's dead. He was supposed to go into hospital for some tests. I...' That was probably enough information, unless I wanted to get Emma involved, and I figured she'd had enough drama in her life over the past couple of months.

'As I said before, the body was found several weeks ago,' said DS Reynolds. 'Which is why I'm surprised you've come in now. But it seems to me you've already had contact with my colleague for something else?'

'There was a burglary at my home,' I said. 'DS Hannah said they'd borrowed him in my borough for the investigation. But in terms of Willie, the doorman at The Dilly saw me walking past, remembered that you were looking for me back then.'

'Mr McTavish's body might have been there for some time even before it was found. It was half buried in a corner the park gardeners use for autumn compost. A dog walker.'

The ubiquitous dog walker. So that kind of discovery didn't just happen on Line of Duty. *A few weeks?*

'Do you know how he died?' I asked.

'A head wound, brain trauma.'

I hauled in a breath. I'd expected DS Reynolds to say liver failure or a heart attack. I couldn't shake the uncomfortable feeling with this last comment that I might actually be a suspect. DS Hannah had already hinted I might be implicated in my own book theft. Why not throw in a homicide, too? It was, after all, this department's speciality.

'My God, was he *murdered*?' I asked.

'I'm not at liberty to say,' repeated DS Reynolds and my annoyance escaped my lips on a puff of air.

'He must never have made it to the hospital,' I murmured.

'Which hospital?' asked Reynolds.

'I don't know.'

Although it was Emma who'd told me about Willie going into hospital, I hadn't wanted to tell her I'd gone searching for him, to avoid any guilt that she hadn't followed up on his health or to re-ignite bad memories of her time on the street following her awful domestic abuse. I couldn't possibly get Emma involved in all this again.

'When did he say he was going to be admitted?' asked Reynolds.

I chewed the inside of my cheek while calculating the days back to the first time I'd set eyes on Emma and considered.

'It was a Monday in the middle of October,' I said, my voice sounding uncertain. I took out my phone and scrolled through my calendar to give him the exact date.

'We had several people in the same circumstances as Mr McTavish confirm that he was residing temporarily on the shop front opposite Waterstones on Piccadilly. It was the doorman at The Dilly who told us about you.'

I held up the card I'd been clutching. This, surely, vindicated me from any wrong-doing. If I'd cold-bloodedly done away with a homeless man, I wouldn't be presenting myself to the police investigating his murder. I inexplicably felt the hot spike of tears threatening behind my eyes. Poor Willie. *Oor Wullie.*

'I'm afraid I can't tell you anymore about the old fellow. I used to bring him food and the occasional article of clothing. I didn't visit him every day. Perhaps once a week or so, sometimes to chat, sometimes just to bring him something. He must have been a drinker at some stage, broken veins on his nose and all that, but he never seemed completely out of it when I stopped by. I don't know if he had friends, don't know who would do something awful like this.'

'There's one thing you could help us with, Mr Marsh. Although we've been able to put a potential name to the body, we need to be absolutely sure. You seem to be the only person we can genuinely trust to identify Mr McTavish,' said DS Reynolds.

I swallowed.

'If he's been dead this long, is he still identifiable? I've never seen a dead body.'

'Any corpse is not a pleasant thing to see, Mr Marsh, but it would help us a great deal if you could do this. He's been in the morgue for some time. The deterioration has been halted by keeping his body at a low temperature. But we need closure. Mr McTavish needs closure.'

'Oh God, do I have to? I'm a bit squeamish. Can't we do this by photo or something.'

'It may not be easy with a one-dimensional shot. As I said, Sir, you're the only one we can trust, and it will take but a moment.'

I thought of the other homeless in the vicinity, the ones who would surely be able to guess Willie's identity.

'But someone obviously knew his name. Surely that person would be better at identifying him?'

'I used the word "trust" in a loose sense, Mr Marsh. Perhaps *compos mentis* would be more accurate.'

It was more likely they didn't want any of those homeless people sitting in the back of one of their patrol cars while they drove them to the mortuary for the purposes of identification, infusing the seats with their grime and odours.

I wondered whether I should tell Emma that Willie was dead. She was feeling bad enough about the outcome of her relationship with Despicable Nick, and this might tip the scales of her mental fragility after having made a miraculous recovery under my care for the past weeks. I wanted her to feel good about herself, feel positive about the future. Our future. Surely ignorance was bliss in Willie's case?

'Okay,' I said, a tremble in my voice.

44

JAMES

'Are you alright, Mr Marsh?' asked DS Reynolds as I returned to his unmarked BMW and settled into the front seat. I rubbed my temple, still sucking the mint the mortuary assistant had offered me.

'I'll be fine. It's a shock, and gruesome with it. I hope he gets a decent send-off. Poor Willie.'

'Well at least he now has a name. We've been burying too many John Doe's recently in the greater metropolitan area.'

I didn't mention the government's policy for the economically challenged homeless or the current reputation of the Met and whether that might have something to do with inefficient practices. I still needed them on my side to try and recover my precious books.

'If we need any further information from you, I'll be in touch. In the meantime, I'm sure your colleague will get back onto your book theft case. I have to say, of all the crime scene investigation teams we have at the Met, it's a right old coincidence you're involved in two completely unrelated cases. Unlucky on your part as the victim, obviously, but identifying Mr McTavish's body has helped us immensely. Are you quite sure you don't want to talk to anyone about how seeing him has affected you?'

I shook my head and DS Reynolds gave me a tight smile before starting the engine and driving out of the building's parking enclosure. I wondered whether DS Hannah who was really a homicide detective was also on the investigating team for what was obviously now the *murder* of Oor Wullie.

I also thought about what might have happened if Emma had stayed more days on Piccadilly. Maybe she would have been a another victim dragged away by an unknown assailant, robbed of... what? Her sleeping bag, maybe? Then strangled, and her body dumped in Green Park. Thank heavens it hadn't been her.

This would be a distressing revelation for Emma. I wondered what the best way of breaking the news to her would be. It felt deceitful not to tell her anything at all, despite the old adage of *what you don't know won't hurt you.*

DS Reynolds dropped me in the centre of Seven Dials, causing the chip of a car horn from a frustrated taxi driver behind us. Everyone in a vehicle needed patience in this part of town as the roads were so narrow. I almost raised both palms to the driver to show how ridiculous I thought he was being. But any small gesture was likely to cause outrage in this day and age, and I was too close to home to want to draw attention to myself, or more importantly, where I lived.

I decided to break the news to Emma about Willie's death gently. I could do with a little of her sympathy and a hug. Her presence would be a breath of proverbial fresh air to take my mind off the vision of Willie McTavish's pasty grey body surrounded by the sickly smell of embalming fluid.

As I let myself into the flat, I heard Emma's voice talking heatedly to someone upstairs in her room. I thought she might have a visitor, but a long pause in the conversation made me realise she was talking to someone on the phone. I frowned and let the front door, now mended with a new lock and a repaired keypad, close loudly in the frame. It was something I usually abhorred, but now subtly announced my presence at home.

Emma must have quickly finished her call, as she came out with a bright smile on her face. Her hair was pulled back into a ponytail, and she wore her old sweats and an oversized pullover I'd picked up from her flat back in October. Warmth filled my heart, replacing a niggling feeling. I felt so lucky she was alive and well and here in my flat. I was in need of her comfort.

'James! I'm so glad you're back. I was just talking to Mum. She's home. We were discussing when would be best for me to visit her. I might wait until the winter break after exams, what with all the studying I still have to do.'

From what I'd heard, the conversation with her mother hadn't sounded harmonious, but I was relieved she'd be around, although I now felt bad, as I was perhaps about to bring her mood down a notch. I took a deep breath.

'Emma, something terrible has happened. Come here, let's sit on the couch.'

'Is it something to do with your books?' she asked hesitantly, sitting beside me. 'Is it bad news from the insurance company?'

'What? No, according to George that process will take weeks, maybe even months to go through. No, this is about Willie.'

'Willie?' she asked, as though she'd already forgotten who he was.

'Willie, whose patch you were occupying on Piccadilly.'

Emma's face blanched. Did she know it was going to be bad news? She must have read my expression and assumed the worst.

'The police found his body in Green Park.'

'Oh no!' Emma put her hand to her mouth.

'I wasn't going to tell you. I didn't want you to feel bad about his disappearance.'

'This is truly terrible news,' she said.

'The police persuaded me to identify his body this afternoon – he was in an awful state – and asked me when I'd last seen him alive. But it's made me wonder which day either of us last saw him. Can you remember? I told them Saturday, a couple of days before I came to talk to you for the first time.'

'The police questioned you?' Emma's voice took on an urgent, almost angry tone, as though just talking to them had been the wrong thing to do.

'Well, I...'

'Oh God, I'm sorry, James.' The anger on her face quickly dropped and she came to hug me, burying her face against my shoulder. I could feel her heart beating. She hadn't answered my question. 'This must be so upsetting for you. I didn't know him very well. But I imagine he must be in a better place now. Living on the street is no life for anyone.'

I wasn't sure how to respond to that comment. It certainly wasn't what I'd expected. However much living on the street was a hardship, there was surely always hope. Death was not the answer, and certainly not at the hands of someone else.

45

EMMA

I stayed quiet for the rest of the afternoon, trying to work out what I should do with this latest news. James assumed I'd gone into a bit of a funk in learning of Willie's death, and I was happy to let him think that. While he was in the kitchen making us dinner, I went up to my room with my phone to sort out a few things and then take a long shower.

James had made an English version of my favourite dish he'd cooked at the chalet in St Moritz – a macaroni cheese made with cheddar – claiming it would be comfort-therapy. We ate from bowls sitting on the sofa, watching a sappy film, accompanied by a bottle of chilled Chablis. Half way through dinner, my phone beeped. I picked it up and opened the message.

'It's my mum,' I said. 'She's sent me a train ticket. For tomorrow!'

James swallowed, and a slight frown appeared on his brow. I felt a rush of affection for him and the first seed of guilt that I would be leaving him so soon after discovering this afternoon's tragedy.

'That's a sudden change of plans,' he said. 'Did you tell her about Willie?

She nodded.

'You should really go, Emma. You haven't seen her for ages. Waiting until February does seem like such a long time. If I had a daughter and hadn't seen her for Christmas, I'd be sending train tickets too.' I said.

'Are you sure about this? I feel bad leaving you.'

'You're not *leaving* me,' he said, smiling. 'When will you be back?'

'The return is for the 30th. I'll be back to celebrate New Year with you,' I said, kissing him on his cheek.

'The last thing I can think about at this point is celebrating anything.'

'New Year, new start and all that,' I said.

James frowned. 'The New Year celebrations will probably put everything on a go-slow as far as the investigation is concerned. DS Hannah and is undoubtedly taking days off.'

I suspected he wanted to ask whether he could come with me. Did he find it odd that I hadn't invited him? I'd just spent a week in his parents' company. He'd undoubtedly hope I might reciprocate, given the depth of our relationship. Before he could voice that thought, I continued. 'My ticket for the train is non-refundable. If you need me around, you know I *could* change it, but it makes things a bit complicated.'

'You must go,' he said. 'It's your mum.'

'Anyway, you'll be able to sort this business out with your books without me bothering you every five minutes,' I said.

He leaned towards me and tucked a stray lock of hair behind my ear, a wistful smile on his face. This, at least, was the truth.

Later that night, I made James feel better by taking his mind off his woes between the sheets. I wanted to leave him with a lasting good memory and I actually felt bad about leaving. James was a thoughtful and considerate lover. I'd actually grown to enjoy these intimate moments as much as his wit and kindness over the past weeks.

In the morning, I lay with my head on his shoulder, the musky smell of our bodies infusing the rumpled sheets.

'I'm not going to change the sheets until the day you come back,' he said. 'So I can be reminded of you while I sleep in your absence. The bed is going to feel way too big.'

I stroked his chest, remembering Marta wasn't due back for at least another week, and that she might be a little pre-occupied with the police for a while on her return. I rolled away from James and stretched, before climbing out of bed and going to my room. I quickly showered and packed, and went back into James's room where he was stirring from a snooze. I pulled on my jacket.

'Do you have to leave *right now*?' he asked, his voice sounding a little whiny.

'Oh, baby. It's only for a couple of days.'

I leaned across the bed and gave him a kiss, my hair falling into his face. He wiped his eye, and my stomach clenched, thinking I might actually have reduced him to tears rather than my hair brushing his eye. I pushed myself off the bed, and began backing out of the room.

'I'll keep in touch,' I said. 'I'm only a phone call away.'

I clattered down the stairs in my favourite pair of boots, dragging my bag behind me, feeling like a naughty child for wearing outdoor footwear in James's flat. I heard no reprimand from his room.

I took one last look at the flat, this amazing oasis in the centre of London. Then I hurried across the courtyard, hauling my bag behind me. The iron gate clunked closed behind me and I walked swiftly to the Covent Garden tube, a tiny grain of regret knocking on my conscience. If I thought deeply about it, James was the man of my dreams, and in any other circumstances, I wouldn't have left his side.

But I had a family commitment to uphold, and blood would always run thicker than water.

46

SALLY

I remembered the day I'd seen Jamie looking out of the window back in October at whom I soon learned was that wretched girl in the doorway, that there was a guy checking *him* out in the bookshop.

Jamie had been up and down that ladder to the shelving unit in Classics all morning, organising the display for the festival. I initially thought the stalker guy had the hots for him, the way his eyes lingered on Jamie who seemed distracted by something outside on Piccadilly. Jamie kept looking out of the window down to the street between his task of attaching the two ends of a banner above the unit.

If it hadn't been for the stalker's creepy behaviour, I'd have found him attractive; tall, strong jaw, remnants of an old tan, dark blond hair with what looked like natural streaks from time spent outdoors. I experienced a tiny spike of jealousy, wanted to tell the guy to take his eyes off Jamie who was swiping a lock of hair away from his temple and trying to get a better view through the window – what *was* he looking at? But then I could have stated the reverse. Why was this guy so pre-occupied with someone like Jamie?

My curiosity to know what had caught Jamie's attention outside almost diverted me from the stalker. But my eyes narrowed when the guy quickly turned away as Jamie climbed down the step ladder. It was obvious the stalker didn't want to be caught. But obvious in a way that was different from creepy. It wasn't an embarrassed duck-out-of-the-way to avoid revealing some kind of sexual attraction. His body language said he was trying to avoid being spotted at all. I felt the frisson of something sinister but also intriguing.

My suspicions were further confirmed by the way the guy moved past the shelves and table displays with complete nonchalance when Jamie left the floor. The man's eyes didn't once stray to any of the hardback display tables we'd all taken great care to arrange for their visual attractiveness. Instead, he slalomed quickly between them to make himself scarce. It was obvious he wasn't there for the love of books. Maybe I'd read too many whodunnits, but he moved with the stealth of a spy.

A few weeks later I saw a guy outside Jamie's place in Seven Dials with *her*. Although I hadn't seen his face, something about his physique and a few locks of hair poking out from under a tight beanie was familiar to me. Back then I couldn't work out where I might have seen him before. I'd been too occupied in my relief that Jamie's girlfriend had moved on to consider I might have indeed seen him before. There seemed to be a familiarity between her and this strange man, perhaps a sexual spark that two people in a long-term relationship might have. It hadn't occurred to me that she might be cheating on Jamie. I simply assumed she was no longer *with* Jamie.

It was only later that it struck me odd that this guy and the girl in the doorway were both still in Jamie's territory, wandering away down Earlham Street, deep in conversation. I thought it might be petty to mention I'd seen them to Jamie. If he was no longer with her, he'd tell me in his own good time. If by any chance he *was* still with her, I didn't want to be the bringer of bad news like a jealously shunned lover. Grassing on his girlfriend now would have only looked spiteful.

When we finally managed to talk at Christmas, it was because I had the excuse of needing to let him know about the pre-auction request at Sotheby's. This was something that could not be ignored. But he annoyingly brushed off the possibility that it could have been his book.

But I knew. Even Fenella, my contact at Sotheby's knew. Was he that blinded by love? I'd thought it was a bit of stupid ignorance. It didn't make him topple from my pedestal then, though. If I could, I'd still help him out any way I could. But it made me realise he might not care as much as I'd previously thought about material objects, specifically his antique books.

But his call three days before New Year was no real surprise.

'Took you long enough,' I teased. 'Are you still smarting over my last 107-pointer?'

'Brava, Sal. God, I'm so, so sorry about all this.' I guessed he wasn't talking about his latest Words-With-Friends loss. 'You were absolutely right, that's very likely my Dickens that Fenella had notice for,' he continued. 'My flat's been broken into. The Tardis has been raided. A few of my books have gone.'

I'd often wondered why Jamie didn't have more security attached to that cabinet. As he'd gone on to explain the break-in, it was apparent the glass wasn't as impenetrable as the specifications and guarantees had originally stated.

'I had a feeling the Dickens was yours. It's a unique edition. The fact that I could only get hold of you through the gaming app is a sure sign that someone didn't want me to connect with you.' I left out the fact that my gut feeling was his new girlfriend might have removed me from his contacts. I was surmising, and maybe even still hoping, that I posed some kind of threat to her. That she thought I might be in the running for Jamie's affections.

'Can you come round, Sal? I feel like I need your wise counsel. Two heads are better than one. The DS on my case normally investigates homicides. He probably doesn't have a clue about the book world.'

This would be the first time in over a month that I would see him. Not that I'd been pining for him. Things at mum's had become a little chaotic with my brother going through a relapse, and I'd had to take a few days unpaid leave off work to help them back in Chelmsford. We were still desperately trying to secure the expensive treatment, but the GoFundMe page hadn't accrued enough funds.

But when he called, I acknowledged to myself I'd definitely been having Jamie withdrawal symptoms. I'd resigned myself to the fact that it might be months before I saw him again, if little miss street girl had anything to do with it.

'Is your girlfriend there?' I had to ask, but still couldn't say her name, in the fear I might say it with a great deal of animosity. As it happened, the word 'girlfriend' came out with an equal amount of suppressed sarcasm.

'She's gone to visit her mum. She'll be gone for a couple of days while I try and sort all this out. Except it's likely to take way longer than that. But at least I should have a handle on this madness by the time she gets back.'

'I'll bunk off early. Oh... wait, where have I heard that before?'

'Jesus, don't you go losing your job as well, Sal. After you've finished work will be fine.'

'Oh, pooh. I'm owed a few hours,' I lied. 'Shop's not busy right now. I'm heading over. A skinny latte for me from that new-fangled coffee machine of yours when I arrive. Have you had lunch yet? I'll bring a few bacon rolls.' I didn't wait for his answer. 'I'll be there in a tick.'

When our call ended, I rushed to the staff cloakroom, shoved my laptop into my backpack and left work, claiming a forgotten dental appointment. I'd used up the credit I had when I'd covered for James Marsh for all those weeks last autumn, but this I would not miss. It was time to put my Miss Marple hat on to help him in his time of need.

47

JAMES

'I should have followed up on your suspicions immediately, although I don't know what I could have done from Switzerland,' I said, preparing coffees for Sal and me.

Sally slid the bacon rolls from a paper bag onto two plates. 'I should have checked up on this place earlier,' she said. 'When Fenella told me about the Dickens. I could easily have found your neighbour's telephone number.'

I reached into the cupboard for my tube of Coleman's mustard and slathered each roll with a healthy, nose-tingling dose, knowing Sal's love of spicy food.

'I did ask Mrs A next door to check my place,' I said. 'But she didn't give the door much of a push to see if it was open, or if she did, she must have only done it timidly. Has George contacted you, yet?'

I meant George Merrison, my antique book insurance rep. Although we were long-time acquaintances, I imagined him desperately seeking a loophole to avoid paying out a significant insurance claim.

'Why would he call me? I'm your friend. I'd be the last person he'd contact if he thought I might be protecting you.'

'I know he's asked your advice before about tracing books. The police are investigating *me*, for Christ's sake. I don't know how much time they're spending on looking for the real thieves.'

'But I'm your ally, so George might think I'd even lie for you if I thought you'd committed fraud.'

I hesitated, the question *well, would you?* was on the tip of my tongue. 'He'd still scope you out though, surely?'

'You're probably the most honest person I know,' said Sal. 'Gullibly honest, if truth be told. How can the police suspect you? You weren't even here! Do they think you got someone else to organise the theft? That feels pretty weird – a 1970s crime thriller movie perhaps – *The Seven Dials Job*. Do you think they'll put *me* on their list of suspects?'

'I don't know,' I said. 'The police say the owners are the first people they investigate in a case like this. They asked for a list of close contacts, so you're on there, but they can't suspect everybody.'

'I haven't received a call yet,' she said. 'They're probably preoccupied with Christmas issues. Filling their holding cells with drunken vandals and domestic violence culprits.'

I raked my fingers through my hair and carried my plate and cup across to the living room. Sal was always able to raise a laugh, but today my sense of humour was sadly lacking. Sal paused briefly to glance at the ravaged Tardis and sat on the sofa next to me.

'Whoever took those books did a poor job of hiding the fact that they already had access to my place and then made the break-in look like a spontaneous theft. The police actually think Marta did it.'

'Lovely Marta? No way! Have they questioned her?' asked Sal.

'They tried to contact her. But she's not due to return from Portugal until the 6th. I hope the bloody police don't arrest her at the airport when she lands.'

'Honestly, James, I don't think Marta could possibly have the know-how to get a pre-notification sent to bidders for Sotheby's.'

'I didn't think so either. I've met her husband. He's a lovely guy too, but as a talented pastry chef, he doesn't strike me as someone who'd have knowledge of antique books. The cops said you never know, though. Maybe someone they know is blackmailing them. She's not hired through an agency. She's been with me forever through a friend of the family. And she's never given any indication that she might have been put under pressure.'

'Whoever is trying to sell your book or books is either trying for a quick sale or scoping the auction climate to set a price on the black market.'

'Did you ask Fenella if she was able to trace the seller? I gave the police her name as well. I hope you don't mind. She'll know it came through your connection with me.'

'She'll be fine with that. She already knows the scoop. This one has stumped us. Fenella hasn't come up with any leads on the origin of the request to auction. Because it's only a request for catalogue inclusion, banking details haven't yet been supplied. It's pretty typical for sellers to remain anonymous, but she says the amount of cover-up in this case means the book's ownership was already in question. Obviously if it had gone for auction, the police would be able to access bank details.'

'Could this really be Marta or her family?' I said as I shook my head.

'I don't believe it either,' she said. 'Let's see whether the cops come up with any other explanation. Maybe someone's aware of your finances and has been stalking you over the past few... oh shit.'

I looked at her, eyebrows raised.

'Do you remember the Greek Classics festival?'

'You mean the one where I was fortunate enough to be fired before I had to take that sodding poster back down at the end of the week? How could I forget?'

A smile touched her mouth, perhaps glad that I hadn't entirely lost my sense of humour, even if it was bitter irony.

'There was this guy checking you out in the shop the day you were setting up the display, when you were struggling to put that *sodding* poster up.'

I pressed my lips together, remembering that was the first day I'd set eyes on Emma across the street from the book store. Sal continued.

'It was rather odd. I couldn't work out whether he fancied you or not. Perhaps he didn't want to ask the shop assistant standing right there in the middle of the shop for help looking for a book, because I was a *woman*. But then I didn't get that vibe, you know, the puppy dog look of repressed passion.'

I snorted. 'You're going to have to show me exactly what *that* looks like.'

'I can't, because I'm not a bloke, but I guess it would go something like this...' Her eyebrows rose into a V above her nose and she pouted.

It was a look I'd already seen from time to time over the past few years, confirming she might have wanted our relationship to develop a little further than our already solid friendship.

'Anyway, he obviously didn't want you to catch him watching you, turned his back as you came down the ladder to pick up a pile of books and climb back up again to put them on the display stands. And then when you came down and went to put the ladder away, he just skulked off through the shop and left. I knew he wasn't a bibliophile, because he ignored my spectacular display of hardbacks at the top of the stairs, went right on past them in his hurry to leave.'

'I guess you'll get to the point of telling me why you thought this was significant.'

'It was like he was *stalking* you, Jamie. Perhaps he was sussing you out. Perhaps he was building a picture of when would be the best time to break into your place and rob you. It looked dead suspicious.'

'Sounds a bit far-fetched to me, Sal. Come on. If it was so significant, why are you only mentioning it now?'

'That night there was a double book launch. The one where Jen went home feeling a bit squiffy. We were run off our feet, and I felt a bit like a wedding planner. I was going to tell you at our regular post-event analysis in some pub or eatery afterwards, but you were distracted, and if I'm honest, I was a bit miffed when you said you had something to do at home. I hadn't realised at that point that something else, or I should say *someone* else, was on your mind.'

'Look, I know Emma's changed so much in my life—'

'It's okay, I'm sorry. I'm sounding grumpy. I've missed our get-togethers.'

This confirmed that Sal was jealous of Emma. I felt a stab of guilt. I'd thought about taking our relationship further many times over the years, and we'd even broached the subject in the pub once after some drunken book event, but she'd stressed that work colleagues should never get romantically involved, so I'd never pursued it. She seemed to be regretting that now.

'I was going to mention the stalker guy to you later that evening,' she said. 'But I only remembered after we parted ways and I was already tucking into a double cheese and bacon burger at Honest Burgers. *On my own.*' She looked at me in mock disapproval, confirming my earlier thought. 'And we didn't really see each other anymore after that.' She was beginning to sound like a disgruntled ex.

I looked at her, my mouth turned down in a frown, returning an expression of mock guilt.

'It could be that the guy who'd been stalking you in the bookshop had some kind of ulterior motive, namely a plan to steal your books. He would definitely be on my list of suspects.'

48

EMMA

I have had to pull out sooner than planned.' I spoke into my mobile as I hurried towards the tube station, my heavy bag already digging painfully into my shoulder. 'I've left the condo. I'm on my way. I'll come straight to you. I'll see if I can get on an EasyJet flight from Gatwick.'

I felt a twinge of remorse as I'd left James in his room, wondering why on earth I suddenly had to leave after my made-up mother living up north had been on a cruise with my made-up aunt and why we felt compelled to see each other *right now*. His confusion elicited a modicum of guilt.

'What? Why?' said the voice on the phone. 'I thought you were going to wait to see about the insurance for the books. That's why you went back to London.'

'Change of plan. That stupid vagabond's body was found in Green Park by a dog,' I said as I pushed my way through the crowds. 'A fucking dog!' I stage whispered to avoid turning any heads. 'Can you believe it? The thwarting of many a murderer's plans.'

There. I'd said it. Murderer. Although that certainly hadn't been our intention. Not even manslaughterer.

'But it was an *accident*!' he said.

'Well, I'm not going to hang around to prove our innocence on that count. The police wouldn't look at it that way if they put two and two together. Don't forget we are now thieves too.'

'How come you've only found out now?' His voice squeaked.

I figured he probably felt worse than I did about the death of the vagabond.

'It was impossible to find out exactly who the vagabond was or where he'd come from. But the fucking doorman at the Dilly was questioned by the police back in autumn and remembered our Good Samaritan taking stuff to the guy. It just so happened that James was walking by yesterday and the doorman recognised him, put him in touch with the cops who were on the case back then. We can be thankful he never told them about me occupying that homeless man's patch. He was protecting me, but not in the legal sense. He was protecting my emotions. Anyway, I've had to leave, things are getting too hot. I don't want *anyone* to think I was somehow responsible for either of these acts.'

'Well...'

'Christ. Don't you start! Come on, it was neither of our faults that the vagabond died. Well, mine just a bit. But I feel really vulnerable now. As though the police will eventually link the two things with the tenuous connection to James. And that bloody friend of his, Sally, has been poking her nose in where it's not wanted. I fixed James's phone so her messages wouldn't get through, but I suspect she's found a way.'

I heard a swallow on the phone. Back in October, we hadn't realised how belligerent the homeless man would be and how protective he was of that doorway in Piccadilly. The promise of money got the old fellow as far as the entrance to Green Park. We'd entered the park to try and avoid being seen by anybody on the street. It was unlit in there and less likely to be covered by security cameras. The strange trio of us stumbled through the night. Both of us had been wearing dark hoodies so we were unlikely to be identified if we were caught on camera. The vagabond was also dark with dirt. And smelly.

It was as we were trying to shuffle the guy westwards to find him new digs in a different borough, he began to protest that we were moving too far away from his food donation sources. Apparently, Mayfair was far more lucrative than Knightsbridge where there had been more tourists and he was less likely to be moved on. When we firmly insisted on him continuing towards Hyde Park Corner, he became quite violent. I didn't think he had it in him. We didn't have much money, but even the promise of a bribe couldn't get the old fellow to comply.

He had wrestled his stinky sleeve from my grasp and staggered sideways with the momentum. He'd suddenly kicked out with his foot. As I was bending to regain my own balance, the edge of his shoe caught me on the side of my face, and I wondered whether he had broken my cheekbone. But it was nothing to do with agility. He'd tripped down some unseen steps in the dark. In surprise I pushed his leg, perhaps a little harder than I meant to, trying to get his stink away from me. He stumbled forward to the ground and fell against a curb hemming in a leaf-strewn flowerbed in the park. His body rolled at a strange angle and he didn't move. With a horrible, sick feeling, before I'd even scrambled for my phone to turn on the flash light, I knew the guy was dead.

Despite this horrible tragedy, that whack ended up being fortuitous. Although it hurt like crazy, it created a shiner that would make the story of Nick's abuse all the more authentic.

'There's a seat on tonight's flight to Zürich. I'm paying through the nose as it's still the most expensive week to fly, but I have to leave,' I spoke into my mobile phone as I came up from the underground at Victoria, hurrying towards the Gatwick Express platforms.

'Why don't you wait a few days? Won't James be suspicious of this sudden departure?'

'I can't risk the police getting leads on the vagabond's death and linking it to the theft. By the way, what the hell were you thinking? A stupid mistake leaving the key lying on the floor. I set everything up for you. You had the keycodes to the door and knew where the cabinet key was hidden. Why didn't you put it back?'

'I thought I did put it back. It must have somehow come away from the magnetic holder,' he said. 'I did what you said, extracted the books first, and then smashed the glass in the cabinet and jimmied the front door of the flat to make it look more like a random break-in.'

'It was imperative that you wouldn't damage the books in any way. That's why I suggested you remove them before smashing the glass of the cabinet, then make it look like a random theft. But that key makes it obvious the cabinet was opened before it was smashed... James is gradually working things out. It's why I had to get the hell out of there.'

'Where did you find the key? I certainly didn't do that on purpose,' he said.

'It must have bounced across the floor to rest underneath the armchair. I thought James was going to go off on one when I reached for it and picked it up before the police arrived, but I didn't want the risk that you might have left your prints on anything.'

'I was wearing gloves. But so what if my prints were found? I'm not traceable. I don't have a record.'

He was right. I figured he couldn't possibly be connected to any of this, and that even if his prints were lifted by the police, he wouldn't appear on any database in the UK. I should have left the damned thing there. I could tell James had been intensely irritated with me for picking it up. Too late now.

With doubts now likely adding up in James's mind, the longer I hung around, the more likely I'd become a suspect. That bookseller friend of his, Sally, had the look of mistrust all over her face from the first day we met. It was time for me to give a hand on the other end, to make sure we at least had the secondary focus of our booty secured in all of this.

'You have the books stored somewhere dry and out of the light, though, right?'

'Yes, Ma'am,' he said. 'They're safe.'

49

SALLY

I had always wondered what an independently wealthy young man was doing working a relatively shitty job in the country's biggest chain book store. I'd rather be seeking employment in the Bodleian or the Gladstone if I'd had the chance. I'm sure with his university degree in library sciences and his family's influence, even that would have been possible. All that peace and quiet, without the bother of having to pander to clients and shoppers all day. Or if it had to be retail, I wondered why he didn't seek employment in one of the more glamorous or eclectic independent book stores. I had every reason to resent him for his station in life. He seemed to be ignorant of the fact that he was richer than anyone I knew.

But annoyingly, it's what made James *him*, that he was so *engaging* with people. He needed lots of booklovers around him to share their passion. Waterstones had a constant stream of book-loving traffic and potential book-lovers ready to be converted. Shoppers in the antique book shops of Cecil's Court already knew what they wanted and were less likely to be wooed by something new.

I didn't let on that I knew he was independently wealthy. But the first time he invited me round to his place for a game of Scrabble, it was pretty obvious he couldn't have paid his rent or acquired his precious objects with the earnings of a mediocre bookseller's salary. I avoided asking him, because I didn't want him to have to admit that he was leading some kind of clandestine lifestyle as a working-class bookseller for reasons he didn't want to reveal. He seemed so happy in his job which appeared so *normal* to me, and I'm sure one of the reasons was that he wanted to appear normal to others. I also imagine it was something he didn't feel he could discuss with me. I must have given the impression of being a little too bohemian to approve of family trust funds and inherited millions.

It was only after our fourth or fifth game of Scrabble that I became curious about his understated wealth, and carried out a little online research. I discovered who his father was, looked up some of the family assets and found out about a bunch of directorships through Companies House. Scouring the Financial Times and a number of trading bulletins further revealed his father's involvement in various funds. I felt guilty doing this, as though I was the type of potential gold-digger girlfriend he'd undoubtedly be trying to avoid.

Back then I valued his friendship more than a romantic interlude that had potential not to last, thinking if I declared my feelings for him, the status of the other part of our relationship in its platonic mode might change. I didn't want anything to change on the friendship front. I just wanted the extra stuff that goes with a romance *on top* of that friendship. But by the time I was ready to make a declaration about my inner feelings, he'd met his girl in the doorway and got himself fired. With the latter event, I was finally mentally free for the pursuit, as we were no longer work colleagues. But his involvement with the person who'd put him in his state of unemployment meant it was too late to do anything about the former.

Jamie had a generous heart. He always gave spare change to the homeless, even took them food. Every book that ever came through the store where the publisher promised to donate a percentage of its profit to some charity or other, he'd buy extra copies, whether he was interested in reading it or not. He also gave off an air of nonchalance, and many people read this as quiet confidence. I'd always worried that someone would take advantage of that. So when we left the bookstore the night of that double book-launch all those weeks ago, he'd stared long and hard at something on the other side of the road in the dark. Of all things, it turned out to be that homeless girl in the doorway of a clothing store that was due to open soon. I'd often seen people sleeping there over the years, mainly drunken old men leering at everyone who walked by.

When he was fired, completely unfairly in my opinion, I couldn't protest too much. I needed my job more than he needed his. But by then I realised that *she* was the object of his newfound affection, I wondered whether she was taking advantage of his vulnerability in the form of his charity.

'Do you think the death of that homeless man is linked to any of this?' I said.

'How did you know about Willie?' he asked.

'Everyone knows you checked up on the guy from time to time. The police came to the shop weeks ago, apparently, when a body was found in Green Park. By then you'd been sacked, but no one linked it to the same guy. I was probably the only one who knew you used to take him stuff. I was on a break when they came.' I laughed. 'Ironically, if they'd interrogated me, you'd probably have been arrested long ago.'

Jamie frowned. 'Willie told me... us, that he was going to hospital for some tests. I went looking for him after she moved in, after I'd lost my job. I was stuck for something to do with my sudden freedom. I wanted to find out if he was okay. I only told Emma that he died yesterday. I thought it might upset her too much. Knowing she'd occupied the place where he used to *live*.' Jamie stood up and walked over to the Tardis. 'I was really sorry to learn about Willie, but I thank my stars every day that it wasn't Emma who'd been dragged off and murdered by some unknown assailant. She managed to get out of there just in time. How do you think it could be linked?'

'I'm not sure.' I paused, thinking. 'Are you certain Willie died after Emma arrived on Piccadilly and not before?'

Jamie's eyebrows creased.

'I'm not sure what you're implying there, Sal, but honestly they are in no way connected. She'd been driven there by a horribly abusive partner.

She had bruises on her face.' He sat down in the armchair and I felt the tiny distance between us was suddenly more emotional than physical.

'I'm not trying to stir trouble, or make you think badly of her, but you've known each other for such a short time, maybe there are things you don't yet know about her,' I said.

'We have no secrets...' Jamie's voice tapered on a sibilant 's' as though he'd remembered something. 'Although she was sneaky enough to mute you on my phone.'

'I knew it. I'm going to sound like I'm just parroting you, but Jamie, do you think Emma has anything to hide?'

'No, I... we trust each other completely. You're making me feel uncomfortable, Sal.'

'I'm not trying to interrogate you or admonish you. Simply trying to work out who might be involved in all this.' I moved my hand in a sweeping arc in front of the broken Tardis.

'Can we stop with the finger-pointing at Emma, though? She couldn't have had anything to do with it because she was with me at the time.'

It was my turn to bite my lip. I could see his point. I'd started piling on her without her being around to defend herself.

'And what about her ex? Maybe he somehow found out she was shacked up with you and took his revenge?'

'I find that hard to believe. He wouldn't have known that I offered her a place to stay or possibly have known where I live. She came to me in the shop after she left their place for the last time, and I only offered her a bed *after* that.'

'Maybe you should still have told DS Hannah about him. They need to examine all possibilities.'

James chewed the inside of his cheek, his look telling me that my theory was very far-fetched.

'Not to be indiscreet, but did Emma have her own room upstairs?'

'Yes. It's not like she jumped into my bed on the very first night.'

'Are you really not tempted to go and look at her things while she's gone?' I asked. 'See if you can discover a bit more about her.'

'Jesus, Sal. That's awful. That screams mistrust to me.'

'Well, I'm sure she scoped out every inch of your flat when you weren't here. Come on, Jamie. Everyone does that. You can't be *that* naïve. If

Marta were here, she'd be going in there anyway.' I raised my eyes to the landing along the gallery upstairs. I knew the first room was the guest room.

'Call me Miss Trust,' I said as I leapt out of the chair and took the stairs two at a time to the landing. I stood beside Emma's door, covered my eyes with my right hand, grabbed the door handle with my left and let it swing open while I faced Jamie. Then I turned to look into her room through a split in my fingers.

'Jamie. She said she'd be back in a couple of days?'

'Yes, why? Sal, what's your bloody problem?'

'She's cleared right out.'

'What do you mean?'

'You'd never know this was her room. It's empty.'

Jamie gave a big sigh, slapped his hands on the top of his knees and stood up. He came up the stairs, his footfalls a little heavy, telling me without words that I should be careful, that I was starting to piss him off. But when he went past me into Emma's room, his hand reached to his head and he massaged the back of his scalp, his fingers slipping through his mop of hair. It was a movement I knew. Confusion had quashed his irritation.

The room was empty, except for the furniture. The sliding door on the wardrobe was open, revealing... empty hangers. No clothes. The bed was neatly made. There were no trinkets on the bedside table, nothing lying across the chair in the corner. I said nothing, watched Jamie walk to the ensuite bathroom, open the door. He turned to face me.

'She didn't have many things to speak of. But *everything* has gone. It's like she was never here.' A note of sadness touched his disbelief.

'Did she keep anything in your room?'

I swallowed the unpleasantness from the back of my throat. The thought of them together in his bed made me feel slightly sick.

'She kept all her things in here,' he said. 'It was unlikely we'd have long-term visitors so rather than making space for her in my wardrobe, we thought the simplest thing would be for her to continue to use this spare room as a kind of dressing room. With the ensuite, she could spread all her stuff out without it getting in the way of my shaving gear in my bathroom. Look, I know it sounds pretentious, but I have all this space and no one using some of it. I left it to her. But... This looks horribly like she's not coming back. She must be coming back, right?'

He posed this last question as though it was rhetorical. Much as I wanted it to be true that she wasn't coming back, I couldn't say a word. I went over to the waste paper bin. There were a few papers in there underneath a couple of eye makeup remover pads and some hair that had probably been pulled from a brush. I gingerly pulled the papers from underneath, shaking off the hair, cotton-wool pads and some eyeliner pencil shavings. There were a couple of Eurostar and TGV tickets, a reservation slip with *Emma Smith* written on it, and an open but empty envelope, stamped and addressed to E.Schmid with an address not far from my place south of the river. The contents of the envelope had been removed.

'Do you recognise this address?' I asked Jamie, as he took the envelope from me.

A look of confusion crumpled his face as he breathed out noisily.

'It's the flat where she used to live,' he said. 'Where I picked up her things.'

'Wait, you've just travelled with her half way across Europe. Did you ever see her passport?'

'We travelled by train, and only had to show our passports on the Eurostar. On the way back, I remember thinking I should ask to see her passport – you know, it's the thing you do – check out the terrible photos. But I missed the opportunity as a family with a bunch of kids was walking through the carriage and there was momentary mayhem when they realised that they were in first class by mistake. The rest of Europe is in the Schengen zone, including Switzerland. Open borders. You don't have to show your passport. Unless you're flying.' He bit his lip.

'Oh Jamie, I'm really sorry. But I'm not sure your Miss Smith is who she really says she is.'

50

JAMES

'She's not answering her mobile.' I took my mobile from my ear and tapped out a message on the screen for Emma to call me. 'It's just so... confusing. This might be nothing, though. I don't want to make her think I'm suspicious, that I'm keeping track, or that I think she might not be invested in our relationship.'

'God, Jamie, I'm so sorry. This wasn't my intention *at all*. I feel like shit now.'

'I know, Sal. It's not like you knew she'd taken *all* her things. I honestly don't know what to think. Maybe she thought Marta would do a deep clean while she was gone? But Marta won't be back until well after the New Year. Emma told me her return ticket is on the 30th. But to take *everything?* I refuse to believe she's... gone.'

I felt a little queasy. I knew Sal wanted to give me a hug, but thought that might actually trigger full-on tears that weren't very far away, so I surreptitiously took a step back out of her reach.

'Do you think Emma Smith is really Emma Schmid?'

'I'm not sure. Why she'd Anglicise her name is beyond me. We're generations away from the post-war trend of wanting to change names because of their origins.'

'It really does look like she's done a runner, though. If I were you my suspicions would be on high alert.' I almost heard a tone of glee in her voice, and swallowed as this possibility had not yet entirely sunk in. Sal put her hand on my arm. 'If there's anything I can do...'

'Actually, there is,' I said, trying to pull myself together. 'Will you come with me to her old place? This address?' I waved the envelope at her. 'The flat she shared with Despicable Nick.'

'Despicable Nick? Sounds like a cartoon villain.'

'He's the partner – the ex-partner – who abused her. The whole reason she ended up on Piccadilly in the first place. Maybe your theory has some glue to it. DS Hannah might not give it a thought, but maybe we can do a bit of digging ourselves. Perhaps this Schmid person was a flatmate.'

Sal gave me a silent look with her lips pulled in. I knew she had a thought she wasn't voicing. Mainly I felt sick that Emma might have gone back to Despicable Nick, after what he supposedly did to her. Hadn't I been enough for her? I would have given her everything she wanted. We'd hadn't yet uttered those three words to each other, but we'd certainly shown each other physically how much we meant to each other. During the moments we'd spent gazing into each other's eyes before, during and after our lovemaking, far more than three words were conveyed in the things that were left unsaid. Unless she was a very good actress.

I knew Sal wanted to ask how serious our relationship had developed in that respect, but also knew that a conversation with her about this would be akin to entering a minefield.

On the train to Clapham Junction, I tried to call Emma again.

'She's still not answering her phone, and I've no idea how to get hold of her. Am I overthinking this? Could her ex have done the dirty deed? It's just... something doesn't seem right.'

'I guess we might find out,' she said.

Once out of the station, we followed the instructions on my Google Maps app to the address on the envelope, where I'd picked up Emma's things that fated week back in autumn.

'We're not far from my place,' Sal said, and I felt a twinge of remorse that I'd never been to her flat. 'I'm half a mile or so in the opposite direction. It's kind of uncanny she lived so close by.'

'It's the next street. I recognise the houses. I remember there was a policeman on the street. I'd wondered whether the ex was expecting Emma to come back and take her things, and had thought she might take more than she was entitled to. I became unnecessarily paranoid but was also worried I was going to run into Nick. He didn't sound like the kind of person who would want to pass the time of day exchanging pleasantries.'

'Despicable Nick,' stated Sal, and I pressed my mouth into a line. 'Well, you may run into him now, but if he's at home, he's hardly going to admit to having stolen your books. Do you even know what this Nick looks like?'

'No... Oh, I hadn't thought of that. This is it,' I said as we passed through the two low brick pillars by the box hedge border that still smelled vaguely of cat wee.

What looked like a child's stroller was tucked into the area beside the front door with a broom handle sticking out of the top. I didn't remember seeing that last time.

'It's a kiddies bike trailer. Must be from the upstairs flat,' I said as my index finger pressed the lower of the two brass bell buttons, neither of which had a name next to it.

We made out the shape of a person dressed in pale clothes through the frosted glass approaching the door. An arm reached up to release the catch. The door swung open to reveal a young, blonde woman wearing rubber gloves, her hair folded into an untidy ponytail.

No hello, she simply raised her eyebrows and pursed her lips.

'Um... Is Nick in?' I asked.

'Nick who? Cave, Kyrgios, Father Christmas?' she asked with an antipodean twang.

I thought, *wow* and wanted to say *no... Nolte, Kershaw, Cage*. That was a lot of Nicks. I was worried Sal was going to say "Despicable," but she didn't.

'The guy who lives in the ground-floor flat *is* called Nick, right?' I asked.

'No one lives in the ground-floor flat,' said the woman who I guessed was Aussie after the mention of the tennis player.

Sal frowned. 'But we can see furniture through the window. A sofa. A TV. It looks lived-in to me,' she said.

'It's an AirBnB rental,' said the woman.

'But... A girl called Emma used to live here. With her boyfriend Nick.' I recognised an empty echo to my voice. I was beginning to feel I could do with that hug from Sal.

'Or Schmid,' said Sal. 'Have you heard of Emma Smith or Emma Schmid who lives, or used to live here with her boyfriend Nick?'

'I don't know any flipping Nicks!' she almost shouted. 'As I said, no one lives here permanently. Was it the last lot that were in? If you find them, you can tell them I hope they rot in hell for the skid marks they left in the dunny.'

'It would have been back in late October,' I said, forcing some calm into my voice. 'When you say AirBnB, was it possible it was rented on a long-term contract?'

'I don't have a clue who stays in any of the lets. But as far as I'm aware, they're all short-term. As I said, I'm just the cleaner. But there've been tons of different tenants over the past year or so.'

'Do you work for a cleaning company or the rental agency?' I asked.

'I work for the agency. My boss takes care of the bookings, but she's an agent, not the owner.'

'Well at least that's one less hoop to jump through,' said Sal. 'What's the name of your agency?' she asked the Aussie.

'Kerry Franklin Services.'

'Could you give me their address?' I asked.

'Their office is up on York Road.'

I typed the address into the maps app on my phone.

'Is that all? Gotta get this place spick and span by 2pm for the next guests,' said the Aussie.

'Wait! Is it worth talking to the people who live upstairs?' I asked, turning to Sal with a *what-the-heck-do-we-do-now?* look on my face.

'That's an AirBnB rental, too,' said the woman.

'Who does the kids trailer belong to?' I asked.

'Oh, that's mine. Got all my cleaning stuff in it. Can never find a bloody parking space round here, so I do all the properties on foot. Keeps me fit.' She pronounced the word 'fit' like 'feet,' and Sal looked down at the pair of Uggs she was wearing.

It was imperative that we find out who exactly I'd taken Emma's things from in Wandsworth.

51

SALLY

We reached the tiny office of Kelly Franklin Services to find a woman locking the door to leave.

'I'm sorry to disturb you. We need some information about one of your rentals,' said James, getting straight down to the nitty-gritty.

'Looks like you'll have to wait til after lunch, love, doesn't it?'

Bless Jamie's cotton socks, his lower lip actually trembled. The thought that his girlfriend might possibly have deceived him was taking its toll. But I was beginning to lose my patience with his constant denial.

'If you don't want the police heavily involved, you'd best give the gentleman the information he needs,' I said. 'There may have been criminal activity conducted from the property we're inquiring about during the tenancy of one of your clients we're investigating.'

The woman stared at me for a full five seconds before wordlessly lifting her key to the door and unlocking it.

'I suppose you'd better come in, then. You know I'm not supposed to give out client information unless you're the police.'

'We're private investigators, actually,' I said, trying to sound convincing. 'We work closely with the Met.'

Jamie looked at me, brows raised. I took my wallet out of my bag and waved my membership card to the Agatha Christie Folio Society in front of the woman, who reached for a glasses case in her handbag. I pocketed the thing and before she could put them on, moved to the other side of James, who quickly picked up on the PI thread.

'Can we at least get a name for a particular booking? It's for a client who believes there's been some wrong-doing,' I said. 'And it might avoid an imminent visit from the Met if an investigation ensues, which I assure you will be time-consuming.'

Out of the corner of my eye I caught Jamie's look of surprise at my forthright interrogation. I was beginning to feel in my element.

The tiny office was mostly crammed with cleaning equipment. There was a computer on the single desk in the corner wedged between two filing cabinets. The woman tapped the mouse to activate the screen.

'And what criminal activity are these tenants suspected of?' she asked.

'Some books have been st—'

'It's perhaps best if that information isn't divulged at this time,' I said, looking sternly at James who bit his lip, ever the honest Joe.

'Which property were you... investigating?' she asked, looking straight at me.

'13 Khyber Road. The downstairs flat.'

'And how do you know it's that particular flat you need this information for?'

'I've—,' began James.

'We've received some confidential information,' I said, shooting another look at him.

The woman, who hadn't yet touched a key on the computer, swung around to face the screen.

'What was the date you needed to know for the occupancy?'

Jamie looked up to the ceiling, as though he needed to consult his memory again about when he'd first met his girl in the doorway. I was sure he knew exactly when. I certainly did. It was beginning to stick in my mind.

'Somewhere in the first three weeks of October, but definitely including the 17th to 19th. You can start there.'

The woman looked long and hard at the two of us then pulled up a schedule with different coloured tabs on a spreadsheet with a heading of *October*. She looked at the screen, her index finger waving between the columns.

'It was a three-week rental, from the 15th. Quite unusual for that length of time. Look, I can't give you the client details; you know that would be violating privacy issues.'

'So then it looks like we'll be calling the Met sooner than we thought. Can you at least give us a name?'

The woman sighed, rightly reluctant to give us any information, but I could see her weighing up the consequences of having to deal with the police, even if she didn't completely believe that we were genuine private investigators.

I leaned in towards the computer, squinting a little to see two names, Rich/Schmid, in the coloured spread sheet column for 13 Khyber Road. I tried to scan the document for any other information, but she quickly clicked the mouse to make the screen go dark. I didn't even get to see either of their full names.

'No, I'm sorry. This is preposterous. I really can't just give you client information. I've already breached several protocols letting you in here in the first place. Not sure why I did, really. If these people have done anything wrong, perhaps it's best the police deal with them anyway. Now, if you'll excuse me, I have a cinnamon roll and an espresso waiting for me at Costa.' She stood up, pushed her chair towards the desk as a further barrier between us and her computer screen. She held her arm out towards the door, palm flat, fingers together, like a warden at a traffic intersection. We dutifully shuffled out to the street.

There were posters on the window of the agency that I hadn't noticed before. As the woman locked the door again, I spotted the house on Khyber Road on one of the TO LET posters. The interiors of the two flats looked standard, Ikea-type furnishings, but bright and clean.

I nudged Jamie and directed his gaze to the poster.

'That's the one,' he said, and the woman narrowed her eyes at Jamie.

'Thanks so much; you've been so helpful,' I said to her and guided Jamie down the street while the woman put her keys in her handbag and walked in the opposite direction.

'The Agatha Christie society?' whispered James, shaking his head with a laugh. 'Who knew? You really are a dark horse, Miss Marple.'

When the agency woman had disappeared, we turned and went back to the poster.

'N. Rich,' I said. 'Nick. Or Nicholas. How the heck would we find him? It's a common name.'

'I just don't understand why Emma would have lied about how long she was living there. It looked exactly the same inside as you saw on that poster. Impersonal. An AirBnB. I can hardly believe it. Why?'

'Did she ever actually tell you how long she'd lived there?'

'No, but it was assumed. I mean, she said they'd been together for a few years. When I picked up her stuff, I did remember thinking it was odd there were no pictures of them in the place. Not that I had the presence of mind to look for those things.' He took a deep breath, and I could see he was holding back a sob. 'Now I'd really like to find Despicable Nick,' he said with more vehemence. 'Perhaps he hasn't moved from the greater London area.'

I was also wondering why his girl would bend the truth. I looked at info-finder and 192 on my phone.

'There are 44 N.Riches in London, 17 of those are a Nick or Nicholas, but none in SW11. He could be anywhere in the UK, considering he doesn't actually live in SW11, if he ever really did.' I looked at Jamie, trying to work out his emotions. 'Do you know where Emma's mum lives?'

'No...'

'Jamie, you'll never make a good detective,' I said, consulting my app. 'Oh, this isn't helpful. Didn't you once say Yorkshire? More than 100 Emma Smiths in that county.'

'Try Northumberland.'

'Six there... but I thought you said she was from North Yorkshire?'

'It was something she said, once. I'm beginning to feel like I'm missing a big piece of a puzzle.' He sounded miserable, and this time I turned and hugged him without thinking, and he rubbed my back.

'Thanks for being here for me, Sal.'

'Of course. That's what best mates are for.'

He gave me a weak smile.

'You'd better try both Smith and Schmid. The latter will be less common.'

I typed the name into both the apps for both North Yorkshire and Northumberland. A gazillion results for Smith, but zero results for Schmid. I shook my head, and Jamie's shoulders slumped just a little, before he raised his head.

'Maybe Emma's real name *is* Smith. Perhaps it's someone else who was living there.'

'You don't want to believe anything is wrong, Jamie. Don't you think it's a bit of a coincidence her initials are the same?'

'I guess…' he said, looking miserable once again.

'Anything else we should be doing this side of the river while we're trying to figure this out?' I asked.

Jamie shook his head. 'Back home to my violated flat, I guess.'

'Let's grab some lunch at the Seven Dials Market.'

'Good idea,' he said, slightly more cheerfully.

But as we headed back to Clapham Junction to travel back to Covent Garden, Jamie's mobile phone rang, and as he answered, the look on his face told me things might be about to get a whole lot more complicated.

52

JAMES

As my phone buzzed in my pocket, my heart lifted. It must finally have been Emma returning my calls and messages. I scrambled for the phone and pulled it out, but instead of her icon we'd uploaded together at Christmas – a photo of her wearing a fluffy Santa hat from the Covent Garden market – 'DAD' was displayed with a generic phone icon on the screen.

'Dad? Hi, what's up?'

'We've been burgled as well, son! This is madness! I don't know the extent of what's missing, but bloody hell, James. We can't do an inventory as we're not there.'

'Wait, what? Slow down. You're not at home in Suffolk? When did this happen?' I asked. Dad must have been really upset to swear like that.

'Not here. Our place in St Moritz. The chalet. I don't quite know what to do.'

'OK. Hang on. Stay calm.'

I guided Sal over to the side of the pavement near a shopfront to shelter from the wind, and pressed the speaker function so she could hear as well.

'We're not the only ones. Next door also has some things missing. Mikael is driving now from Schaffhausen to Chalet Edelweiss. It's not clear how the buggers got in to ours. Nothing was forced.'

'How did you even know?' I asked.

'The cleaning company who does for all of us on the street discovered the break-in at ours first. Then Chalet Edelweiss. From the outside, there was no evidence that either place had been touched. It's snowed over any footprints around the house.'

'How much of a coincidence is this?' I said, more to Sal than my dad, exasperation in my voice.

'I know you have your own troubles at the moment, but I'd appreciate it if you could fly out and sort out the police report,' said Dad. 'I have an MRI booked for my knee the day after tomorrow, and I'm not sure I will get back in time. I've been waiting months for this damned leg to be looked at. Your mother is completely exhausted after all the Christmas festivities. I cannot possibly ask her to go.'

'Dad, I can't leave. I need to be around in case the police find anything out about my books.'

Something was niggling me. This was sounding all too familiar. *Coincidences* indeed.

'Please, James. You know I wouldn't normally ask you. It'll only be for a day or two. It's not like the police will need you in situ for their investigation. You'll be contactable by phone.'

'They might not even let me leave. I think I'm on their list of suspects.'

'Oh, Christ,' said Dad. 'Is no one safe from the suspicion of fraud these days? I'm sure they'll understand if you tell them what's happened.'

'Do you know what's missing from St Moritz?' I asked.

'No. The cleaners just said it was obvious some objects had been taken. Gaps on the sideboards. There was no damage to the property. Next door had gone back to Schaffhausen and weren't due to return until after the New Year. I really need someone to check this for the police and do an inventory for the insurance.'

'I'm not sure if I would even know what's missing. I've only been there for a few short stays over the past few years.'

'You know it hasn't changed for at least two decades, James. But it's imperative we work out if anything of significant value disappeared in the theft. You can call me when you're there and walk me around the chalet with your FaceTube or whatever it's called.'

'Okay, Dad. I'll call the DS in charge of my case here and see if it's alright for me to leave. I guess it won't hurt for a couple of days. There's not much I can do anyway at the moment.'

'I knew you'd understand. Thank you, my boy. It's your future as well, you know.'

'I'll call you when I've spoken to the police. But in the meantime, let me know who I need to contact at the *Graubündner Kantonspolizei* in St Moritz.'

'A break-in in Covent Garden and two break-ins in St Moritz? Do you think they're connected?' Sal asked when I'd pocketed my phone again.

'I'm not sure how they could be. One theft here in London while we were gone, and the other in St Moritz only moments after we'd left. How could they be connected when they're a thousand miles from each other? It sounds like we've just been unlucky, that my parents' chalet was in a row of unfortunate targets for a gang of thieves. It's not the first time this has happened in Switzerland. The most common multiple thefts of this kind are bicycles.' I paused. 'Would you like to spend a couple of days in the Alps?'

'Oh, God, I'd love to. Didn't you have plans here for New Years' Eve?'

'I *did* have plans. With Emma. But I really have to go and check my parents' place as soon as possible. If Emma comes back in the meantime, I'm sure she'll understand. I'll text her.'

'You'd better not tell her I'm with you,' she said.

I looked at Sal. 'Why?'

'I've never felt the friendliest of vibes from her whenever we've met.'

I frowned.

'I'm not sure what I'm going to tell them at work,' she continued. 'I guess I'll have to call in sick at such short notice. It's a pretty busy time, what with the post-Christmas sales and a higher volume of shoppers. But you know that.'

'Please,' I said.

I could see her calculating several undisclosed options in her mind. It might be that she didn't want to help because of the feelings I admitted I still had for Emma. I knew she'd want to help recover the books, perhaps even more than I did. But now I wondered what she thought about me walking away from an investigation into the theft of my books at the whim of my father. To her, it was probably like abandoning your own child to go and help someone else's.

'Okay,' she said. 'You book the tickets and I'll grab a bag of stuff from home.'

53

SALLY

We picked up a rental car at Zürich Airport, a smart Range Rover Sport.

'Well you certainly don't hold back on the expenses,' I said. 'I think it's the first time I've seen you truly flaunt your wealth, Mr Marsh. Apart from what was on display in your Tardis, of course.'

'Safest vehicle for the roads up to St Moritz. There might be a lot of snow on the Julier Pass.'

'Will the town still be decorated for Christmas?' I could hardly believe I was on the way to one of the glitziest resorts in the Alps. A holiday in Switzerland, even though it was going to be an abridged version, was something I'd only ever dreamed about on a bookseller's salary.

'Once the lights go up on the chalets for Christmas, they generally stay up all season. It does look lovely against the snowy backdrop. The Christmas tree in town stays at least until the end of January. We may not have much time to enjoy it, if the police get their way with their endless red tape in this country.'

'This already feels so different from soggy old London,' I said, looking at a spectacular snow-spattered cliff across a narrow blue-green lake. We were speeding along a gently curving autobahn slipping in and out of a series of tunnels.

'This is the Wallensee,' said Jamie, my instant tour guide. 'There's some great mountain biking over those peaks. And this lake is full of kite surfers in the summer. I was going to bring Emma here; she said she liked mountain biking...' His voice dropped to match the sudden melancholy. 'It still feels odd that she cleared everything out of her room just to visit her mum for a few days. You'd think she would have left something there – perhaps her artwork or some books.'

'Jamie, I...'

'I know it seems strange, but I refuse to believe she's not coming back.'

I chewed the inside of my cheek, feeling my mouth go askew with my Marple hat on. Having her own space in his flat would have given her the perfect opportunity to keep her affairs private. Messages, phone calls, any conniving she might get up to could all be done in the relatively private space of her room. I was still sure she'd been the one to delete my presence from Jamie's mobile phone, but thought the act was a bit extreme if jealousy was the motive.

'I told her the guest room was her retreat,' said James, as though he'd read my mind. 'That I'd never interfere if she felt she needed time to herself within our living space. It was just easier, Sal, don't look at me like that. I didn't think it was weird at the time. And then we got back from the Christmas trip, and well... The books, the news about Willie, and then – *poof* – gone.'

'*Is* there even a mother up north?' I said, and James shot me a glance. 'Don't you find it odd that Emma didn't tell you where her mum lived? The town, I mean?'

James shrugged.

'I mean, if someone asks me where I'm from, I say I live in London, but I almost always say I grew up in Chelmsford.'

'I didn't know you grew up in Chelmsford.'

'Okay, point taken.' It was on the tip of my tongue to say: *But if we were sleeping together, you'd know that sort of thing about me.*

'The books are actually nothing, you know. I would have given her everything.'

'James Marsh! That's blasphemy! Are you seriously saying you would give up the books to have her back?'

'Well, not if she's deceived me, of course, but...'

'I don't want to hear any more of this. Stop that thought right now.'

It sickened me to think he might seriously take her back, even if she had something to do with all this. *Give up those priceless books?*

After another series of tunnels, we entered a wide valley leading up to some impressive snow-clad Alps in the distance. The traffic intensified, and for a while we were stuck behind a lorry that was carrying refrigerated produce with *Schmid Lebensmittel* marked on the back. James didn't seem to have noticed the name of the company on the truck.

I pulled out my mobile phone and searched for *Swiss Phonebook* on Google. It came up with *TelSearch.ch*. I tried to recall the spelling of the two names I'd seen on the rental agency's computer screen.

'If that envelope you found in the rubbish bin was addressed to your Emma, was the surname of her alter-ego with or without the "t" at the end?' I asked, pointing towards the truck.

'Oh, I didn't see that. Schmid. Without, actually, like that. Both are as common as Smith here.'

'Do you think her origins are Swiss?' I asked, looking at Jamie, and in one brief moment it was as though a load of connections were aligning like cherries on a slot machine behind his eyes. I tapped the link on the phone app, then typed in *Schmid* and *St Moritz*.

As James flicked the indicator to overtake the lorry, I put my hand on his thigh. I hadn't meant this to be in any way sexual, but wanted to warn him he might not want to hear what I had to say. He moved his thigh slightly away, like a leg shrug, and I flushed with disappointment before reading out the search result.

'Schmid, E. Via Tegia—'

'Via Tegiatscha,' interrupted James. 'Oh good God, I have to get to St Moritz as soon as possible.' The car accelerated. 'Bugger the speed cameras.'

I raised my eyebrows.

'And after I've worked out what's missing from the chalet, I have to call DS Hannah.'

54

JAMES

Clues were connecting like synapses in my mind. The extent of the deception was blowing open like a super nova. I couldn't even begin to voice the possibilities and my disbelief. After several more kilometres the valley narrowed, with snow-clad mountains rising either side, giving the impression that the sky was darkening over us.

'Looks like we're going to get more snow, damn it,' I said.

'Are you worried about the roads?' asked Sal.

'Not really. This car can get through anything. If I wasn't so busy with all that's been going on, I'd love to get some skiing done.'

We passed the autobahn rest-stop called *Heidiland* which caused Sal to snort, and she turned to me.

'Okay, Jamie, spill.'

'Something is bothering me about the day we discovered the cabinet was broken into,' I said. Sal raised her eyebrows, sensing my hesitation, but waited for me to continue. 'I don't want to diss her, because she's not here to defend herself, but Emma did something really bizarre.'

'Go on.'

'Now we've discovered a link, albeit tenuous, I suspect Emma had been polishing someone's fingerprints off the antique book cabinet key that day.'

'Flippin' heck, Jamie, why didn't you say? Did you tell the police? That sounds dead suspicious to me.'

'I just didn't want to believe she would have had anything to do with the theft. She seemed so helpless and innocent when I met her. But I'm beginning to feel more and more like a fool. If she does have something to do with this, I can't believe the complicated way she wormed her way into my life. That we had...'

I had to stop myself. I could already hear the thoughts going through Sal's mind. *Gullible*. I'd been about to blurt information that she definitely didn't want to hear. 'I can't believe she would do this to me,' I said, almost a whisper.

My eyes were hot with unshed tears. My shoulders dropped and for a moment I thought I might slump over the steering wheel with some kind of bizarre turn. As I felt the car drifting towards the middle of the road, I mentally shook myself. At over 140 kilometres an hour, Sal would be fearing for her safety.

'James!' she chirped, and I relaxed my foot on the accelerator, concentrating once more on my driving. 'I'm sure you would have told me, but has Emma contacted you at all?' she asked.

'Do you realise that's the first time you've called her by her name.'

'Yeah. Sorry. I can finally think of her as Emma, now that I know it might not be her real name. Before, she was *That Girl in the Doorway*.' She was sounding like the scorned girlfriend now. Or the scorned *almost*-girlfriend. 'I'm sorry, but it confirms my belief that she somehow intercepted my messages on your phone or deleted my texts to avoid us having contact. I initially thought she might be jealous of me, but maybe she had an ulterior motive. Maybe she didn't want a curious friend asking too many questions about her.'

I shook my head. 'It's not looking good, is it, Sal?'

'Remember when I couldn't get hold of you at Christmas? You'd timed out on our Words-With-Friends games, so I sent you another invitation to play. You must have been a little distracted and I was surprised you didn't play back. But Jamie, I was already convinced back then that she'd somehow wiped my WhatsApp and text messages, and I must have been right. If she was monitoring your apps on your phone, she probably didn't realise that the username JMarple on Words-With-Friends was me. Why would someone go that far to stop us from talking to each other?'

'Perhaps she's seen your bookshelves.' I tried a little wry humour to get Sal off slamming Emma. Even though it could be true, I wasn't enjoying this at all.

'So what was the epiphany back there when I mentioned the E.Schmid in St Moritz? Miss Marple here says you can never rely on coincidences, but this is close to the bone. How can you be so sure it's *her*?'

Her question was now almost rhetorical. Common sense was now knocking very loudly on both our consciences.

'The thing is, if all this *is* connected, and *she's* connected, I can think of only one reason why my family, or more specifically, *I* would have been targeted,' I said.

55

SALLY

When I was a teenager,' said Jamie, 'A whole group of us used to ski together in St Moritz when our families were out there for holidays. Christmas, half term, Easter, etcetera. One February, there was an accident on the ski slope. We were all terrors back then, racing each other down the red and black runs, taking risks. Lawrence and Tristan had wanted to try out snowboarding and had rented boards for the day. Tristan got the hang of it really quickly, but Lawrence was being reckless on the slopes, should really have hired a snowboarding instructor at least for his first day. He lost control in the middle of a red run and crashed into a girl who couldn't get up. She'd been knocked out.'

'Holy shit,' I said, putting my hand over my mouth.

'Her name was Claudia. I recognised her from sometimes hanging out at the bar at the sports centre. She was always on the ice rink, had potential to become a world-class figure skater. She was well-known and loved in the community. Lawrence had a minor injury, a cut he needed tending to, but didn't need to be hospitalised, so he snowboarded down to the ski lift station to alert ski patrol and get a dab of antiseptic and a plaster. I stayed with Claudia, who came around, but was groggy and said her leg was giving her excruciating pain, that perhaps something was broken.

'I ended up following the ski patrol, skiing down behind the luge, and rode with the girl in the ambulance to the hospital. I stayed with her until her parents arrived. She was incredibly distraught. It turned out she had broken her foot in three places and needed a plate in her ankle. But the thing she was most upset about was that it marked the end of her professional figure-skating career before it had even started. And because I rode with her in the ambulance, I later found out that they all thought I was the one who'd caused the accident.'

'Oh God, that's awful, James. But didn't you ever straighten that out? Tell the family, and Claudia, that it wasn't you who caused the accident?'

'I didn't find out until we were back in England. It was the talk of the town back in St Moritz, apparently. And no matter how much I protested my innocence, I wasn't there until the following Easter to plead my case. I did go back and see Claudia, but the mother sent me away, saying I couldn't mend anything with my guilt-trip to see how she was.'

'But how is this connected?' I asked.

'I know the address because that's where I went when I tried to explain to Claudia. It's kind of imprinted in my memory.'

I looked at Jamie with furrowed brow. Now it was me who wasn't joining the dots.

'Claudia lived with her mother then, and had taken her mother's last name as the father had left and was no longer in the picture. I only knew that because I helped fill out the admission forms at the hospital and was surprised she had such an English name – Johnson I think it was. She explained that her mother was English, had been living in St Moritz since coming to Switzerland as an au pair in the eighties and then met the father. I didn't know much else about Claudia. Except that she had a sister I'd never met. Back then.'

'Oh, let me guess. The sister who still had the last name of the father? Whose name was Schmid?'

'Yes, but that's not all, Sal. When we were at my parents' chalet at Christmas, Emma had a book with her. It was a Highsmith.'

Sal drew in her breath. 'One of your rare titles?'

'No, no, not at all. I thought she might have bought it at a second-hand book market, because it had a dedication on the title page.'

'And...'

'It said: *To Eva, Happy studying. Love always, C.* But now it has clicked. Eva is Claudia's sister. Emma Smith is Eva Schmid.'

56

EVA

The plane from Gatwick to Zürich had been full the night before; I must have taken the last available seat and was stuck at the rear of the cabin in the middle of a row amongst a rowdy group of young male English skiers. They were heading to Interlaken, or more precisely the resort of Grindelwald, in the shadow of the Eiger, for a week's holiday.

As I took my seat, the group was already working out how many bottles of spirits they could purchase between them from the duty-free magazine. They were complaining about the exchange rate, which had strengthened even more for the Swiss franc since the pandemic. It hadn't deterred the ski tourists who were clamouring to get back to the slopes after a couple of seasons in lockdown. The money they'd saved by not going on holiday back then wasn't an object when it came to destination choices. But the English will always be fussy about how much they pay for drinks or food, whatever their destination, and the conversations about the price of alcoholic beverages was one I was familiar with, especially in St Moritz.

I was glad there was no risk of travelling with them on the train to Graubünden. I'd be heading to the eastern corner of the country, while they would head south towards the Bernese Oberland. The group was already well-oiled with beers by the time we took off, and I had to move to let one of them access the toilets twice before I gently suggested that I sit in the window seat so they didn't need to disturb me. They tried to chat me up, but I pulled down the blind, balled up my jacket, and leaned my head against the window. I feigned sleep, listening to their infantile promises of conquering black ski runs and chatting up barmaids.

It was past midnight when I'd arrived in St Moritz. Mama picked me up from the train station, still confused as to why I had not been able to spend Christmas with her.

'I like what you've done to your hair,' she said after we'd hugged. 'You've let it grow, and the blond highlights suit you.'

I had done that in an attempt to avoid being recognised by acquaintances in the village, especially when we were in town at the Christmas market.

In the car on the way home to our modest little chalet on Via Tegiatscha she told me about her Christmas spent with the neighbours. 'Vreni said she thought she saw you on the ski slopes on *Stephanstag*,' she said, using the German term for Boxing Day, the English one having long been discarded in our household. 'I told her it couldn't have been you; you've been in London for so long. But now why have you suddenly come back? I thought you were going to stay in London through the new year? Soak up the atmosphere of a celebration within chiming distance of Big Ben. There'll be fireworks here, though, and the usual parties down by the lake.'

I wished I could have told her I was sick of travelling back and forth to the UK, even though James and I had travelled first class on the train. Airports and train stations at Christmas were not the easiest of places, even if one had access to a premium passenger lounge.

'Mama, I won't be staying here for New Year, either.'

She tutted in a way that belied her Anglophone roots. 'But you've been away for so long. I haven't seen you! Spend a little time with Mama. I always miss Claudia so much at this time of year. I need you.'

I felt guilty at that, but I had to carry out our plan.

'I'm going to Venice to spend it with friends. I'll be back on the 4th or 5th. And I won't be going anywhere after that,' I assured her.

I made a mental note that the first treat I would bestow with the earnings from the sale of our contraband, would be the tasting menu at Ecco in the Giardino Hotel. I'd find some excuse for coming up with the money to be able to afford it, perhaps that I'd been saving since last Christmas to treat her for this Christmas.

It was too late for my meeting that night, and I was too tired anyway to go over the plans for the next few days. The weather was still socked in, and although we had a trusty four-wheel drive Subaru available, we figured it was better to let the municipal road clearers do their job and go over the roads a second time with their salt trucks once the surface of the roads had hardened under the plough blades.

But the next morning, I was raring to go. I wanted to get this thing over and done with, this thing that we thought would make us feel better about the injustices done to someone we loved so much, and still loved. All the way through the months of studying James and his family, pandering to his charitable weaknesses and then finding the perfect way of seducing him and securing an important place in his heart, I had kept the memory of Claudia alive in my mind.

And each time I thought I could simply integrate myself into this new life in London, I conjured the face of my happy, ambitious sister, and the depression that the ski accident had put her into over the past years.

I'd sent a text and agreed to meet my accomplice for coffee at the Art Café in town. As I crossed the road towards the café I looked up at the sky and pulled my collar close as a sharp breeze carried a flurry of snow on the air. The last thing we needed was another snowfall. I'd never seen so much snow before the new year in the Alps before. I silently cursed

'Have you kept the books wrapped like I told you?' I asked.

'Of course. After I photographed them for you, I carefully re-wrapped them, placed them back in the hard-shell cabin suitcase and have already put them in the trunk of the Subaru so we can leave straight away if we need to. The car is parked in the underground garage where the temperature shouldn't go below freezing. The Somerset Maugham is on the top, so we can set up the video to film the burning of it as soon as we're over the border.'

'Have you seen the weather forecast?'

'Yes. More snow. Maybe we wait another night,' he said.

'Did you check the street last night?'

'Both places are definitely uninhabited. But, Eva, the weather—'

'I'm not thinking about our drive. I think we should take the other stuff now, while we're sure there's no one there. We can store it in your car. There aren't any cameras on the street. I checked thoroughly when I was there last week, between the cocktail parties and the invitations. I know the Marsh's place will be empty until mid-season, but we don't know anything about the one next door.'

'I'm pretty sure they vacated yesterday morning. I've been keeping regular watch,' he said.

'It's mid-week. It's possible they'll come back up from Schaffhausen for the weekend and the new year celebrations. And if not them, then they might have friends who visit. These places are often borrowed by work colleagues or friends of the family. I think we have to do it tonight. It gives us the best chance of not getting caught.'

'OK, if you're sure.'

'Are you getting cold feet?' I asked.

'No… but however this is going to make you feel, don't forget that all this won't bring her back.'

'I know. But I'm sure it will help ease the anger I still feel.'

'Tonight, then,' he'd said. 'Bring your backpack. We don't want the car to be seen anywhere near that road. I'll park by the lift station. It won't look out of place there.'

57

JAMES

Bingo. Eva Schmid,' I said miserably. 'And now I'm assuming that was her father's surname.'

'It seems like a convoluted way of involving herself in your life, but what for? Revenge for a ski accident that happened years ago?'

'And if this burglary at the chalet is connected somehow, why involve my parents? I should be the one she's targeting.'

'I suppose indirectly she still is. For one thing you care for your parents very much and for another, you'll be inheriting their wealth at some point in the future.'

'That's why we have to get to St Moritz quickly. I've no idea what's missing from the chalet.'

'How much further to go?' asked Sal, gazing at the imposing steep mountains as we headed further into eastern Switzerland. She sounded like a bored child on the way to visiting an old relative.

'We still have to get over the Julier Pass. St Moritz is really in the back of beyond. In the summer I often come in from the other side, from Davos, but that pass could be impassable with all this snow. We still have some distance to go.'

'Just make sure you get me there safely, Jamie. All this snow and ice is making me a little nervous. I find it hard to believe a resort that has become so popular with wealthy British tourists is so far from Zürich Airport.'

'There's an airport at St Moritz,' I said. 'It's only big enough to take small planes and jets. Some of the wealthier tourists fly directly from London in their private jets.'

'But not the Marshes,' said Sal with a smile.

'Not the Marshes,' I said. 'Except of course right now I almost wish we *had* taken a private jet. Time could be of the essence.'

'Do you think you should call DI Hannah now?'

'I want to see what's been taken from our chalet first. By the way, he's only a DS. Which makes me think my case isn't so important. I'd like to be able to give him something to get his teeth into though.'

At Landquart we turned southwards and began a long climb up the mountain road towards Lenzerheide, the first of the ski areas we would pass through to our destination. The higher we climbed, the thicker the snow clung to the pines, weighing the branches down like great globs of icing on an over-decorated cake. Occasionally a branch would release its hold on its heavy load and a cloud of powder drifted to the ground, spindrift winking in the weak sun, now low in the sky.

'It snowed a lot again since we left a few days ago,' I said. 'This is unprecedented around Christmas. It's often cold, but the mountain resorts usually have their canons working full time because there's not enough snow. Business will be good. Even the Swiss will be flooding to the slopes for the rest of the school holidays.'

As we drove on the winding switchbacks towards the Julier Pass, it was as though we were driving through a roofless tunnel as the snow piled up on the verges either side of the car. The road had been cleared with a giant snow blower with a rotating cutter that had left circular lines on the vertical walls of packed white. As we levelled out at the top of the pass above the treeline, the snow was windblown into crests of frozen waves to either side which resembled a static photo of frothing ocean surf across the landscape.

'Shame there's no time to teach me skiing,' said Sal.

I couldn't work out whether she sounded relieved or disappointed.

'Not far now,' I said as we descended into a valley with a long flat white area under which lay the frozen Silverplaner Lake, the middle of the three lakes in the St Moritz Valley. Ant-sized figures were moving along the lake's edge.

'A few cross-country skate skiers out too. They'll also be happy for the early snow.'

At the mention of skaters, I thought of Claudia.

'I guess you'd never seen Claudia's sister Eva before?' said Sal, as though she'd read my mind.

'No. But it's pretty obvious this must be the same person. In a way, it's a clever revenge. Rather than creating the scene for a complicated accident where the results might or might not end up with my broken leg on a ski slope, hit the victim where it would hurt in a way that avoids any contact at all.' I suddenly thought of the avalanche incident, but before I could ponder on it, Sal continued.

'You would presumably have had no idea that she was feeling so bitter about what happened all those years ago. That's a long time to hold a grudge. It's a shame no one ever put the true facts right for the family.'

I nodded, my lips pressed into a line.

'Why would she feel so desperate to avenge her sister, and so many years after it happened?' asked Sal. 'That's surely risky. And how on earth would she have known that you wouldn't recognise her?'

'I guess that was the whole ruse with her settling in across the street from the bookstore. If I'd recognised her, even given an inkling that I somehow knew her from somewhere but didn't know where, it would have been easy for her to abort her mission, or find another way at least.'

'Do you think she would have been cruel enough to murder your homeless man Willie?'

'I just can't believe she would have done that. That's surely one thing too far. There was no reason for her to do so. Another mystery, though. Don't forget she was cruel enough to sleep with me while still holding that grudge.'

'We're coming up with too many coincidences, Jamie. Just an hour ago in the car you couldn't believe that your girlfriend would have anything to do with this. What did you say Claudia's surname was again? Johnson?'

I nodded. 'Are you Googling her? Perhaps add St Moritz to the narrow down the possibilities.'

'There are a few entries that include the name Johnson, but they don't mention Claudia. Oh, wait!'

My heart pounded. I still wanted to believe that my Emma, Eva, or whoever she was, had no connection to all this, but in reality I'd passed the point of ignoring the obvious.

'There's an article in something called the *Bündner Tagesblatt*.'

'That's the local newspaper,' I said.

In my periphery, Sal clicked open the article.

'There's an image – a photograph – of an ice skater doing a pirouette, or axel-spin or whatever they call those jumps ice dancers do.'

I glanced quickly at the image Sal had zoomed in on with her splayed fingers. The photo was of a young woman in mid-air above above the ice, her short skirt splayed like a ballerina tutu with the force of the twirl. I fixed my eyes back on the road again.

'The caption has only two phrases I can understand "Claudia Johnson" and "Swiss Ice Skating." Here, I'll stick it in Google translate.

I imagined Sal scrolling down the article and highlighting the text on her screen, then copying it into Google translate. A feeling of foreboding came over me as Sal drew in her breath.

'Oh, Jamie, I think you should pull over. You're going to need to read this. It's shocking.'

58

SALLY

James gave me a side-long glance, saw the horror on my face and checked the rearview mirror. We'd already entered the town.

'I can't stop here. There's nowhere to park,' he said, looking for a space on the edge of an already full street of parked cars in vain. The traffic was slow ahead of us, others also looking for parking spaces and driving carefully on the snow-packed main street.

Through the middle of town, people were walking home from the lifts and the bottom of the runs with skis balanced on their shoulders, their faces ruddy from the cold, vapour puffing out of their smiling mouths. The entire village was a precarious obstacle course.

'Let's get up to the chalet,' he said. 'We're almost there. You can show me what you've found when we're safe inside.'

He navigated some steep curves up through the village away from the main lake and turned onto a narrow lane with a row of three chalets. He pulled into a driveway where a snowplough had recently swept in an arc to clear a small area in front of an impressive chalet.

'The plough has pushed the snow up against the garage door,' said James. 'I'll leave the car out until I've cleared the snow away. I don't want to break the mechanism. It must have snowed since the cleaners and the police were here. It doesn't look like they've been back. No crime scene tape or anything. I guess I can go in, but I'd better check.'

'Nice place,' I said, as he pulled out his mobile.

'I just want to check whether the occupants of the other chalet that were burgled are home.' He walked along the lane a little way, then came back shaking his head. No one seemed to be home.

He called a number on his mobile I guessed his father had given him for the person in charge of the investigation, and spoke briefly to someone in German before ending the call and turning to the entrance of the chalet.

'The detective told me to get an inventory of what might be missing and meet him later at the police station in the village.'

He keyed open the front door and switched off the alarm.

'I'll turned up the heating, too,' he said, tapping some additional symbols on the screen on the wall.

We took off our boots, and each put on a pair of sheepskin slippers that were lined up near the front door. This felt laughably Swiss.

'I think you should see this before we do anything else,' I said, pulling my phone from my pocket and scrolling to the translation of the news article I'd seen in the car earlier.

He took the phone from me and walked towards the kitchen island.

St Moritz. 18th September 2024.

Mother of ex-ice-skating star makes a plea to parents to pay more attention to the mental health of their children after her daughter takes her life...

'Oh my God,' he said, his finger moving up the screen of my phone as he read the headline, then scrolled through the rest of the translation. I sat next to him on a bar stool at the island as he read the article out loud.

'Claudia Johnson was a well-known, bright young personality in the community of St Moritz. Her development as a professional figure skater was cut short several years ago when she sustained injuries in a ski accident which ended her ambitions. Her mother, Claire Johnson-Schmid said she'd shown no signs of still being troubled by the fact that her career had been destroyed by a collision with a snowboarder that broke her leg in three places, requiring a metal plate which restricted the flexibility of her ankle.

She had seen a psychologist in the months following the accident, but had appeared to accept her career would take a different direction. She'd been working in the hospitality industry linked to many sporting events in the community and had recently worked closely with Swiss Ice Skating for the junior championships which are to be held in St Moritz early next year. Her mother said it was perhaps this close contact with the team of young talented figure skaters that reminded Claudia of what she had lost, and that any young person who has been unsuccessful in qualifying for a national team or an important event should be closely monitored for the effects such a blow could have on their mental health months or years afterwards. The funeral will take place at St John's Anglican Church in St Moritz on Friday 20th September. No flowers, but donations can be sent to the Dr Hans Durrer Foundation for young sports hopefuls.'

'So Claudia took her life! That's truly terrible. I know she was distraught at the time of the accident, as anyone would be, but it's such a shock her depression about it wasn't monitored further and simmered for so long. This pretty much confirms the involvement of her sister Emma, or Eva, or whatever she wants to call herself, in some kind of weird revenge.'

Eva Schmid had been emotionally driven to seek revenge on something that would have most certainly affected the mental health of her sister Claudia Johnson since that fateful day on the ski slopes some years before.

'But what on earth had she been planning?' I asked. 'This all feels too elaborate for a simple household burglary, or burglaries.'

'I agree. Let me show you your room,' said James, mounting the stairs. I followed behind, and he opened one of the guest rooms. 'You can have this one. Make yourself at home. It's a little bit smaller than the others, but has its own ensuite bathroom and the best view over the village and mountains. I'm upstairs in the attic room. I'll just dump my bag, then I need to call Dad to do a thorough inspection. Maybe there'll be a clue or clues in what has gone missing.'

59

EVA

Every year we used to wait for them to come – *Die Engländer* – the English. Depending on the weather, some years they might already have started arriving for long weekends in November, to take advantage of the first fresh snow before the busy Christmas period.

When I was old enough, although still at school, I took on part-time jobs at any one of the luxurious hotels in St Moritz on weekends and holidays, either in the kitchen or amongst the housekeeping staff, to earn enough money to buy myself a regional season pass. At that stage, my parents were sinking all their funds into my sister Claudia for her figure-skating career. They paid for her travel and hotels to national and international competitions and training camps. There wasn't much left over for me. But that was okay. I wanted Claudia to do well. She was incredibly talented, and I knew at some stage she might sweep us all along with her medals, fame and prize money. We often talked about where the world champs would be each season and how when I'd finished school, I could accompany her as her official assistant, do her hair, mend her outfits, give her pep talks.

Our mother was English, but not part of the elite tourist invasion of the 1970s and 80s. She'd come to Switzerland to work as an au pair for a wealthy family. Their main residence had been in Zürich, but they also owned a holiday penthouse apartment in St Moritz.

Fate had thrown Mama and Papa together in the local supermarket while she was shopping for supplies for the family – they'd never given her time off to ski. The couple began seeing each other any moment they could steal during the weekends and holidays. They married so she could escape a job she didn't particularly like and secure a work permit to stay in St Moritz. A marriage of convenience, perhaps a little hastier than they would have ordinarily wished for, but they were in love back then.

Papa was the concierge and handyman at the Lyceum Alpinum in Zuoz – an international boarding school. When he met Mama, he'd already been working there for many years, having started at sixteen as an apprentice with plumbing and electrician skills. A few years after they married, they decided to have children. I was the firstborn and Claudia followed less than two years later. As Papa was a valued employee of the school, we were both offered bursaries to attend for our secondary education until graduation.

I had a natural talent for English as the older child, as I had spoken only Mama's mother tongue at home until I attended play group and later primary school. English therefore remained my first language. Claudia always preferred to speak in the same dialect of the Bündner native children. She ended up speaking English with a slightly clipped accent. A native English speaker might question whether Claudia's mother tongue was English. By the time I'd graduated from high school, my own English was completely fluent. Although I'd never lived in the UK as a child, no native English speaker ever guessed that I hadn't been born and brought up there.

When she was barely sixteen, Claudia hooked up with a guy she'd met at the Ludains synthetic skating rink who worked part time and used to sharpen her skates when her technician wasn't available. When she graduated from the juniors to the senior Swiss figure skating team, I began planning a year or two of work and study in the UK. Now that she had a serious boyfriend, I became less of an emotional support for my sister. He went with her to her major tournaments, and there was talk that if she qualified for the worlds one day, he would become her manager. But before they even had the chance to go beyond their starry-eyed engagement, Claudia's dreams were dashed by the accident on the ski slopes.

60

SALLY

The heavy door to my room opened on its forged iron hinges revealing rough-hewn wooden planks on the walls. They were gnarled and cracked, giving the room, like the rest of the house, a comfortably rustic feel. The floors and ceiling were of a paler hardwood, with exposed beams crossing the latter. Two giant silver-grey sheepskin rugs lay on each side of the bed. The twin light fittings were made out of the horns of two miniature slain alpine beasts. The soft beige and burgundy tones on the bed linen made the room feel instantly warm, although the heating hadn't yet fully kicked in. I put my pack on a chair, took out my toilet bag and put it in the bathroom. I didn't need to hang stuff up in the wardrobe. It felt less invasive to leave my clothes in my pack, and I was dying for a cup of tea after our journey.

'Jamie!' I called up the stairs to his attic room.

I jumped as he came through the door to my left at the end of the hallway, which must have been his parents' room judging by its size. He was holding his phone in front of him, and I realised he was guiding his father virtually round the house. He had a notebook and pen in his other hand. He saw me, and raised his eyebrows. I made the sign of holding a tea cup up to my lips. He gave me the thumbs up.

'Am I allowed to touch stuff? Do you want a cuppa?' I whispered, and he nodded.

'Is that Emma with you?' I heard his dad ask.

Jamie sucked in his breath. Her name coming from his father must have been a shock. It certainly was for me. *I am not, and will never be, like Emma*, I wanted to shout.

'No... My friend Sally from the bookshop is with me. She's been helping sort details of the theft at home. We thought... You've never met Sal, have you, Dad?' He wandered over to me and swung the phone between us. 'Dad, meet Sally. Sally, meet Dad... Frank Marsh.'

'You're the young lady whose reputation with words precedes you, my dear. It's a pleasure to meet someone who can keep young James on his lexicological toes.'

'Likewise,' I said, chuckling, wishing I'd checked what I looked like before being introduced to Jamie's father. I hadn't even glanced at myself in the mirror in my ensuite bathroom. No make-up, definitely. Scraggy hair, certainly. I probably had spinach in my teeth or something, though why I should feel the need to look perfect in front of Jamie's father rather than Jamie himself was beyond me.

'Ok, let's get on with it,' said Jamie as I glanced at the notebook. There were already a few items listed. I wondered what they might be. His mother's jewellery, artwork, precious ornaments, more books? He wandered down the hallway and opened another door at the end, to a bedroom, perhaps. 'They've dusted for prints everywhere,' Jamie said to his father. 'If I have time, I'll clean up a bit. It's left everything looking so grubby.' His voice faded as he went deeper into the room.

I was tempted to follow him, offer to write items in his notebook like a faithful secretary while he showed his father each new corner with his phone. Instead, I went downstairs to the kitchen, an ultra-modern blend of technology against the thick-beamed timbers of the ceiling and walls. Through the window the sun was sinking lower in the sky, tucked between the two slopes of the snowy valley to the west. A sunset glow shed light on the granite tops and modernised wood-burning stove. It was a luxury version of the vision I'd previously conjured with tightly-bunned lasses in gingham blouses and dirndls cooking on tiny pot-bellied stoves in high mountain chalets. The price of installing that thing this high in the Alps would probably have made Willie's eyes water.

I found the kettle, filled it with water, placed it on its stand and flicked the switch. I searched the cupboards for tea bags, but suddenly realised there'd probably be no milk. I opened the fridge. There was some salad sauce, a couple of jars of jam and half a jar of olives. I wondered how far away the supermarket or the shops were.

'No milk!' I called out, as I heard Jamie's footfall on the stairs. 'Are you okay with black tea?'

'There should be some small long-life cartons in the cupboard above the kettle,' said Jamie's Dad, his voice distant and husky on the FaceTime app on Jamie's phone.

'Thanks, Mr. M!' I sounded perhaps too jolly given the circumstances.

As the kettle rumbled towards boiling, I remembered from a science class that water boiled at a much lower temperature at altitude. Rather than snatching it from its stand as I would have done at home, I let it rumble on with steam gathering in a great cloud under the kitchen unit until the lever clicked off.

Jamie had already finished the call with his father and was speaking German to someone else I assumed was the police. The call didn't last long, and Jamie reached for his jacket lying on a chair in the hallway. He pulled his keys out of the pocket.

'Going to the police station?' I asked.

'I have to take them the full list of missing stuff. There's not much, but they have to register it for the insurance company. And I want to find out whether they have any leads on who this might have been. *We* have our suspicions, but I wonder if they've come to their own conclusions. To be honest, we're more likely to get this stuff back than those books.'

'Really? You think there's no hope? If it *was* your girlfriend who took them, I'm not sure she would have the market knowhow,' I said.

'In my head I've kind of written them off now. It would be so easy to make them disappear.'

'Will you tell DS Hannah about this connection as well? I'm even more convinced she was also involved in your theft.'

'Damn! I need to call DS Hannah, too. I'll do that after I've been to the police station in town. I'm not sure how long the detective there will wait for me. It's getting late. Do you want to come with me? I don't mind if you wait here. There won't be much you can do.'

'Perhaps I can pick up something for dinner while you're with the police?' I said, eyeing the two mugs of tea I'd just poured.

'Good idea. Come on, let's go.'

I sighed and followed Jamie out of the chalet. As we climbed back into the rental Range Rover parked outside the garage, Jamie paused for a moment before pressing the button to start the engine.

'Emma-Eva was here with me when the books went missing in London. If she had a hand in the theft at my place, she must have had a collaborator.'

'Despicable Nick,' we said simultaneously.

Jamie dropped me off at the Co-Op supermarket by the lake and drove to the police station down the street. I told him I'd meet him there.

I picked up some food for dinner – a couple of chicken breasts and some mixed veggies. I'd seen a box of rice I could use in the cupboard in the kitchen earlier. I also bought some fruit, muesli and yoghurt for breakfast, and milk for the tea and coffee, after a conversation earlier that long life milk with tea definitely didn't cut it. And a reasonable bottle of Spanish red. Then I paid for it all, expecting to be asked something at the checkout that I couldn't possibly answer in Swiss German. The checkout lady spoke impeccable English and was mega friendly, and I was pleasantly surprised I didn't need to mortgage an arm or a leg for the bill. Everyone was always ranting on about how expensive Switzerland was, but honestly, I would definitely have paid more for that lot in a central London Tesco Metro.

In the lobby of the supermarket, I sat on a bench and brought up Google Search on my phone. I went back into the TelSearch website and typed Nick, then Nicholas, then Rich; nothing. Then when I re-typed N.Rich, the app asked me: *Did you mean N.Reich?* I looked at the address and frowned. According to Google maps, it was very close. The centre of town wasn't huge. I could wander by and take a look and be back at the police station by the time James had finished.

I arrived outside a large wooden building with a pitched, chalet-style roof. There were several mailboxes with a list of door buzzers beside them. Reich was third from the top. I pressed the buzzer.

'Ja,' came a slow drawl through the speaker.

'Hi,' I said. 'Is this Nick?'

'No... Well... I'm— Who is this?' His voice was deep, accented, immediately wary.

'My name is Sally. I'm a colleague of James Marsh. I've come from London. He doesn't know I'm here, but I need to talk to you,' I said in a rush, and then added: 'Only if you're alone.'

There was an intake of breath and then silence, and then a click as the connection cut. I suddenly felt vulnerable; this might not have been such a clever idea. At any moment I could be faced with not one, but two cold-blooded murderers. If he released the door for me to enter, I decided I wouldn't go in. I would say my piece and be on my way.

Through the square frosted window in the main door of the building, I saw a light come on in the hallway, and before I'd even reacted to the flight adrenalin now pumping through my veins, the door swung open.

There he stood, all six feet of him. Hair dampened from a recent shower, those wide shoulders, blue eyes, full lips slightly open with unspoken curiosity. Not at all stalker-like. Although he should have been worried about my presence, and I about his potential reaction, he smiled at me, and I felt immediately at ease.

'Hi Sally, I'm Klaus,' he said. 'You'd better come in.'

And I stepped into his home without a second thought.

61

JAMES

As I came out of the *Kantonspolizei* building Sal was waiting by the Range Rover which I'd parked on a spot normally reserved for a police car. She was chewing her lip, her gaze tracking several SUVs of luxury model cars as they drove past.

She jumped when she saw me.

'Lost in thought there, Sal.'

'How ugly they all look compared to their super-model relatives,' she said, pointing her chin at a Porsche Cayenne crunching past on the fresh snow. 'I imagine these people all have sleek Lamborghinis and Ferraris in their garages waiting for the summer months. Range Rover Sports are a dime a dozen, James. Your rental car isn't exclusive here.'

'But more practical, perhaps, than some of these vehicles. There's more money here per square metre than the centre of Mayfair. And everyone is happy to show it off.' I cast a look across to the opulent Kempinski Hotel and to Badrutt's Palace on the hill above the lake.

'The cops must be used to dealing with rich owners' chalets being broken into,' she said.

I shrugged. 'Let's get out of here before I get a hefty fine for parking in the wrong spot.' I clicked the key fob to open the boot, took the shopping bag from Sal and put it in before we both climbed into the front.

'I gave them the whole story,' I said gripping the steering wheel. In my frustration I gave it a little shake, only managing to sway myself against the weight of the heavy car. 'I'm not sure how much they believed me, or how much they would follow up on it. There's no single person in charge of these break-ins on our road, which seems odd. But two of them knew Claudia, remembered the tragedy of her suicide last autumn. They told me under no circumstances should I go and visit the mother. The policeman I spoke to said "*Nicht den Bock zum Gärtner machen*" the German version of "don't set the cat amongst the pigeons."'

'Shouldn't you call DS Hannah, now?' asked Sal. 'It's getting late, although they're an hour behind in the UK.'

'You're right. Sooner rather than later,' I said, looking for the detective's number on my mobile phone and pressing the dial and the speaker buttons one after the other.

'Mr Marsh,' said DS Hannah. 'What news from the Alps?'

I recounted what had been stolen from my parents' chalet. Then I told him about the connection to Claudia's sister Emma-Eva.

'So you've changed your tune about her,' said the detective. 'You were all lovey-dovey last week.'

Ouch. I thought that was a bit cruel. My heart was still full of her, despite the deception.

'Well, I didn't know I'd been swindled at that point,' I said, a slice of anger finally slipping off my tongue. I'd felt miserable until now; perhaps this new emotion was healthier for my state of mind. 'Anyway, because she has family here, we think the robberies might be connected. And even if she's managed to disappear, it's obvious she had a collaborator. It's important you try and find this Nick Rich she was living with. He must be the one who broke in while we were on holiday at Christmas. I think it's also important you look for Eva Schmid rather than Emma Smith. That's her real name.'

'And how did you find that out?' asked the detective.

I clenched my jaw and sucked in a whisper of air between my teeth.

'I saw it written on some correspondence she left behind in her room a couple of days ago.'

'And you didn't think to call us and tell us about this immediately?'

'I... no. She wasn't a suspect at the time. It didn't occur to me until after she'd gone.'

'Everyone was a suspect at the time, Mr Marsh. How can I be sure that she's not *your* partner in crime?'

'Oh, for Pete's sake,' I said.

Sal put her hand on my arm. Although I'd turned my misery to anger two minutes previously, it was imperative I didn't piss off the detective. I looked at Sal and pressed my mouth into a firm line before continuing.

'I think it's important we find her ex-boyfriend.'

'Your young lady could still be coming back from visiting her mother,' said DS Hannah. 'I find it odd that you've no way of getting hold of her, though.'

'She kept some truths from me, DS Hannah. It's not sitting very well with me at the moment, I can assure you.'

'Well, finding this Nicholas Rich might be an equally big problem. The Met can't put energy or resources into looking for someone because of a gut feeling. That type of thing only happens on TV shows. And whatever impression Ms Smith, or Ms Schmid if you think that's her real name, has given you about her past, there may be a number of reasons she's kept this information from you.'

'So, you think all these are just coincidences?' My voice was hard, frustration coming off me in waves. Didn't they want to catch the perpetrator? How many leads were ignored in police cases because they were hunches? I was angry for the system, but wondered how hard they would actually look for my books. It would probably be up to the insurance assessor in the end. 'The police here are going to question the Schmids. I've been told to stay away from the family. I'm not sure how convinced they are either of my story, but they are being cooperative.' I wanted to say they were being more cooperative than *he* was, but held my tongue.

'If they find out anything significant, I'd appreciate you sharing that information with me,' said DS Hannah.

That was good, surely? He didn't completely discount the story I'd told him.

'I'll text you the *Kantonspolizei* contact details, too,' I said. 'Until I clear up the burglary here, I'll be in St Moritz for a few more days.'

'Enjoy your holiday,' said DS Hannah sarcastically.

'It's not...' Sal put her hand on my arm again to stop what she knew was coming. 'We'll speak soon,' I said, and stabbed the end call button on my mobile phone screen.

I scrolled to Emma Smith in my contacts, and tried to call her again, not caring that Sal was in the car with me. The phone went to voicemail "Hi, this is Emma, I'm not available right now..." and my throat tightened as I stabbed the end call button again and threw my phone into the tray in the centre console.

'She went to some trouble to set this all up,' said Sal. 'A UK mobile phone number with a message for her Emma Smith persona, the whole shebang luring you in with her domestic abuse and student poverty story.'

I didn't say anything, but bit my lip and started the car. We drove back to the chalet in silence. I pulled up to one side of the driveway.

'I'd better clear the drive properly so I can open the garage door and put the car away, in case it snows again tonight. You can come in through here,' I said, leading the way to an entrance beside the double-sized tilting garage door. 'I'll find you a bottle from the wine cellar to take upstairs and I can fetch the shovel,' 'I bought a rioja at the supermarket,' said Sal.

'Good idea,' I said, keying the code for the side door and opening it. 'Although I've a feeling one bottle might not get me through the evening, oh... shit!'

'What?' asked Sal, as I was already keying another number into my phone. 'What is it?'

I raked my fingers through my hair and pulled at the roots on the crown of my head. My frustration had just ramped up tenfold. I listened to the long ring-tone on the other end, not the double tone of a UK mobile.

'Herr Vögel?' I asked, 'You need to add another item to the list of stolen objects. My father's Bentley.'

Sal cleared her throat and looked into the darkness of the garage. Mum's BMW was parked to one side. The truck-sized gap on the other side was where the Bentley was usually parked.

'Vögel's coming up,' I said to Sal when I'd finished the call. 'More papers to fill in. Shit, I didn't even think to look in the garage. This is the single most expensive item on the list.'

'Including the books?' Sal asked.

'A different kind of value. My dad... The books are very likely already beyond our reach. If they've already left the UK, God knows who they've been sold to. Some Russian Oligarch, a Middle Eastern oil tycoon or an African dictator. If Fenella is right, I think they would have simply used the potential valuation they were trying to ascertain from Sotheby's. I'm sure whoever took them has no knowledge of the antique book market, but it's not that hard to find buyers illegally for priceless things when money is no object. And objects like that disappear without trace very quickly. The car, the Bentley, it's far more traceable.'

'Out of curiosity, what's worth more to you?'

'Financially, the books, I guess. But Dad loves that car. It's a special edition, almost an antique or an "old timer" as the Swiss locals would say. He's not the type of rich old guy to just up and buy something that takes his fancy. He has a real passion for the Bentley. My books, they're probably worth more than three of Dad's cars. But his passion is worth more to me than any of those.'

Sal sighed deeply, possibly mirroring my additional frustration, but sounding, I wasn't sure, relieved, perhaps?

'Where was the key kept?' she asked.

The police would be asking exactly the same question.

'There's a hidden key cabinet in the hallway cupboard. Whoever took it, probably knew where to find the key.'

'Little Miss Street Lady certainly did her homework,' she said, sounding almost impressed, and I darted her a look that said she shouldn't be rubbing salt in any wounds. I gripped my forehead, digging my thumb and middle finger into the soft sides of my temples.

'That way will take you up to the hallway outside the kitchen.' I pointed to the inside door and picked up a large orange snow shovel leaning against the wall.

Sal stood at the door for a moment, watching me push the first shovel of snow down towards the road, leaving a dark path of tarmac behind me. She turned to cross the garage with the shopping bag and climbed the stairs to the kitchen. I'd suddenly lost my appetite.

62

JAMES

I was talking to my father again when Detective Vögel arrived. Sal let the policeman in through the front door and showed him through to the kitchen-diner.

'The Bentley has a tracker in its computer system.' Dad was talking on the mobile phone's loud speaker sitting on the marble island top in front of me. 'But I'll need to contact the company. It's only automatically activated if the car is stolen without the key fob. Otherwise, privacy issues and all that. They don't track the car all the time.'

'Unfortunately. Well, they have the key. It was removed from the key box in the hallway here,' I said.

'You'll have to convince someone there that the car's been stolen. Maybe the St Moritz police can help,' said Dad.

Standing beside me, Detective Vögel nodded to say he'd understood.

'How the hell did they know where to find the key? It's not obviously a key box.' It was the first time I'd heard real concern in my father's voice. The car was truly his pride and joy. He'd sounded annoyed but not quite as desperate as this about the other stolen objects, only that the house had been broken into, his holiday space violated.

'It's a long story,' I said. 'But I think I know who did this, or at least I think I know who they were connected to.'

'And who might that be, Sherlock?' Dad's anger now held a tiny tone of sarcasm I had been on the receiving end of a few times in my teens.

'We think Emma might have something to do with this.'

'*Your* Emma?' Dad sounded surprised, as though that possibility would never had entered his head, and I felt an unwarranted spike of shame, that I'd been duped by someone I'd fallen in love with.

'Her real name is not Emma,' I said, 'It's Eva. Eva Schmid. And her sister's name is... was Claudia Johnson.'

'The figure skater?'

'Yes.'

There was silence on my mobile phone while Dad registered this new information.

'Oh...' he said after a few moments.

'Look, Dad, I have to go. The detective is here for the theft of the Bentley. Where are the papers for the car?'

'They'll be in the safe. With the spare key. They won't be able to sell it on easily without either of those.'

'OK. As soon as you have that tracer link to Bentley, send it through. I'm sure the police here will want it.'

Detective Vögel nodded, indicating he'd understood my conversation with Dad in English.

'Oh, and Jamie?' said Dad. 'You might just want to check that your mother's diamond choker is still in that safe.'

'You didn't tell me about that when we were doing the inventory,' I said, picking up my phone and heading for the stairs. The detective followed me up to my parents' room. He didn't need to ask. Sal tagged along behind, her interest obviously piqued.

'Emma asked me if she could borrow some cash,' said my father. 'Said she'd seen something at the market she wanted to get you for Christmas but that they would only take cash because their credit card machine was broken.'

'Oh God, Dad, you're saying she watched you open the safe?'

'No... well, I can't be sure. She might have been lurking in the hallway. It was all a bit of a rush. The girls were back and forth from town. A taxi was waiting. I just remember being surprised that she was on the landing when I came out...'

The policeman rubbed his jaw, and I wondered if I'd just seen him rolling his eyes.

'Call me back when you've contacted Bentley,' I said, exasperated.

I didn't wait for an answer, threw the phone onto my parents' bed and entered their walk-in wardrobe. I slid aside an all-in-one ski suit and a fur coat I knew Sal would freak out if she knew it was real, exposing the safe in the corner. I bent down to open it.

Sal reversed back towards the door of the room and I could tell she was calculating whether someone could see the safe being opened from the doorway. Six numbers. Probably not hard to work out if you were standing in the hallway and had good eyesight. But who knew the extent my deceiving girlfriend had gone to? Maybe she'd had binoculars, or set up a camera.

The door of the safe swung open exposing a gaping dark hole.

'Everything's gone,' I said, no longer shocked.

'*Verdammt*,' said Vögel quietly, at the same time as Sal said: 'Wow.'

'How could she do this when she was already back in London with you?' asked the detective in English.

'She wasn't. I thought she was visiting her mother. But she must have come back here. To do this. What I can't work out is, who took my books?'

'One thing at a time,' said Sal. 'I think if you can track her down, you might get a few answers.'

'Despicable Nick,' I mused. 'Who the hell is this guy?'

I called my father back to give him the latest on the stolen items while the policeman waited patiently.

I then told the policeman everything that Dad remembered having been in the safe. We both spoke in English now, for Sal's benefit. Now she knew the cop spoke the language faultlessly, I wondered whether she thought I might have been showing off before with my language skills.

'There is already a notice out for the vehicle, especially with our colleagues in Italy. It's unlikely the car will stay in Switzerland for very long. These things move fast, especially with such high profile vehicles like this, but so far nothing has been seen on the cameras crossing the local borders on the main roads.'

'Do you think they'd risk the Bernina? It'll be super dangerous in these conditions. It's an awkward beast to drive at the best of times. Dad never drives the thing in winter.'

The policeman nodded thoughtfully.

'*Wahrscheinlich*,' he said. Probably.

63

EVA

After Claudia's death, I was compelled to find out what would hurt James Marsh most of all. How could we execute the ultimate revenge? By destroying the one thing he was most passionate about, of course.

Integrating myself into his life, my goal was to find out what that one thing was from the beginning. James didn't have a girlfriend, so I couldn't break them up, although I did a pretty good job of destroying his friendship with Sally Crime. There was no point in getting him fired from his job because he was going to inherit more money than he could ever spend, and therefore didn't need to work.

When he introduced me to those books, I realised they were like his babies, and I knew for sure they were what mattered to him most. His manky old copy of *Of Human Bondage* was like the love of his life. It would be the ultimate satisfaction to place it on the top of a pyre and watch its pages burn, film the act and send it to him. I was trying to work out if there was a way we could watch James as he witnessed his precious book burn, but we would have to be content with knowing how distressed he would be.

There was potentially a major setback at the beginning when the stupid vagabond fell and hit his head while we were trying to move him off that spot opposite the bookstore, but they didn't find his body until my relationship with James was well and truly established. And by then we had everything we needed. Including those bonuses that began to present themselves.

For a man who made his fortune in finance and economics, Frank Marsh wasn't terribly clever when it came to protecting his domestic valuables. I'd followed him the day we went shopping at the Christmas market to the door of his bedroom after the excuse of needing to borrow some cash to buy James's gift. I assumed Mr Marsh was going to fetch his wallet. But my heart leapt when I saw the safe in his walk-in wardrobe.

It was a keypad affair, like the small metal boxes you find in hotel rooms, not a giant metal safe with a sensitive dial ring, drive pin and door-locking wheel you might see in rich guys' offices or banks on TV programmes. I couldn't see the entire sequence on the buttons from where I was standing in the doorway, but the way his fingers moved across them, when I saw the last three of those numbers, I knew straight away that the code was James's birth date. The cliché made me smile.

He moved his body across the open safe as I heard the rustle of paper – an envelope perhaps. I couldn't see what else was in there, but filed its presence for our imminent plans. He closed the door, beeped in the code, and turned around to face me, two crisp hundred-franc notes between the thumb and forefinger of his outstretched hand as though offering a small child a lollipop.

Our booty was getting larger. Who the hell still kept cash in their safe in that day and age? It would be yet another bonus on top of the books. The artefacts on display in the rooms of the chalet would be fairly easy to sell at a flea market or an antique fair in Italy. The cash would be an even easier haul, though it was impossible to know how much was in that safe. We'd recently added all but one of his books to the booty, but they would be a little more difficult to shift. I had my eye on The Antiquarian Book Fair in Venice in the new year and had already contacted the organisers at the Palazzo Pisano to request a stall, using James's membership card. They were dubious as to the eclectic items, but when I sent them photos of the collection, they promised to issue me with a table number.

It was as I was emptying the safe that night, that the final object of our growing haul for re-sale was offered to us on a platter. The cash had been a moderate sum. I'd initially been disappointed at the thickness of the brown envelope I pulled out. But as I slid the notes out and fanned a few hundred and two-hundred-franc notes, my excitement spiked as I saw several purple bank notes bearing the image of a giant ant – the graphic depicting the industrious mentality of the Swiss workers which adorned the ridiculously high thousand-franc denomination.

As I counted the notes, I wondered not for the first time why old people still insisted on hiding money under their mattresses, or in this case in the house safe, for an unsure future. It was as though the fear of a world war was still imminent, but ignorant of the fact that paper money wouldn't be worth anything at all if the world's markets should crash. A big denomination of cash was the last thing anyone would be able to use to barter, despite the fact that up until the middle of the last century, properties were sometimes traded with cash on the real estate market in Switzerland, hence those massively valued bank notes.

Still kneeling in front of the open safe, my gaze flickered to something glinting in the rear corner. Thinking it might be a piece of jewellery that had fallen from the pouch with the diamond choker I'd removed earlier, I reached back and grappled for the thing, my hand slipping across the blue carpeted interior of the little safe. My fingers closed around the object and I pulled it out. I opened my hand, and sitting in my palm was a car key fob with the spread of a raptors' wings and a B in the centre. It was the spare key for Frank Marsh's Bentley. I'd completely forgotten about this gem of a car sitting in the garage downstairs.

Everyone knew about Mr Marsh's Bentley in St Moritz. 'Sir Marsh,' we used to say, when we saw him gliding past in the monstrosity. In summer he drove Mrs Marsh to the Co-Op to buy the groceries. We never saw her driving that big old car, and seldom saw her driving her own BMW. Mr Marsh looked more like a chauffeur than a husband. A kind of Parker to an aging Miss Penelope.

After seeing the opulence of James's flat in Seven Dials, all that space hidden inside the discreet row of condominiums off one of the most high-end real estate areas of Covent Garden, I'd expected him to also have an expensive car, perhaps some kind of vintage soft-top you could drive out to the country on the weekends, an MG or an Austin Healy. But I soon found out he hadn't inherited his father's passion and wasn't really interested in cars. It turns out his passion was in boring books.

It made sense though, the non-car thing. London had slapped all those emission charges on anyone who had an environmentally unfriendly vehicle and there was a lack of parking spaces in the area. James had become a bit obsessed with walking everywhere. He said everything he needed was within a stone's throw of his home, so what was the point?

He didn't even use London Transport unless it was absolutely necessary, and only travelled on the train for his journeys outside the city, including to his parents. Granted he always travelled First Class, but it didn't seem in keeping after I'd seen his digs in Covent Garden. It would have been nice to hop into a Porsche or a Ferrari and head out to the country for a weekend drive. But it was the middle of winter when we met, so I wasn't really missing out on any roofless car rides in that respect. The only time he got into a car was a taxi to and from the airport with luggage.

It hadn't even occurred to us to target the Bentley in St Moritz at the beginning. But when I took that spare key from the safe, along with its papers, an idea began forming in my mind. The old classic must be worth a mint on the black market.

I knew the Bentley would be in the garage downstairs because James' parents had taken the train back to the airport after Christmas when they'd seen the forecast for more snow.

64

JAMES

After Vögel left, I set a fire in the lounge at the chalet and within minutes had it crackling and roaring. Sal put some rice on to boil and sprinkled the chicken breasts liberally with herbs and spices she'd found in the rack above the hob. I couldn't face food at first, but as Sal sautéed the chicken in a pan on the convection hob next to the Aga, the smell of the food began to whet my appetite. With the steam and heat from the cooking pots on the stove, the chalet was warming up and felt cosy.

I looked at the label of the rioja Sal had bought and nodded my approval. Leaning past her I slid open a draw to take out a corkscrew. I wasn't a heavy drinker in general, but a glass of red wine was the thing I needed most in the world right now. I almost smiled as I held the corkscrew aloft, this simple pleasure becoming a necessity in the face of disaster.

As Sal continued to work at the hob, I took two glasses from an oak and glass cabinet by the dining room table. As the cork slid out with a satisfying *thwock*, I began to relax. It seemed there was nothing we could really do while waiting for news from the police and the tracker information for Dad's car.

After we'd eaten at the kitchen island, I took the bottle of wine to the low table in front of the fire and we sank into the comfy couches swathed in sheepskin rugs. I noticed Sal had switched to water, and she poured me a generous glass of the wine. We were warm now, and the alcohol had given me a soft fuzzy feeling.

'I guess you must be an expert skier after so many seasons holidaying here,' said Sal, sinking back into the couch.

'After my last escapade on the slopes, I thought I might be losing my touch.'

'What do you mean?'

'I was caught in an avalanche at Christmas during our trip.'

'Oh, wow! You didn't say. That must have been scary.'

'It was a bit. It was a gorgeous day. Conditions can be so deceiving. Check this out.' I shifted and took my mobile phone out of my back pocket, and put my wineglass down on the table. Sal leaned over and topped it up, finishing the bottle.

I scrolled through my photos to the video showing bright white snow and a cyan blue sky.

'Look at that slope,' I said. 'You'd never think it could be so dangerous...'

Sal paused, and made a little humming sound. 'Who's that?' she asked, looking at the skier on the edge of what looked like a dangerous cornice of snow high up above where I'd been filming. The skier's face was hidden behind a helmet and goggles.

'It's my mate Klaus. In your opinion, what does it look like he's doing?'

I zoomed in on the figure, moving my fingers apart on the screen to magnify Klaus.

'Is he cold? He's stamping his feet. Can't be easy wearing skis.'

'I thought he was creating a platform to launch his descent, but that looks like quite the determined stamping,' I mused.

'Tell me about Klaus?' Her comment was posed like a question. I wasn't sure how much information she wanted.

'He's my mate from the old days. A skiing buddy. We made a date to ski that day, after I'd run into him a couple of days' previously. This was the last moment before I got caught in that avalanche.'

'Shit,' she said. 'His might have been the last face you ever saw.'

'Don't joke. As he pulled me out of the avalanche, he did say: "Come on, James. We don't want to lose you just yet."'

'Oh!'

'The whole group of us were always a bit casual about the dangers on the mountain.'

'Some of you too much, judging by Claudia's experiences,' she said.

I grimaced, then looked at Sal for her insensitive comment. It seemed a little cruel for her to be pointing out the obvious at this stage.

65

SALLY

'Do you honestly think it was Klaus's *intention* to get you caught in an avalanche?' I asked.

'I'm beginning to think he may have a connection to Claudia Johnson,' said James.

'But that he might actually have tried to *kill* you seems a bit far-fetched. Appearances can be deceiving.'

'Well yes, precisely. He and Emma-Eva didn't *appear* to know each other when we met at the ski hut, but I don't know what to believe any more. Maybe she and Klaus are an item.'

I remembered that's what I'd thought when I'd first seen Klaus embracing Eva outside Jamie's condo all those weeks ago. It had been hard to tell back then whether it was the embrace of lovers, good friends, or siblings. Now I knew it was no longer any of those options, I wanted to voice the thought: *She was living with you! You must have known!* But Jamie probably thought that too, as his faced crumpled a little, which I assumed was a combination of heartbreak and humiliation.

Jamie's mobile buzzed and 'DAD' came up on the screen.

'Oh! That was quick,' I said, surprised, and James looked at me with a frown.

'I'm sending you a link via email,' said his father when James answered on speaker. 'It's an activation code for the tracker on the Bentley's chassis. It should work even if the vehicle runs out of fuel and the computer shuts down. The car's too old to have a modern IT system.'

'OK, hold on. Stay on the line to make sure I can get it to work on my phone. I'm putting you on the coffee table.'

Jamie put the phone down, swiped his father's name off the screen and opened his email app.

'Got it,' he said. 'I'll just see if the link works. Yep. Looks like it. I need a password though.'

'A bit complicated, I received that by separate text message. I'll put it on our family WhatsApp chat.'

The message dropped down from the top of Jamie's screen. He opened it and copied the password, which seemed to be a hundred symbols long.

'I'm in. Oh, wow. The car's still in the valley!' he exclaimed. 'It seems to be somewhere to the East, in Zuoz. The tracking beacon's not moving, so it must be parked there.'

'Unless they found and removed the tracker,' said his dad.

James gave his mobile a despairing look. 'I'd better go. I need to call Vögel,' he said.

I looked out of the window. The sky was now a deep cobalt – *Bleu Majorelle* – I remembered from my visit to the spectacular gardens of the same name in Marrakech. The winter heavens were juxtaposed against the rosy alpenglow-tipped mountain ridge across the valley, a world away from the Atlas Mountains. Darkness was imminent.

'Maybe they're waiting for nightfall. To make their escape,' said James as he dialled Vögel's number.'

'It's going on four days now since the theft, right?' I asked.

'We're not even sure about that. The cleaners came in on Tuesday, but the break-ins could have been long before that.'

'Not too long after you returned to London, then.'

Jamie nodded. 'They must be waiting for the roads to be cleared,' he said. 'Shit, Vögel's not answering his mobile.'

He stood up and headed for the hallway, leaving a message on Detective Vögel's voicemail asking him to call back as soon as possible and that the Bentley appeared to still be in the vicinity. This time he spoke in English, any attempt to impress me with his language skills overriding the urgency to get his message across to Vögel. He came back with his ski jacket tucked under his arm.

'I can't just wait until he calls. He might have turned his phone off for the night. I've no idea where he lives. And the reason the car is still here is undoubtedly due to the bad weather. That beast is a nightmare – it's like a tank in snowy conditions.'

'So why does your dad have such an impractical car here?'

'It's just a passion of his. Big old cars. My parents drive the Beemer in winter. It has four-wheel drive. But the Bentley... This is the first time the roads will have been clear enough for the thieves to drive it safely out of here. They'll have waited for night to avoid attracting attention. No one in their sane mind would want to drive a car like that at this time of the year.'

'Jamie, you should wait for the police to intervene. It could be dangerous. Desperate people do desperate things.' I couldn't help thinking I sounded like a prude, but I had to try and stop him going after that car. In normal circumstances I would be thinking more like James Bond than Miss Marple.

'If my suspicions are correct, they'll try and head over the Bernina Pass to avoid being spotted at the border, especially now that the cops are aware the car's been stolen. They may know we're here, somehow, but that puts more urgency into this.'

'Why the Bernina Pass? Is it the only way out of here?' I knew it wasn't, but wanted to hear his logic.

'No, but I think any thieves will be wanting to head out of Switzerland as quickly as possible. The Bernina Pass is open all year, but can be treacherous in the snow. The biggest advantage to anyone stealing a valuable vehicle is that the border control isn't manned at night. By the time anyone has registered their movement on CCTV, the car will have disappeared into the mysteries of illegal Italian car thievery.

'Doesn't the police station have someone on duty 24/7?'

'I doubt I'm going to get hold of anyone who knows what's going on. I have to find Dad's car. At least then I can let the police know where it is and they can intervene. The weather has only been clear for a few hours. I'm sure someone has been waiting for this window to move it out of the valley.'

I glanced pointedly at the empty wine bottle on the table. 'You shouldn't be driving.'

'A quick espresso and a glass of water should do the trick.'

I bit my lip. I knew his capacity to absorb alcohol had never hampered his Scrabble-playing ability, so he was bound to know his limitations as far as driving was concerned, but it was imperative he didn't get behind the wheel of the car.

'Let me just pop to the loo, and I'll drive,' I said, grabbing my mobile and heading down the hallway to the privacy of the downstairs cloakroom.

Once I'd sent my text, I collected my own coat and boots from the rack next to the door.

'You definitely shouldn't drive,' I repeated, not mentioning that I probably shouldn't be driving either, with my inexperience in winter conditions. But James had mentioned so often that the Range Rover could handle anything, I felt reassured. 'You navigate' I said. 'You know the area better than me.'

66

EVA

Once I'd established how to get back at James, it was as though we'd been offered the chance of a reward on a platter for having gone to all that trouble. After initially thinking he was some over-the-top book geek, the day James put on those white gloves and handled his books with such care, I realised they all must be worth a fortune. The one he most cared about probably wasn't going to fetch as much as some of the others, so it was worth relinquishing the Maugham to the sacrificial pyre.

I'd called Klaus straight away.

'You'll have to get over here, though, just before Christmas. James and I are leaving for St Moritz on the 21st. It'll be the perfect opportunity. He won't discover the books are missing until after he returns, and we'll be long gone by then. There are no cameras or alarms on the cabinet, and only an alarm on the front door of the condo. I have the codes. It'll be a doddle for you.'

'Do you think those books are insured?' Klaus had asked thoughtfully a few days later, after we'd fixed further plans for the theft.

'For sure! They could be worth a fortune. There's no way he'd keep them on display in his own home without having them insured. Otherwise, they'd be in a book vault.'

'Then maybe you could also work out how the insurance pay-out finds its way into our wallets.'

'Ooh, good thinking, although I'm not sure how. I don't have access to his bank accounts. It's something I can work on though. It'll be risky. It means I'll have to come back from Switzerland after Christmas. You'll have to do the burglaries in St Moritz on your own. It's not like there's any urgency. If no one is at the chalet, it'll give you more time to carry out the break-in at the Marsh's place.'

The door downstairs in the condo had clunked closed at that point in our conversation. I was getting careless with my calls to Klaus. I already suspected James had heard me on the phone a couple of times. And Klaus had asked me on more than one occasion if I thought we were becoming too greedy.

'I have to go,' I'd whispered to Klaus. 'He's just come back from work.'

I remember looking around my room, by then so familiar and comfortable. I'd been getting used to living in the centre of London in James's luxury pad. Back in October after Klaus and I had put this whole plan into action, I'd spent days dreaming of getting off that street and back into a warm environment with a roof over my head. At that time, I hadn't cared what James Marsh's living situation was. I just needed to woo him and get him to invite me to his family's chalet for Christmas. We knew his parents were loaded, but it was possible all he had was a crappy bedsit in the East End. At that point, anything was better than that godforsaken doorway on Piccadilly.

'It's not a bad plan anyway,' I said to Klaus, looking forward to spending a few extra days in Seven Dials. 'As long as I don't come under any suspicion, it would be good to be here to keep an eye on the books on the pre-auction site. As soon as I know a realistic number for their worth, I'll withdraw the request and we can look at selling them on. I'll try and find a way to get that insurance payout, but I'm not sure that will be so easy. James doesn't have a great sense of financial security. I'd have to find a way to get into his personal account, unless the compensation would go to some family trust.'

'Poor, gullible James Marsh. He has a swamp of money he probably doesn't know he can access,' Klaus said.

'Honestly, Klaus. I don't think he cares. He's so frugal, doesn't throw money about at all. When he bought me all those new clothes, he didn't want to buy anything for himself, and although his walk-in wardrobe is huge, there's not a great deal in it.'

'Burning that book and selling the others will likely hurt him more than ransacking a few *objets d'art* and jewels from his family's chalet. This is working out better than we could have hoped,' Klaus had said.

'A double heist.' I already imagined us toasting our winnings with a glass of bubbles.

The day James and I left for the Christmas holidays, I'd disengaged the alarm, claiming the need for one last visit to the loo. I'd hovered by the keypad next to the door pretending to key in the alarm while James waited in the courtyard outside at the top of the steps leading down to our taxi waiting in Shortland Gardens.

But by the time we returned together after our little Christmas break to find James' books missing, any joyfulness in the planning of what was initially an act of simple revenge, was soon thrown into turmoil when our reputations risked turning from those of petty thieves to potential murderers. After I'd voiced my suspicions about Marta the cleaning lady to both James and the police, to throw them off the scent of the book theft, I knew I had to get the hell out of there.

Then there was the Bentley.

'I know a place I can park it until the weather improves,' Klaus had said when I showed him the key and suggested we add it to our takings.

'That's good. If we parked it on the street outside your house, we'd be arrested faster than a tax-dodging immigrant,' I said with a laugh.

We'd found the main key in a key box beside the coat rack in the stone-tiled hallway amongst an assortment of keys that were labelled things like "Wine Cellar" and "Boot Locker." I remembered Frank Marsh accessing the cellar key at Christmas.

'Woah. That's a monster car,' Klaus had said, as we descended the stairs together to the garage.

'So where are you thinking of hiding it? We can't possibly drive it over any of the passes in the current weather conditions. We'll have to wait until a break in the storm.'

We stood admiring the massive maroon and gold car, its bulk and gleam even more intimidating in the confines of the garage.

'A mate of mine keeps his snowmobile in one of the outbuildings at the school where your dad used to work. I often wax my skis there in preparation for working at the ski school. I still have a key. There's enough room in there for the car. Are you really up for this?'

'I know stealing the Bentley isn't going to directly hurt James. He's a bit of a greenie, and never drives anywhere in London. But the angst he'll experience for his father will be enough additional payback for me.'

'And the books,' said Klaus.

'And the books,' I agreed. 'The question is, how do we trade *this* thing?'

'There's a massive market in stolen cars in Eastern Europe,' said Klaus. 'But I might have an idea. I once gave a guy private ski lessons whose daughter went to the Lyceum. He hired me for a couple of seasons. He often shouted me lunch on the slopes and talked about all kinds of shit. He's a car freak, a real petrol head, and loaded. I remember him saying he collected Jags, Ferraris, Porsches, even a Lamborghini. He lives in Dubai. Runs an import-export business. He once joked with me that he'd like to fill one of his regular shipping containers with Swiss cheese.'

'Do you think he'd be interested in the Bentley? Could you convince him you were acting as a kind of agent for the car?'

'I can give it a go.'

'That sounds almost too good to be true.'

I'd been thinking more on the lines of driving to southern Italy or even the Balkans to get rid of the Bentley. I was dubious about this. Surely a mega-rich business man would still want to know that a vehicle had been legally sourced?

'I'll dig out his number, call him later.'

'Ask him if he knows anyone who wants to buy a few antique books too,' I said with a laugh.

Klaus frowned.

'It's okay. I'm kidding,' I said. 'I'll very likely get a seller's ticket for the Antiquarian Book Fair in Venice. You don't need to be doing *all* the homework.'

'Let's get the stuff you wanted to target here and in Chalet Edelweiss, then we'll get the car out of here,' he said.

After we'd bagged up Mrs Marsh's jewellery and the money, we gathered some other objects I'd already targeted at Christmas. And because we had the giant boot of the Bentley to fit more in, we took three paintings of mountain scenes by a local artist who was making a name for himself in the East of Switzerland, and a snow scene that looked like a genuine Turner, a possible Picasso, a couple of medium-sized sculptures, and a dragon-decorated vase that could have been Qing.

We took everything down to the garage, wrapped the fragile things in the bubble-wrap I'd brought along, and loaded them into the back of the Bentley. Then with the security code swiped open on my phone, we visited the neighbouring chalet to plunder the watches Petra had showed me the night of the Christmas Eve drinks party. We also took a few other things of significant value, including two hand-blown Murano vases and a trinket box delicately carved out of a lacquered tropical wood with ivory marquetry. I'd looked all these things up on line when I'd got back to London after Christmas, but would only know their true market value once we reached Italy.

By the time everything was packed and ready, it was close to midnight. There'd be hardly anyone on the street to notice the Bentley. Klaus drove it timidly down to the village. I followed behind in his old Subaru, and noted that he only touched the Bentley's brakes fleetingly, worried the heavy vehicle would slide round the curves like a tank with slick tracks. He'd inspected the tyres before driving the car out of the garage and said with relief that they seemed to be all-weather. Otherwise, we would have had to try and find some chains, though I doubted we'd source a set big enough for those massive wheels.

Once down to the flat of the village by the lake, it was a relatively easy, level journey along to Zuoz. We drove up the lane past the school to one of the outbuildings where Klaus said we could keep the car.

'Do you think we should try and hide it, cover it with something?'

'No one else will come in here, but here's an old tarp,' he said, pulling a tatty green cover from the back of the room. 'It won't cover the car completely, but should at least act as a deterrent if anyone is being nosy.'

After drawing the cover up over the bonnet and the windscreen, Klaus closed and locked the door of the building and we drove back to St Moritz together in his Subaru. To avoid Mama asking any more questions about my sudden reappearance and impending disappearance to Italy, I stayed in the studio of a friend who'd gone to Australia for the season. She'd always said I could stay there in case things got too emotional with my mother. There was a keylock inside her mailbox she'd given me the code to before she left. Klaus dropped me off and agreed to touch base in the morning.

'It's too late to call this guy in Dubai now,' he said. 'They're three hours ahead. Let's get a good night's sleep and we'll see what the weather's doing in the morning.'

I fell asleep with the sound of the snowploughs scraping the roads outside the apartment building and hoped Klaus and I would be able to make our getaway soon.

67

EVA

After waking the next morning, I'd pulled on all the warm clothes I had in my bag and went to the bakery to pick up some fresh *Gipfeli* – croissants still warm from the oven. This was mainly to check on the weather, but also to give Klaus a little extra time to call his contact in Dubai. He'd told me he preferred not to make the call while I was hanging around listening to his every word. It wasn't the first time I suspected he still felt self-conscious about speaking English in front of me.

My thoughts turned inexplicably to my father, comparing him to Klaus. Back when I was spending so much time in the UK, Claudia had experienced the brunt of his vitriol when he was still living at home. Claudia was the one who suffered the most out of the two of us and resented my father in ways I had not. She must have seen things between him and my mother that I was never a party to. Were there things she hadn't told me? Secrets that might have been eating at her? They might have added to her state of mind over the years. It was all so convenient for us to assume her mental health had taken a long slow decline in the years following her accident. But I sometimes wondered whether my parents' split had anything to do with her depression.

When Papa moved out, the tension in our household suddenly dissipated. Klaus became the son Mama had secretly always wanted, and the brother I'd never had. He took over the position of the alpha male in our lives, with a generous and tolerant personality our father had never possessed.

Which was why we were all so shocked at Claudia's death. No matter how much one thinks a bunch of pills and a few swigs of alcohol might be the best way to go, it was never going to be pretty. Choking on one's own vomit was an option I could never have imagined, or would ever have had the courage to do. But Claudia simply couldn't see a life without skating.

It would have been a slap in the face for Klaus. Not only could she not live a life without skating, she chose to leave him behind as well. So he had to blame someone. And that someone was the person who'd taken away Claudia's professional chances on the ski slope several years before. The more his disappointment and anger was fuelled, the more I realised his sense of revenge was contagious. In the end, he had me fired up more than he ever would be. But months had now gone by since Claudia's suicide, and despite our plans, I felt that maybe, just maybe, his appetite for revenge was waning.

Outside it didn't look good. Blue-black clouds were gathering on the horizon to the east, where the sun would normally be rising. A chill breeze swirled a few random snowflakes around, and I could tell yet another heavy fall was on the way. I checked the weather app on my phone and saw that with Swiss precision, it would be snowing by 10:15 am. We wouldn't be able to drive the Bentley away today. This dampened my mood even further.

But I knew we couldn't back out now. We had a boot full of stolen goods. Putting them all back was not an option. We likely had time on our side, as it might be days, even weeks, before the burglaries were discovered, depending when the chalets would next be inhabited. All I had to do, was think of my sister, but I couldn't help hearing Klaus's voice: *This won't bring Claudia back.*

As I entered the bakery, the head baker was bringing a tray of *Gipfeli* and freshly baked *Zopf* – plaited bread – out of the kitchen to store in the baskets at the front of the shop. I bit my lip as he greeted me with a jovial *Gruezi!* I should have gone somewhere I was less likely to be recognised. My new hairstyle wasn't going to foil people I knew this close up. I hoped my mother wouldn't come in to this particular baker today and learn from him that he'd seen me. The assistant took my order and placed a few warm *Gipfeli* into a paper bag with her tongs. She folded the edges of the bag inside, leaving a gap for the warm air to escape and stop the buttery croissants going soggy. I paid and left hastily, making my way back to Klaus's place.

I walked into the apartment to see Klaus with a smug expression on his face.

'You're kidding me! It's a go?' I asked.

'He has a shipment leaving from Trieste to Dubai on the first Monday of every month. You're not going to believe it, but he told me there's often a car in it, a new one or an antique or special edition, either for himself or a client.'

'And the deal? He saw the photos you took yesterday in the garage? Did he make an offer?'

'He wasn't fazed at all by my request, but there was quite a bit of haggling. He has no idea of the state of the vehicle, even though I sent him detailed photos of the engine and the bodywork I took in the garage yesterday. It's a trust thing, but he's a trader. He knows where I live.' Klaus said this last comment with a hint of humour that had been missing for the past months. 'I've been trawling the Auto Scout website for a price comparison, and I realise it's half of what it might sell for here, but he offered a hundred grand.'

I thought about the little chalet Mama currently lived in, and wondered how much money we might need to change the kitchen that was over half a century old. And then I wondered if I even wanted to stay in St Moritz after all that had gone on over the past few years.

'Imagine how many months that will buy us on a tropical island,' I said, and Klaus chewed his lip. I don't think he'd even thought about his own future at this stage. 'So, what's the plan?'

'Payment will be into the bank account I set up in London. Half now and half on delivery once he sees the car.'

'Can we trust him?'

'I believe so. But Eva, even fifty grand is fifty grand more than we thought we might get at the beginning. We just need to get rid of the car without a trace.'

'What did you tell him about the ownership?'

'I said it belonged to someone in town who died, and the family asked my help in getting rid of it for them. That's pretty standard. So the name on the papers we send with it won't set off any alarm bells with him.'

'And the delivery?'

'There's a guy at the port authority in Trieste who deals with his company's admin, papers for export, port fees, loading, etc. By the time we get there, the funds should be in the account we set up in London and we can hand it over to the shipping company. He said there'd be room in the next container, but not the one after.'

'Monday,' I mused. 'That's only two days away. 'The only thing we need to worry about now, is the damned weather. We'll have to leave tonight.'

68

JAMES

The gutsy motor of the Range Rover roared to life as Sal pressed the start button, reminding me that the button on the Nespresso machine had never been pushed for my caffeine shot. I wondered whether Sal was over the limit too. I hadn't seen how much wine she'd drunk, but it was obviously less than me. It was too late to worry about that now. The garage door slid open to reveal my earlier labour of neat, wide rows of snow-clearing.

'Top marks for the shovelling task,' said Sal, braking tentatively at the bottom of the driveway onto the narrow lane. The car skidded a little and she pulled in a sharp breath. I didn't say anything, knowing I shouldn't be behind the wheel if we were stopped. I propped my phone on the dashboard, the signal for the tracker on the Bentley flashing a little red target on the map on my screen like something from a spy movie rather than a glorified Find-My-Phone app.

'Shall I drive past the police station to see if anyone is there first?' she asked.

As much as I was impatient to get to the Bentley, I conceded this was sensible.

'I guess it would make it easier to explain all this face to face. The app is showing that the car is situated somewhere in Zuoz.'

'Is that far from here?' asked Sal.

'No, it's just along the valley. It's almost a suburb of St Moritz. There's a famous boarding school there – the Lyceum Alpinum. My parents almost sent me there when I was a kid, but given the choice, I decided to stay in England with my friends. Going to school in the Alps was appealing, but the friendships I had at home were more important to me.'

She took her hand off the steering wheel to pat my thigh gently. Her physical display surprised me, after all we'd been through and I almost read it as a patronising gesture, but it must have been triggered by the word *friendships*. I was making a bit of a mess of this one.

Sal navigated the Range Rover down the winding road to the centre of town and on towards the lake, back to the police station where we'd been that afternoon. The building was in darkness, but she parked right in front and I leapt out. I peered at a notice on the door, then walked briskly back to the car.

'It's closed. There must be a police presence somewhere in the region, but the number they've put for emergencies is a number in Chur. That's miles away. It will take them ages to get here.'

'Isn't there a 999 number for emergencies in Switzerland?' Sal asked. 'How long would it take the police to drive from Chur to where we're heading?'

I rubbed my cheek. '117 is the number for the emergency police service, and I'm not sure about the distance... Look, we'll just try and work out exactly where the car is parked and then I'll send Vögel another message with the address. I'll drop him a pin and he and his merry men can investigate in the morning.'

'Sounds like a plan,' she said. 'Let's go.'

I climbed back into the car as Sal started the engine and we drove off into the night, the smoothness of the frozen lake to our right resembling the surface of a vast iced Christmas cake with a velvet covering of snow. Sal drove carefully, obviously not used to these conditions.

'It feels like we're heading downhill again,' she said. 'I thought you mentioned a mountain pass. Didn't we come up from the other direction when we first arrived?'

'St Moritz is in a high valley. There are several ways to get to the resort. This road will eventually take us down to a valley leading into Austria. We're following the River Inn, which ends up in the Danube.' I wanted to tell her she could put her foot down a bit, but didn't want to panic her.

'It feels like we're still heading into the Alps somehow, not coming out of them.'

'We're surrounded by them. This next town is Samedan. A lot of people I used to know when we were regular winter visitors lived there, probably still do. It's a lot more economical, cheaper rents. They commute to St Moritz to work. Ski teachers, barmen, waiters and chamber maids don't have the salaries enabling them to work *and* live in glitzy St Moritz. It's like that commuter town of Montadon that no one's ever heard of next to Monte Carlo.'

'Sounds like you're familiar with Monte Carlo too. Oh, for the life of the rich,' she said. She would now be fully aware how much money my family had amalgamated.

'Monte Carlo's an awful place. Especially during events like the Formula 1. Full of people showing off their money. It's crass. They want everyone to know they're rich.'

'What about the polo games on the frozen lake here? And the notorious Cresta Run? They're all for the mega rich too, right?' she asked.

I tipped my head in acknowledgement. Sal had now seen my big flat in Covent Garden, my family's chalet on the slopes above St Moritz, and now knew that my father had one of those wretched objects of ostentation – a Bentley. She didn't seem to bat an eyelid that we were now on the road trying to find out where it now was and by whom it had been taken. By somebody or somebodies who undoubtedly did not have nearly as much to live off as me. Sal would now be seeing that there was rich, and there was ostentatiously rich. Both came with some morally questionable values. She had likely grown up in the section of society where some people really resented that.

'There's something coming at us with bright lights!' she squealed suddenly, tapping the brakes and pointing up. 'My God, is that a UFO?'

'It's a private jet. The airport is just here. Probably from London. Some of *those* people.'

'James, you know you are one of those people, don't you?' she said with a smile in her voice. Then to herself: 'What a fool. A flipping UFO.'

I felt a stab of nostalgia, wishing we could go back to our innocent Scrabble-playing days. We'd often had conversations about the imbalance of the world's wealth, but that was before Sal knew that my family was probably in the top one percent of *those* people.

Sal drove on, and I resisted the urge to press my own foot on an imaginary accelerator on the passenger side's footwell. I silently urged Sal to feel my urgency without provoking a feeling of danger on the icy, snow-packed road. As we passed through the village of Madulain, I detected the slightest movement of the flashing red blip on my phone. I narrowed my eyes, concentrating on the blinking dot.

'It's on the move!' I said, pointing redundantly at my phone on the dashboard.

'Yeah,' said Sal, and the car slewed slightly on the slippery road as she momentarily hit the brakes.

I couldn't fathom her "yeah." She'd uttered it in almost a triumphant tone. Her glance slid to the screen on the phone, then to my face.

'I mean, at least we know the tracker is working,' she said. 'I'll try to speed up so we can intercept it.

And in true Bond style she accelerated, the conservatism of Miss Marple left far behind in St Moritz.

69

SALLY

James leaned towards his phone on the dash holder and spread two fingers on the screen to magnify the map area.

'It's coming down through the village to the main road,' he said. 'It looks like it was parked at the international school I told you about. That cluster of large buildings on the map is the school. I'll find Vögel's number.'

He unhooked his phone from the dash, pressed the phone icon, then 'recents,' and hit the call and speaker functions. It went to Vögel's voice-mail again. I imagined the policeman enjoying a Sunday evening fondue with his family.

'This is James Marsh again,' he said into the phone. 'My father's Bentley appears to be on the move. We're just outside Zuoz where I told you it had registered on the beacon location app. We're going to follow, and hope there's a patrol car or something in the area who can intercept. We have hands free in the car. I don't know which direction they'll be heading, but please, please call me.'

'Until that last part, you sounded like a 00 agent,' I said with a laugh, trying to lighten the mood.

'They haven't reached the village yet, but I assume they'll come down to the Kantonstrasse. They could still be planning to take the Bernina Pass, in which case, they'll come towards us, and we'll be heading in the wrong direction. Find a place to pull over, and we'll wait and see which road they take.'

After a mile or so, there was a wide area to the right that had been cleared by a snowplough. There was some kind of warehouse where there was snow-clearing equipment and large containers lined up against a wall.

'Salt,' said Jamie, answering my unasked question. 'And that building is where the *Gemeinde* keeps all their road-cleaning equipment. All their vehicles will have been busy here up until this afternoon. This'll be a good place to wait.'

I pulled over and the Range Rover came to a halt with a creaking squelch of tyres on the packed snow. James's gaze was fixed on the blinking spot on his phone.

'They're down to the village now. Oh! They're heading to S-chanf. I wouldn't have expected that.'

'Where?' I asked, trying to fathom the impossible sounding name. If Swiss German wasn't already a challenge, it seemed like this forgotten end of Switzerland had an even more complicated dialect.

'S-chanf. It's the next village along. They must be heading for Zernez on the minor roads. Less chance of being spotted so close to St Moritz. Come on.'

I started the engine again. I pulled out of the lay-by, the wheels spinning briefly before gripping the snow with the four-wheel drive, and accelerated into the night.

'We'll keep track of them on the main road. The roads converge once we cross the River Inn. I should have realised – they're already this far along the valley, so they must be heading towards Zernez where they have a few choices of routes to take. Hopefully Vögel has realised that too, if he's even seen my message.'

'Maybe he'll have a patrol car waiting?' I asked doubtfully.

'Well, yes, but he should have called me by now, damn it. I'm beginning to wonder whether he's taking this whole thing seriously.'

'Or purposely ignoring you. How corrupt are the Swiss police?'

Jamie looked at me as though I'd just declared that pigs could fly, then creased his brow and shook his head. I hoped he wasn't being too naïve. Chasing any number of criminals over an international mountain pass in the dead of night screamed madness born of naïvety to me. And here I was, taking him along for the ride.

'Anything is possible, but I wouldn't have thought... Maybe they're planning to take the Bentley into the South Tyrol over the Ofenpass. I must have been wrong about the Bernina. It makes sense now I think about it. Probably still no camera coverage at the border, certainly no physical presence at this hour. They've allowed a couple of days for the roads to be clear enough to take that big car over. And once in Italy they'll be further east, better roads towards the Balkans. Bosnia, maybe, Monte Negro, Albania.'

'Europe is an open playground for these people now,' I said. 'No border control surely makes it harder to catch thieves.'

'Switzerland isn't part of the European Union, but they're not as strict as they used to be about border crossings. Even the main ones just let the traffic flow through freely during busy holiday periods. They're only quick to close things down if it involves a drug heist, a money laundering operation, or there's a human trafficking alert. Stolen cars are less interesting, not worth engaging extra personnel.'

In my periphery he swiped open the map app on his phone to check the various routes he'd mentioned. The little blue dot of our presence moved steadily along the road we were on. I compared the map on our satnav to the one on Jamie's phone, and saw we were parallel to the Bentley on the minor road somewhere beside us out there in the dark.

'Ironically, Mum was stopped by the police once driving her BMW over the Brenner Pass from Austria to Italy. As the car had Swiss plates, the police simply wanted to check the papers, to make sure she was the rightful owner. But the Brenner has a strong police presence. These other passes in winter don't. Maybe the Austrians care more than the Italians about stopping car theft.'

We both watched as the blinking red target continued along the road parallel to ours, and I strained to see if any car headlights were visible in the snowy landscape rushing past us to the left. Snow laden trees and icy rock verges appeared between the slices of blue-white walls created by the road-clearing equipment.

The red dot slowed as it approached the next village. For a moment it hesitated, and I wondered whether the passenger was arguing about the route they should take. Then the car turned onto the road we were currently on some way ahead of us and accelerated. Jamie seemed determined for me to keep up with the Bentley so I was happy to comply.

'I assume you'll wait to see which direction they take before alerting the police,' I said, the crack in my voice belying my nervousness about the anticipation of driving increasingly faster on the snowy road. 'When will you know their destination?'

'There's a junction in Zernez, but feasibly only one of the roads leads safely into Italy. Once I know for sure which direction they're heading in, I'll call Vögel again. From what I understood, he could have a colleague waiting on the Italian side of any of the passes to arrest these guys.'

I swallowed, knowing we were all going to converge at some point. My eyes strained in the beam of the headlights against the whiteness of the snowy road, made even more ghostly with the darkness of night all around us.

'We need to stop those bastards getting away with Dad's car,' said Jamie.

There it was again. The vehemence that maybe his books had taken a back seat in the importance of this recovery operation. But I was worried, despite what I already knew about what was ahead of us. It was so easy to ruin antique rare editions, especially once they'd been removed from the perfect environment of the Tardis. The thought that Jamie would place the feelings of his father over any of his own material objects made me feel slightly better about the eventual outcome of this chase.

'If you're not feeling up to it, please let me drive,' he said. 'My head is clear, honestly.'

Although it made my heartbeat quicken with the fear that we might slide off the icy road at any moment, I accelerated, to prove to Jamie that I could do this.

'I'm fine,' I said, glancing quickly at his phone.

I saw we were now matching the red blip of the Bentley for speed on the road.

'I can't let these bastards get away with it,' he muttered.

That one of these bastards might be the girlfriend *he* rescued all those months ago didn't lessen his intensity. I applauded him inwardly for finally becoming angry about the extent of her deception. But I urged him silently to stay calm, knowing that although this car chase was about to come to a climax, it would be a long while before the police made it to the pass. My knuckles grew white as I gripped the steering wheel, and I sent a silent apology to Jamie for what was about to happen.

70

JAMES

Our vision was limited to the double funnel of bright blue-white LED headlights ahead of us on the road. As we raced along, tiny whorls of snow floated on the air in front of us. For a moment it appeared to be snowing upwards. I briefly admired Sal's driving ability in conditions she must be facing for the first time.

'We're catching up; the powder snow they're kicking up is light enough to hang in the air for quite a while,' I said, glancing from the road ahead to my phone. 'We can't see their tail lights yet, but they must know there's a car behind them now. Our presence is like a beacon over this landscape. Don't get too close. I don't want them to feel threatened, and certainly don't want them to *think* that they're being followed. It's unusual, but not unheard of, for tourists to be travelling at this time of night.'

'You'd think they might suspect their vehicle has a tracker on it. Don't all expensive cars have that?'

'Normally, yes, but the Bentley is an older model, before they built such things into modern car computers. Putting a tracker on the chassis was the idea of a friend of dad's who did the same on his old Morgan. These classic old cars are easy to steal.'

Sal snorted. I turned to her and raised my eyebrows.

'I'm just thinking of my old Peugeot 305 I left behind in Chelmsford before moving up to London. My little brother used to drive it for short journeys back and forth from college. He can't trust it now, and anyway he's not supposed to drive, with his illness and everything. I once left the car unlocked for weeks on mum and dad's driveway hoping it would be stolen and we could get something back for the insurance.'

'I feel kind of sorry for your Peugeot. If it's done you well, it should be treated with respect,' I said with a little smile. As much as I hardly ever drove, I did have respect for all old cars. 'It wouldn't fare well here though. I'm sorry to hear about your brother. His latest treatment didn't go well?'

'I thought I told you some time ago,' she said. 'His is such a rare form of cancer, the only thing left is some immunotherapy treatment in the US. We've been trying to raise funds to send him to a special clinic in Stanford.'

I felt another stab of guilt for not having kept in touch with her over the past weeks.

'I'm sure I would have remembered if you'd told me. You know, I could help if you need funding.'

I watched Sal bite her lip, and her fingers tightened on the steering wheel as she negotiated another steep corner. I imagined her little Peugeot pirouetting daintily on this icy road before crunching into one of the ice walls at our side. She glanced briefly at me, then back to the road to concentrate on her driving.

I looked up through my window. Myriad stars pocked the sky. It was a moonless night. The headlights reflected off the white brilliance of a smoothly scraped road with alarming patches of black ice showing through. I was in two minds about pointing this out to Sal. Despite the danger, her angst would only slow down our pursuit. The occasional movement of air as we passed through the half tunnels of snow walls formed by the snow ploughs at either side of the road kicked up white clouds in our wake. It was though we were sandwiched between two spinning candy floss wheels.

As we came into the village of Zernez, Sal hardly slowed, exceeding the speed limit to keep up with the Bentley. I hoped there was nobody about on the streets at this time of night, someone wanting to traverse the road on an unseen crossing in the centre of town. I had no idea how good the brakes would be in these conditions.

As the red blip on my phone took a right turn, I scrolled to find Vögel's number again. The call still went to voicemail.

'They're heading through the National Park to the Ofenpass,' I said, leaning towards the phone to bring my mouth closer, as though this might make it more likely Vögel would pick up with the urgency of it. 'If they make it, your *colleagues* should meet them as they hit the Val Mustair.' I said the word "colleagues" as though it was a promise the policeman wouldn't likely keep.

I ended the call. After navigating the narrow road through the village, I pointed to the approaching right-hand turn, and Sal pulled on the Range Rover's steering wheel, following the signs to the Ofenpass. The brightness of the headlights swung onto the smaller road heading south. Like the beam from a lighthouse, it swept over the sign for the Wildenburg Castle, and its bare stone walled tower loomed ahead. As we drove past the ancient building and out of the village, I pressed 117 on the keypad of my phone. It was finally time to call in the Swiss emergency services.

Sal frowned as she understood none of what I was telling the lady at emergency services in German. I explained the situation, giving my father's name, our address in St Moritz and the model of the Bentley. I urged them to coordinate with the police bureau in St Moritz. It was now the middle of the night, there wasn't much more I could do. But they must at least have had a skeleton staff on duty, either in St Moritz itself, or one of the surrounding towns or villages.

The road began to rise ahead, winding up to the mountain pass some distance above us. Sal deftly negotiated a particularly tight hairpin bend, and I grabbed the dashboard in front of me for fear that we would roll off into a void that we couldn't see. I made out the two red rear lights of the Bentley in the distance. At least that would give Sal something to concentrate on other than the snow, the ice, and the narrow, winding road rising to the pass.

'Step on the gas,' I said. Things could get rocky.'

'Yup,' she said confidently, like a racing driver accepting instructions from her director, and I felt the car accelerate.

71

EVA

I can't be sure, but it's possible we're being followed,' I said.

'Come on. Are you sure you're not being paranoid? There are bound to be people out here like us who've waited for the roads to be clear on the pass.'

'No, but I think the car behind us was on the main road as we were driving on through S-Chanf way back. I could see headlights between the trees. When you slowed right down in the village because of the reduced winter service, it slowed on the main road too.'

'Yeah. Less salt grit. Less grip.'

'The point is, they slowed down as well.'

'It's probably coincidence, Eva. I have to say, this car isn't easy to drive.'

'Comfortable though. I could see us doing a Grand Tour through southern Europe in June, acting like royalty,' I said, but Klaus ignored my comment. I was probably the last person he wanted to spend his summer holidays with by now. After a few moments I turned in my seat.

'I'm pretty sure they're the same lights behind us,' I said. 'Bright LEDs. A modern car. Aren't you curious as to why were they driving so slowly on the main road while we were navigating the minor lane? And can't you go any faster? I mean, isn't this thing supposed to have a mega powerful engine?'

'It does, but it doesn't have *mega-safe* winter gears and tyres. There are some sharp bends coming up. I can pick it up a little, but don't want to risk our safety later on the downhill section over the pass.'

'There's nothing we can do at this point. Maybe you can stop somewhere up towards the pass on one of the turns into a forest road and kill the lights. Let them go past us.'

'Did you bring your girl guide's shovel with you? I already checked back in the garage and this thing didn't have chains. The worst thing we could possibly do now is get stuck in the snow.'

'Let's not argue, Klaus. Just keep driving. We'll be over the pass in an hour, if my memory serves me right, and then it should be an easy drive all the way to Trieste.'

Klaus took a deep breath. I had the feeling he had begun to change his mind about this whole thing some time back. Especially after I reminded him a man died at our expense, and the least we could do was finish this thing we had started. That was probably a mistake.

I was keeping the burning of the Somerset Maugham book until we'd safely made our getaway. I had the feeling that this was the one thing that was keeping Klaus going, as it had been the primary act on our thirst for revenge. Once I saw inside those chalets, though, it was me who was keen to plan the burglaries.

Klaus told me there was a moment at Christmas when he'd had the perfect opportunity for a more sinister act of revenge, but that in the end he simply didn't have the heart to do away with James Marsh that day on the mountain. He'd always liked the guy, especially back when the Marsh family had welcomed him into their home, up until the point that their son had ruined Claudia's career. But one person had already died at our hands, even if it wasn't entirely our fault. With our extra booty in the back of the car, I couldn't imagine what was going through his mind at this point. But something was telling me it might have been: *Has this revenge gone too far?*

'When this is over, we won't have to worry about our finances for a very long time,' I said. 'I know you've said it won't bring Claudia back, but it will help us both to live comfortably in whatever capacity we choose. We can go our separate ways. I know it must feel weird for you. I must remind you of her all the time.'

Klaus bit his lip, and in the ghostly blue light from the dashboard, I thought I saw the glint of a tear in his eye.

It won't bring Claudia back.

72

EVA

My hearing came back first. Or maybe my sight had come back too, but it was too dark to see anything. I heard rapid breathing that I soon realised was not my own, so Klaus must be alive. The only other sound was the regular ticking of the Bentley's stalled engine as it cooled in the sub-zero night.

I reached up and touched a point of throbbing pain on my forehead. It must have hit the dashboard. The point of impact had swollen into an egg-sized lump. But it was dry, no blood. The car was too old to have air bags, which I'd never considered, as it was in such good condition and was one of those timeless designs. This meant it could have been considered an antique. I wondered whether Klaus's man in Dubai knew this might be a collector's item. Klaus would surely have done his research. Would that have made a difference to the value?

And then I remembered that we were actually *in* the car, and that whatever had just happened, whether we'd crashed into a snow drift, or an avalanche had hit us, it was unlikely the car would now be worth anything at all.

I recalled turning in my seat to check whether the car behind us had followed us into the parking area. I'd slipped the seat belt off my shoulder to be able to do so, which was precisely when I'd been thrown forward with the sudden impact of the car against... something. I hoped it was only soft snow.

Klaus's seatbelt unclicked and I felt him lean towards me, touch my shoulder.

'*Scheisse*, Eva, I didn't mean— Are you okay?'

'I think so,' I croaked.

'*Scheisse*,' said Klaus again, but not in a way that expressed pain, so I assumed he was uninjured.

I tried to open the door, but snow had packed in around the car. The lower half of the belt was tight across my lap in the passenger seat. I touched my hair. It was still falling around my face, so I knew we hadn't flipped. I was the right way up. I looked around me although I could make out very little in the dark. I put out my hands, waved them through the space in front of me, touched my legs. The space inside the car felt the same as before; my instincts told me it hadn't been crushed on impact. Had we fallen off the edge of a cliff?

I thought of the Murano glass objects in the boot, and that although we'd packed them well, it was unlikely that any of them had survived.

Then I heard voices. English voices. God, was that James? *James!* What was *he* doing here?

I watched helplessly as an area began clearing on the window next to Klaus's head. A pair of stationary car headlights illuminated the interior of the Bentley through the gradually increasing space, as the heavily-gloved fingers of a hand wiped more snow away from the door. Weirdly, Klaus still had his hands on the steering wheel, as if he was going to drive out of our predicament at any moment.

'Start the engine again! Try to reverse!' I yelled at him.

He remained catatonic, staring ahead at the snow-covered windscreen.

'Are you all right in there?' It was a woman's voice.

'Yes,' said Klaus, his voice flat, seemingly empty of emotion.

Conversely, a whole heat of emotions was currently raging through me. Anger that Klaus hadn't been more careful when driving into the uncleared parking area, wretchedness that we had been caught, confusion that James had somehow been following us, and despair that we might have become a little too greedy in our plans for revenge.

Klaus's little four-wheel-drive Subaru would have easily made the journey over any of the passes surrounding the St Moritz valley without a problem, and we wouldn't have attracted any attention at all. We wouldn't have been able to take the big stuff, but the books and smaller objects could all have been sold at their various markets and fairs and our bank account in the UK would be brimming with holiday funds. I put my head into my hands with a quiet *ouch* as my fingers met the lump on my forehead.

As the snow fell away from the windows on Klaus's side of the car, I realised it was the woman who'd spoken who was clearing the snow. I squinted at her; she was wearing a bobble hat, with a scarf wrapped several times round her throat. It was that meddling friend of his, Sally Crime. Blast her. I'd tried my best to keep her and James from communicating with each other, but she must have found a way. Behind her, James was on his mobile phone.

I reached across to seek out the central locking button on the console but there wasn't any. I wasn't sure what locking us inside the car would have achieved, other than delaying the moment that I would have to talk to James. I turned to press the lock beside me on the door, but as I fumbled to reach it, Sally Crime ripped the driver's door open and a rush of freezing air entered the car.

'What the hell?' I shouted, panicked. 'How did you...?'

'I knew you were trouble from the beginning,' said Sally, eyes flashing at me with anger.

Behind her, James slipped his mobile phone into his pocket and waded through the deep snow towards us.

'Are you tracking me or something?' I shouted, as though *they* were somehow the bad guys in all of this.

James pressed his lips together and patted the roof of the Bentley twice, as though praising a horse. Of course! The car must have had some kind of tracing system. He didn't need to say anything. I felt stupid then, after all the luck we'd had finding a buyer so soon. I should have known something would go pear-shaped when everything was running so smoothly.

James looked at me with such disappointment, I immediately felt abashed. There wasn't even any regret in that look. He'd been duped in love, and I now didn't blame him one little bit. Sally Crime stood right next to him, perhaps worried that he might find enough anger in himself to take a swipe at these two evil passengers now sitting in the front of his father's beloved car.

'The police are on their way,' James said. 'Do either of you need an ambulance?'

'No. Nothing seriously damaged,' said Klaus in that deflated voice of his. Where had his gumption gone?

'You *knew* each other!' James said with vehemence. 'Even when we met that day on the ski slopes. Why did you pretend? Why have you joined forces to target me and my family?'

'Don't you know?' I said. 'Don't you know what you did to my—our Claudia?'

'*Our* Claudia?' asked James, confused.

'Klaus was engaged to my sister,' I said.

James put his hand to his forehead and in a gesture that had become so familiar to me, raked his fingers through his hair.

'Oh it all makes sense now, I've just realised. You were Nick. Niklaus. They wrote your surname wrong in the computer at the rental agency. Not Rich, but Reich.' He pronounced the soft *hh* of Reich correctly, but it sounded like the hiss of an angry cat.

'Here's your Despicable Nick,' said Sally Crime, and I frowned as I actually saw Klaus smile.

So, she'd been James's little detective lady since I disappeared after Christmas. That didn't take him long. I felt a flash of anger, until I remembered all the deceiving I'd done before that.

'Look, I didn't do *anything* to Claudia,' James said, exasperated. 'Are you talking about the ski accident a decade ago? I tried to *help* her, for God's sake!'

'You broke her, and you broke her career chances of continuing her success as a highly talented figure skater,' I said, my voice cracking a little. 'You broke her so far, she took her life.'

Klaus reached over, put his hand on my arm as though to comfort me, or at least stop me from speaking. It occurred to me he was no longer angry, just very sad. I needed him to find that anger again. We had to get away from these people.

'You're wrong about me,' said James. 'I know there were many others who were also misinformed. I've heard the rumours over the years. But this? Do you think I'd really still come back here every year if I'd had anything to do with destroying your sister's career? You can thank Sal, here, by the way for helping me understand your connection.' James looked directly at me with that penetrating stare of his, and I suddenly felt a hot wave of shame. I *had* deceived him. Made him believe I was in love with him. What was he saying. That Claudia's accident was nothing to do with him?

'James was not the one who collided with your sister that day on the ski slopes, Emma-Eva, or whatever you want to call yourself,' said Sally, looking directly at me.

I glanced at the girl who was now in cahoots with James, knowing my face must have looked ugly, that the grain of jealousy I now felt was likely affecting my expression.

'I arrived on the scene shortly after the accident,' said James. 'I rode in the ambulance with Claudia to the hospital and during the journey she regained consciousness. She had no idea exactly *who* had skied recklessly into her that day. But it wasn't me. It was Lawrence. I'm not sure how it happened, but they'd collided on the slope. I don't know whose fault it was. Lawrence was also injured, but only mildly. He needed a plaster for a cut on his chin, so went to the cable car station where they had a first-aid kit, while I accompanied Claudia with the ski patrol down to the ambulance and then to the hospital. You've had it wrong all this time. I didn't deserve this.' James swept his hand in front of the car. 'And my dad certainly didn't deserve this.'

I remembered the name Lawrence. James had wanted to introduce me to him at the Christmas Eve cocktail party. I swallowed. It's possible if we'd met, something might have triggered his memory. It's possible I'd met the guy before, but wouldn't have paid any attention because we were concentrating on getting back at James. A feeling of cold dread swept in with the frozen night air, that we'd been targeting the wrong person all this time.

73

JAMES

'Where are my books?' I asked. 'What have you done with my books?' Although at this point, that was actually the last thing I wanted to know. I wanted to ask: *Why did you make me fall in love with you?*

Klaus didn't say anything, but I saw his eyes flick to the rear-view mirror.

'I'm going to check the boot,' I shouted to Sal. 'Keep an eye on these bandits.'

I closed the driver's door with enough force to alter the pressure in their ears without damaging the Bentley. I wanted to cause them discomfort in any way I could at this point. I moved towards the rear of the car through the deep snow. As I worked my way back, I forged a path, grabbing armfuls of the snow and intentionally piling it behind me to block the driver's door.

'Quick, get out, Klaus!' came the muffled shout from Emma-Eva within the car. 'Get out! We have to make a run for it. Come on!'

Klaus tried to open his door, but it wedged against the snow that I'd piled behind me against the side of the car. They were trapped.

I wanted to transfer everything as soon as possible from the boot of the Bentley to the Range Rover, but knew I should really wait for the cops. We'd parked up on the bend leading into the car park, the furthest point where the plough had cleared the road, and it was imperative that the books didn't drop in the snow. There were a couple of framed canvasses in the boot, and I let them fall back onto the other things underneath. They'd all be safer in the boot for now. I returned to the driver's window with a wheel jack raised in my hand. Eva flinched as I knocked on the window with my other hand. Klaus wound it down a few centimetres.

'You're not going anywhere until the police get here,' I said. 'But I still have a thousand questions, and I may not get a chance once you're arrested.'

Klaus sighed and chewed on his lip. I couldn't read his expression. I thought he might be holding back tears. A muscle ticked in his jaw. I wanted to make him believe it wasn't me. I wanted him to acknowledge that I wasn't responsible for Claudia's death, but it was hard to know how to deliver and receive any messages when both Claudia's lover and her sister were sitting in front of me.

'The first burning question I have is, was it your intention to *kill* me on the slope on Christmas Eve, Klaus?'

Klaus cleared his throat. 'At that stage I was still angry enough to consider it. When I realised you would likely survive the avalanche, I had to dig you out otherwise you would have become suspicious. It would have made things easier for us. I guess you can consider yourself lucky to have survived.'

I laughed cynically. Klaus looked directly at Sal, and I turned to face her. I couldn't be sure, but I thought I saw the twitch of a smile on her face. She must have been relieved for me.

'And why Edelweiss. Why the chalet next door to ours?'

'A bonus,' said Eva. 'I'd seen those watches when Petra and I smoked a joint together.'

I crouched slightly so I could make eye contact with her in the passenger seat. 'Your slyness knows no bounds. They are also innocent in all this. They had nothing to do with what happened all those years ago.'

'It doesn't really matter, James. I know you were all members of that ski gang. The rich young English who came every year to take over the village.'

'Petra and her parents are Swiss. I'm sure they'll make sure you hang for this, even if *we* weren't going to press charges. I'm so shocked at how you put all this together. Why did you come back with me to England after Christmas? Why didn't you just disappear then, with your stolen goods?'

'Insurance,' said Eva. 'Which was Klaus's idea. It hadn't even occurred to me until then that we might be able to benefit twofold. Selling the books, and somehow stealing your insurance pay out as well. It set my mind a whirring about how we could funnel those additional funds into our account.'

'Bloody hell. You thought of everything,' I said.

'In the end, I shouldn't have bothered. When the DS questioned you about the theft, he mentioned how collectors themselves are usually the first to be investigated for insurance fraud. And then I realised that the insurance claim was going to take too much time. You talked about the process possibly taking years to complete.'

Hearing her say this, I realised their initial plan may have been solid, but the additional greed that drove them to scheme an increase in takings was too complicated. These guys weren't professional thieves. They were acting on pure emotion.

'I'm going to repeat this: Although I was the one who took Claudia to the hospital that day, it wasn't me who caused the accident!'

Klaus looked down into his lap and Eva gave him a long stare.

'Knowing I shouldn't have been the focus of your revenge isn't the worst of it. Emma, you made me believe we were perfect for each other. That deception makes me feel quite sick. You were better than any Hollywood actress. You had me fooled. Now I also feel like the wrongly accused in some murder case.'

Emma-Eva stared at me, her beautiful mouth hanging open. But I also saw something in her look, in her shining eyes. Regret maybe?

'Oh, God! I wished I'd known,' she finally said. 'I would have marched right over to that Lawrence person at the Christmas Eve party and punched his lights out.'

'But the deception... What we did—' I sucked in my bottom lip, afraid my emotions might get the better of me. To stop that train of thought I changed the subject. 'Where were you going to sell the books? They would have made a fortune at auction. But surely you couldn't do that if it was known they were stolen?'

There was a look, then, that passed between Sal and Klaus. It stopped me in my tracks. A tiny connection. A stone suddenly formed in the pit of my stomach.

'Klaus was planning to use your credentials,' said Eva. 'I found your ILAB identity card in your office. Klaus would only have to dye his hair to vaguely look like you in the photo on the card.'

'And you wanted to kill me for all this?

'No... I couldn't kill you, James, after all your family did for me,' said Klaus. 'But if you had died in the avalanche, Eva wouldn't have gone back with you to England and we would have gone straight to the book fair in Venice.'

'You're both heartless. This is unbelievable.'

'Despicable,' said Sally.

She actually huffed a half-laugh, and exchanged a look with Klaus I couldn't fathom. Then she tipped her head to the side, and something passed between them which made that stone in my stomach flip over.

74

EVA

My gaze was pulled to James as he shouted again, with an anger I didn't think was possible. 'And talking of murder, did you kill that poor homeless man? Did you kill Willie?'

I couldn't speak and instead turned to try and access the back seat, thinking I could escape through one of the rear doors. But I was restrained by the seatbelt at my hips, the thing finally doing its job at the wrong moment. With my heart racing, I stabbed the release button several times with my thumb until it sprang open, and I crawled through the gap.

As I used my elbows to push myself through, I turned to see Sally Crime standing beside Klaus's window. I paused. Klaus's window was slowly opening. His shoulders and head moved rhythmically as he calmly wound the handle. No electric mechanism on this car. The wind blew freezing air into the muggy interior.

'What are you doing?' I asked.

I stared. Sally was holding out her gloved hand. Klaus raised himself out of his seat, levered himself against the door frame and his head and torso disappeared through the window. I expected to see Sally push him back inside, yell at him to stay put. Keeping us in the car until the police arrived would have been the easiest option for them. But to my surprise, she helped Klaus out through the tight space, making sure he didn't fall head first into the snow.

'What the—?'

I tried to turn around, but everything was stuck, my boot wedged underneath the back of the passenger seat in the rear footwell. My unzipped ski jacket had caught on one of the armrests.

'Hey,' shouted James, his voice muffled from behind the Bentley where he'd been looking in the boot. He must have been taking an inventory of the items in there. 'Klaus, get back in the car! Sal! What the hell?'

I watched helplessly from inside the car. Sally pushed James in his chest with her hands as he came towards them. James lost his balance and fell backwards into the snow. Sally and Klaus ran up the slope, taking giant exaggerated steps into the footprints she and James had left on the way down to us where the Bentley had come to a standstill.

What were they playing at? Running away? *Together*?

James scrambled up, but it took him precious seconds in the deep snow. He looked at me in the back of the Bentley, then looked towards Sally and Klaus who'd disappeared round the corner of the Buffalora Guesthouse above us. James ran up towards the mountain restaurant.

A set of headlights illuminated the bank of snow on the opposite side of the road as an engine started. A small car pulled out and accelerated away down the road, back towards Zernez, or perhaps Livigno, or perhaps – who knows where they were going? It was taking a while for this to compute.

Their escape car must have been parked on the other side of the Buffalora building. In the weak light cast from a quarter moon now peeking out between the clouds, I recognised Klaus's Subaru, the draining properties of a winter night rendering the red paintwork purple. He must have driven it up there earlier that day. Part of a sneaky plan I knew nothing about. What the hell was his connection with Sally Crime? I'd never trusted that witch. She was certainly living up to her name now.

James yelled something incomprehensible and ran towards the Range Rover. I could tell he was torn. Should he chase Sally and Klaus or stay with his father's car and the stolen objects? Both of us had been foiled. Sally had made that decision for him, as James stopped suddenly, patted his pockets, then put both hands to his head. She must have been driving, as he didn't appear to have the key. She would have made sure it wasn't easy to find, perhaps took it with her, or threw it in the snow, giving them time to get away.

75

SALLY

I had been desperately in love with James for years, but the moment he snubbed me for a homeless girl on the street, I felt a stab of pain bitter enough to make me want to take my revenge too. I was too deeply in love with him to choose to carry on a friendship where I was constantly denying my feelings. It wasn't healthy. He'd forsaken the pastimes we used to enjoy anyway – our love of books and playing word games, for someone he appeared to have very little in common with.

When I stepped into Klaus's apartment that afternoon in St Moritz, he listened to my explanation about the misunderstanding surrounding Claudia's accident. I had no expectations about our meeting. I even thought at the beginning when I knocked on his door, that I might be in mortal danger. But he was kind, and repentant. He'd had such a conflict for all those years, hating James for what he thought he'd done to Claudia, and yet respecting him for including Klaus in their gang all those years ago.

'I was going along with the plan because I wanted to help Eva get revenge for her sister,' he'd said. 'But then her plot escalated to not only burning James's favourite book, but also stealing the others, and then more things from the chalets of those rich people. She became fixated on the financial gain and was becoming more and more greedy. In the end my heart wasn't in it, but I was finding it harder and harder to pull out.'

I told him about my little brother Rory, about how he needed to get that special immunotherapy treatment in the US. I relayed what James had told me about the recovery of his father's precious Bentley, that it was more important than the books.

'You're in too deep now, though,' I explained to Klaus. 'The police will know it's you and Eva who stole those things from those chalets once James has worked it out, and he *will* work it out. But I can help you shift the books. I have contacts who won't question their origin. Look, leave the other stuff, and we'll take the books. It means you won't have done anything more than aiding a burglary in the eyes of the Swiss law.'

'I've no intention of staying in St Moritz anyway. I only came back to help Eva with her plan. There are too many tragic memories for me here. I need to find somewhere new to live. A new horizon.'

He had very little time to embellish the whole story of the heist, and we had even less time to formulate a plan to rescue the books, as I needed to get back to the police station to meet James. But after he'd listened to my story, and after I'd heard that his heart was no longer in it for the bigger booty that Eva had become so obsessed with, everything fell together.

Klaus would drive to the Ofenpass with Eva in the Bentley, then drive into the snow-filled parking area below the Buffalora Guesthouse. He would leave Eva there and drive his own car back down to St Moritz to pick me up. I had a contact in Bucharest I knew would be discreet in shifting the books, and in order to get the money onto the account in the UK for Rory, that needed to happen as quickly as possible.

When we found out the Bentley had a tracking device on it, I didn't think it made much difference. The police were being lethargic about following the car, so I didn't text Klaus to change the plans. But then James insisted on chasing the Bentley, even though I'd plied him with wine. The idea was to prevent him getting into the Range Rover and let the police do their job, by which time Klaus would have driven his own car away from the pass and the police would find Eva on her own with the Bentley and the stolen goods from St Moritz. But with James insisting on the chase, I figured if something went wrong at the pass, it would be good for me to be there too. So I offered to drive.

As we drove off in the little Subaru, the books secured carefully in their case in the boot, Klaus said it looked like the Bentley had suffered minimal damage, even though they'd hit the snow drift quite hard. He seemed to think that if there was any repair work to be carried out at all, a Swiss carrosserie expert would have no problem smoothing out the dents in the bodywork.

Frank Marsh would have his precious car back.

Eva would most likely serve some time in prison.

Rory would get his life-saving cancer treatment.

Klaus would have a little pocket money to start a new life wherever he wished.

And James would lick his wounds, carry on being a mini-philanthropist, and perhaps have learned a well overdue lesson about his naïveté.

76

JAMES

I opened the door and sat in the driver's seat, still slightly warm from Klaus's presence. The rear of the Bentley was wedged in the snow and any attempt to open the back doors would likely cause some damage to the bodywork, if it hadn't already suffered from the impact.

Eva was still struggling to find a comfortable position in the back of the car and I momentarily felt sorry for her. I was tempted to wait for the police in the comfort of the Range Rover with its heated seats and modern luxury. But then I remembered I didn't have the key. Eva-Emma had nowhere to run to, on the top of this snowed-in mountain pass.

'For God's sake, keep your filthy boots off my father's upholstery,' I said, as though to a recalcitrant child. There was no love left in my voice.

Eva looked at me warily, then re-arranged her feet in their sheep-skin-lined Sorels into the footwell at the back.

'I just don't want you hurting my dad's car more than you already have,' I said, looking out into the night through the windscreen. 'It was a stupid move from Klaus, to drive into an uncleared car park.'

'Well, it was obviously planned on his part. Now we've both been left in the lurch. I honestly had no idea, and frankly didn't think he had the balls to do something like this.'

I looked at her, anger and sadness scything through me in equal measure. She looked back at me with a touch of defiance still on her face, but guilt was starting to show in her eyes.

'I guess if you'd known from the beginning that I had nothing to do with Claudia's accident, we might never have met,' I said.

'I'm not sure it would have been so easy to snag Lawrence, given he has a wife and family now.' Finally, a remorseful tone in her voice. 'What I'd like to know, is when the hell did Klaus and your friend Sally Crime come up with this new plan? She's certainly living up to her name now.'

'I don't know. She's supposed to be a dab-hand at solving crimes, not committing them. I can only think they somehow hooked up when I was at the police station back in St Moritz,' I paused. 'She saw you together, you know. Outside my place in Seven Dials.'

'God, she's been a right love-sick nosy parker.'

'*Love sick*? She was looking after my interests at that point, Ev... So what do I call you? Have you ever used the name Emma?'

'Never. I just thought it sounded more English. Less chance of suspicion. I knew if I used Eva, I'd probably forget to use that awful English pronunciation Ee-va if I had to introduce myself to anyone.'

'You must have realised there was a risk I'd see your passport at some stage.'

'I was convinced you wouldn't. I knew you wouldn't go through my stuff, and anyway I had it hidden. There would have been no clues in anything you retrieved from the flat in Wandsworth. We'd been studying you for weeks. You were so trustworthy, so bloody *honest*. My mistake was forgetting to empty the bin in my room before I left that day. You might not have been so lucky in your detection.'

'So you were studying me for weeks!'

'We found out where you worked from the staff roster at Waterstones. It's online. Senior Bookseller. Then Klaus followed you home so we knew where you lived. The seduction would take a little longer, but we knew your habits, likes, dislikes. I just needed to become involved with you to find out what you were passionate about. What you couldn't bear to lose. It turned out to be those old books. It was a risk to come back with you to St Moritz for Christmas, so I was determined to make that trip worthwhile too.

'Was it Klaus with his camera that day I took your things from the flat?' I asked.

'We needed a reverse plan in case anything went wrong. By that time I had access to your condo, and even if you were only arrested temporarily for "stealing" from the Wandsworth flat, it would give us a chance to access anything of value in your place.'

'You had it all planned out. And Klaus had been carrying this anger for so many years. We'd been good to him when we hung out as kids. He never told me about his girlfriend – your sister. I guess that's because they met in the years when I didn't come here so much in the ski season.'

'They were the talk of the town, the dream couple. Although Klaus taught skiing in winter, in the summer he worked at the tourist office and was sometimes assigned shifts at the Ludains synthetic skating rink. One day Claudia didn't have her technician on hand to sharpen her skates, so she asked Klaus, and that's how it started. Claudia's film-star good looks, Klaus's rugged handsomeness. People began calling them Clausia – or was that Klausia with a K? We always joked about that.' Eva swallowed, and I figured sorrow must still be finding its way into her memories. 'When she qualified for the worlds, and it had been pretty certain she would before the accident, Klaus was going to become her manager so they could stay together on the competition circuit. It meant Klaus could be with Claudia when she needed him most. It would have cemented their relationship more than a marriage could.'

'I'm truly sorry,' I said. 'I initially thought you and Klaus might be an item, and had no clue as to why you would target me and my family.'

She lowered her head. 'For what it's worth, James, I really like you. I think that was obvious from our relationship. I was never meant to sleep with you at the beginning. It happened because I wanted to get closer to your family. But in the end, it was fun sleeping with you. Now I know the truth, I wish... I wish things had been different.'

I laughed bitterly.

'I bet you do! I can't get over the fact that we were so... intimate, and all the time you had this convoluted agenda going on in the background. If it was money you wanted, I'd have given you anything.'

Eva bit her lip.

'Bit of a sting in the end, though, *gal*?' Eva used the Swiss-German phrase meaning *hey* and I marvelled at how her English accent and vocabulary were flawless. It was easy to forget she was born and bred in Switzerland. 'I'm guessing you didn't find the case of books in the boot.'

'I don't understand why Sal would do this to me,' I said. 'If she needed money for something, I thought she knew she could always ask.' I thought of her little brother, his rare form of cancer. Why had she never been more vocal about it before?

'Oh come on, James. Don't you know the old tale about a woman scorned?'

'What do you mean? Apart from a few weeks where I missed her messages – no thanks to you, mind – and omitted to call her...'

'You didn't ever see it?'

'See what?'

'That she was so desperately in love with you.'

'What? No, I... Oh.' I paused. 'But, *scorned*? I never did anything to hurt her.'

'Perhaps she thought you did, just by being with me.'

'Oh, Sal,' I said quietly to myself. 'What will you do with those books?'

'Probably sell them at some private auction,' said Eva, butting in on my thoughts.

'If she needed money, all she had to do was ask,' I said.

'Given she couldn't even declare her undying love for you, I think she might have been too proud to do that.'

'Pride goes before the fall,' I mused.

'It looks like we're the only fallen ones right now though,' said Eva.

I thought of Sal's little brother and mentally crossed my fingers that she could sell the books as quickly as possible. It wasn't a particularly good time of year for the antique book market.

77

EVA

In the distance I heard a siren. As the police car zig-zagged its way up the mountain, the sound faded and strengthened as it passed gulleys and steep cliffs. It was silenced altogether when the vehicle's journey towards us was cut off by the steep snow-ploughed walls on the hairpin bends. The Doppler effect occasionally made the two-tone siren drop half an octave as it headed away from us on the snaking curves.

James climbed out of the Bentley and stood by the open boot. I knew there must be many items still in there, as I could hear him rummaging around. But I also knew without looking that the hard carry-on case containing the well-packed books definitely would not be in the back of the car. Sally Crime had seen to that. That's what she'd come for.

Two police cars finally arrived and swept in to park beside the Range Rover up near the road. Lights still flashing, the sirens echoed between the mountains long after they'd been turned off. A couple of policemen dressed in heavy winter gear made their way towards us in the snow-drowned parking area.

They discussed something I couldn't hear at the back of the car with James, then one of them spoke into his radio, and the other began clearing the snow from around the car.

'Thank goodness I don't see any damage,' I heard James tell the cops as he opened the rear door.

One cop stood next to him and bent down to look at me in the back. I must have looked a sight, half fallen into the footwell behind the driver's seat, my booted legs sticking inelegantly through the gap. I sat in the back, waiting like a naughty child.

Surrounded by snow, James's chagrin, the police, and the shock that my dead sister's fiancé and Sally Crime had suddenly become complicit in something I was only just starting to understand, I finally conceded there was nowhere to go.

A policeman took me firmly by the arm to pull me out of the Bentley. They didn't cuff me straight away, but led me up the slope to one of the police cars. Cuffing me might have impeded my movement through the deep snow. The cop opened the rear of his car, made me sit inside, and only then cuffed my hand to the door handle. I was shivering now, the biting cold bringing back the memory of a few long nights in a London doorway on Piccadilly.

How different things would have been if James hadn't been interested in saving the poor student on the street. We'd even thought the idea was crazy ourselves. But amazingly he'd taken the bait almost immediately, so we never had to go to Plan B. But then again, how different things would have been if I'd known James was innocent in Claudia's case from the start. I was glad I'd told him I'd become fond of him, though I don't suppose that was going to help him in his misery at that moment. And it probably wouldn't help me out of my current predicament..

When we were dreaming up our revenge, Klaus had always thought it was odd that I ended up sleeping with James. I hadn't intended to, but it served to hurry along the invitation to stay at the chalet for Christmas. We didn't want to wait until later in the winter for the annual ski visit. Becoming lovers secured his infatuation of me, in case I hadn't previously been sure. And it wasn't hard. He was attractive, witty, and his understated class was different from those of the boisterous loud tourists we had to put up with in the ski seasons of our youth.

His kindness made it easy and I now imagined the conversation between him and Claudia in the ambulance. Perhaps he'd been protecting his friend Lawrence by not revealing who had collided with her on the slope that day. He would have had no idea that this small clemency would come back to bite him. We'd all naturally assumed that James had been the culprit.

I remembered something my father telling me when he said I should take responsibility for my life. *Trust is beautiful. Control is better.* Always check. Always check when you've been told something that might not be the whole truth. And always check when you've instructed someone else to do something important for you. Those books were never in the back of the Bentley. They'd stayed in Klaus's Subaru. It was unlikely Sally and Klaus would be stupid enough to attend the antiques book fair in Venice. There were plenty more of those to be found, and Sally probably knew of them all. Paris, Vienna, Münich. Even New York. They could sell them anywhere and be gone before alarm bells rang.

These Swiss policemen wouldn't be concerned with James's books. I didn't know how far the jurisdiction of the British law enforcement would reach. Since Brexit, Europe had become a black hole for anyone in the UK. Even Switzerland, which benefited from most of the privileges of the EU. But my fingerprints were all over the other goods in the boot of that Bentley, and that's what the Swiss police were now concerned about, along with the money. They'd be content with recovering goods that were reported stolen in Switzerland. Protecting their own. Klaus had been my accomplice, but I knew we wouldn't be able to find him now. I wondered whether he had made up that whole phone conversation to his contact in Dubai, whether he even *had* a contact in Dubai. But more importantly, when exactly had he met up with Sally Crime to plan their counter-heist?

The Swiss theft wouldn't involve a life sentence, and I prayed they'd let me serve my prison sentence in Switzerland for the more minor of the crimes I'd committed. If I were to be extradited to the UK to stand trial for the stolen books, and then try to plea accidental manslaughter for the death of that homeless man, who knows how long I would be incarcerated, and where?

It was now up to James. He'd seen Klaus at the wheel of the Bentley, knew he'd been complicit. But now Klaus knew James had been the wrong target, I wondered how far the kind-hearted victim would press for a resolution on the Bentley. His father now had his precious car back, hopefully with minimal damage. That seemed to be more important to James than the books.

Did he now want to see Sally Crime held accountable? What had truly been her motivation? James might not know, but I certainly suspected. Love. Or lack of reciprocated love. It was amazing how much a human being could take revenge for lost or misplaced love. In the end, it was love for our siblings, or fiancées, or best friends, either unrequited or cut off in their prime, that had got us into this mess in the first place.

78

JAMES

In the end I decided not to tell DS Steven Hannah the whole truth. When Sal had set up a GoFundMe page for her brother Rory a few years back after he was first diagnosed, I'd made a donation of a couple of hundred quid. But because I'd been so distracted from the very first day I'd met Emma-Eva, I'd ignored the latest developments in his deteriorating health and hadn't realised the costs of Rory's new proposed medical treatment had escalated to dizzying amounts.

Sal had always been a good friend. I'd also misread the signs with her. When she practically told me during the extraordinary time of the pandemic that she didn't think we should get involved because we'd still be working together when everyone came off furlough, I believed her, and backed off from any romantic notion.

As I reflected on this, after I'd seen them disappear down the road in Klaus's car that night on the Ofenpass, it was possible that she'd had a thing for me for longer than I was aware. It was Eva's comments that alerted me to the fact. But by then it was way too late. If we'd got together during the time we were all in lockdown, it was quite possible we would both still be together, and none of this would have happened, or at least not in the way Eva and Klaus had planned.

Gullible. I could hear Tristan's voice in my head as I prepared to tell him the whole story when I arrived back in London. I gullibly believed that Sal only wanted a platonic relationship. Not as serious, though, as gullibly believing Eva was a poor art student who'd been abused by her boyfriend and desperately needed saving. It was a story I'd always be ashamed to recount, as it was too unbelievable.

But I would do something to make Sal think better of me now. With Eva in handcuffs, the police were unlikely to listen seriously to her stories. She would inevitably end up contradicting herself, unless she was heartless enough to implicate Klaus as well. She had been with me in St Moritz when the books were stolen from my flat, and the police had already said they wouldn't put their resources behind looking for a an ex-partner no one was sure existed. Nick Rich. We never got any further with that. But what would make sense to both DS Hannah in London and Herr Vögel in St Moritz is that during her crazy plan to embroil herself in my life, Emma Smith/Eva Schmid killed Willie the homeless man, accidentally or otherwise. It was up to the police to find the links to his death, if the weather hadn't already eliminated the evidence after all this time. And she deserved to be punished for that, perhaps even handed over to the CID in the UK, rather than spending a few months in a comfy Swiss prison for the theft of a few *objets d'art* in St Moritz.

DS Hannah didn't need to know that I knew where the books were. I would let Sally Crime take them and sell them on, so she would have the funds for her brother's life-saving treatment. Maybe I'd contact her at some point in the future. She wouldn't know at this stage that I'd keep her secret. I suspect she wouldn't have the heart to sell the Maugham, having been saved from incineration. Maybe I hadn't seen the last of my favourite book.

Through a Facebook page that Sal's mum had set up for Rory, I decided to follow the developments through his treatment that would surely go ahead once Sal had sold those books. Once I knew everything had been set in motion for Rory, I'd contact Sal somehow and tell her it was safe for her to come back to the UK, that I wouldn't dob her in to the police. She might change her mobile and hence her WhatsApp contact numbers, but I knew I could tempt her into communicating through a new game of Words-With-Friends if she didn't change her player ID. With her Marple mind, she wouldn't be able to resist. I wondered whether she'd toyed with striking up a relationship with Klaus. She'd said she found him attractive. I was pretty sure he'd be still hurting too much about Claudia to think about any romantic relationship with anyone, let alone Sal. Pot, kettle, and all that. The heat still rose to my face each time I thought how I'd been duped by him and Eva. But Sally Crime's deception was something I never could have predicted.

They say truth is stranger than fiction, but as I boarded my flight back to London, going over in my head just how much information I would choose to impart to DS Hannah, one thing was sure. I'd certainly gathered enough material for that novel I wanted to write.

ACKNOWLEDGEMENTS

Several people had eyes on this novel in its various stages. A handful of my fellow masters from my time at UEA gave useful feedback in the novel's early form: Natasha Hutcheson, Bridget Walsh, Jayne Farnworth, and later Antony Dunford who is always keen to see me dig myself out of a plot hole. Thanks also to Diane Jeffrey, valued reader, for her keen eye and fabulous suggestions. Thanks to Graham Bartlett for his police procedural advice, and if I have gone off piste with this in my later drafts, I apologise! Scott Pack has been with me for several novels, and I am grateful for his structural editing prowess, and being able to fit me in for a tight turnaround. I'm also grateful to Julia Gibb for her proofreading. And once again the members of my book club in Aegeri who supplied the final critiques before the line edits and proofread. And lastly, much love and gratefulness to my husband Chris for his continued support of my writing.

About the author

Louise Mangos writes novels, short stories and flash fiction, which have won prizes, been placed on shortlists, and have been narrated on BBC radio. Her short fiction appears in more than twenty print anthologies. She holds an MA in crime writing from the University of East Anglia in the UK.

You can connect with Louise on Facebook —/LouiseMangosBooks, or Twitter @LouiseMangos, and Instagram as @louisemangos, or visit her website https://louisemangos.com/ where there are links to some of her short fiction. If you'd like to receive information about new releases and be in with a chance of winning the occasional giveaway, subscribe to her newsletter on her homepage.

Having grown up in North Hertfordshire in rural England, Louise worked for a time in the West End of London. She now lives at the foot of the Swiss Alps with her Kiwi husband and two sons and leads an active life in the mountains in all seasons. When she's not writing, she enjoys skate skiing in winter, and wild swimming, cycling and kayaking in the summer.

Dear Reader,

Thank you so much for buying and reading *The Girl in the Doorway*. In what started out as a cliché, this title was the one I worked with throughout the myriad drafts and edits of the novel. It was a nod to one of the most popular psychological suspense twists in *The Girl on the Train*. At the end of all the hard graft, the title stuck, and I have embraced it as the final one.

I grew up in rural Hertfordshire close to London, and used to work and play in the West End until I left the UK in my early twenties. I'm lucky enough to now live in central Switzerland at the foot of the Alps, and often visit the stunning Eastern region of Switzerland that still has some of the most unspoiled areas in the Alps, including the Swiss National Park with the quirky town of Zernez at its centre.

The most important people in an author's career are you, the readers, whether you're a blogger, a reviewer, or someone who simply enjoys a good yarn. A fellow author once told me that reviews are like coins in a busker's hat. I'd like to use that analogy and encourage you to leave your review on the platform of your choice. Each of those coins contributes towards an author's bread and butter.

If you enjoyed my writing, you might like to try one of my other psychological suspense novels, or if you enjoy historical fiction, perhaps you'd like to read my medieval mystery. Details of all these are on the following pages.

I hope to bring you many more tales for your enjoyment in the future.

Cheers,

Louise

MORE BOOKS BY THE AUTHOR

Strangers on a Bridge

How far would you go to protect your family? While Alice Reed is on her morning jog in the peaceful Swiss Alps, she unexpectedly saves a stranger on a notorious suicide bridge. But could her Samaritan deed turn out to be the first of many mistakes?

Adamant they have an instant connection, Manfred's charm gradually darkens and his obsession with Alice grows stronger.

In a country far from home, where the police don't believe her, the locals don't trust her and even her husband questions the truth about Manfred, Alice has nowhere to turn.

And she begins to think she should never have saved him that day on the bridge...

FINALIST in the EXETER NOVEL PRIZE

LONG LISTED for the BATH NOVEL AWARD

The Art of Deception

She must prove her innocence to save her son... but time is running out.

Art school dropout Lucie is on a backpacking trip across Europe when she arrives in the idyllic Swiss Alps. A holiday romance with ski instructor Mathieu takes a crucial turn when Lucie discovers she is pregnant. Spiralling into a relationship of coercion and dark domestic abuse, Lucie is powerless to escape her marriage without losing her son.

Seven years on, Lucie is serving a sentence in a Swiss prison for a murder she insists she did not commit. Surrounded by an eclectic group of inmates, Lucie must summon all her strength and intuition to uncover long-kept secrets and fight for her freedom to be reunited with her son before he is abducted by her husband's family.

The clock is ticking . . . but who can she trust?

The Beaten Track

After her stalker takes his life and she's jilted by a holiday lover, Sandrine comes home from her round-the-world backpacking trip perturbed, penniless and pregnant. She meets handsome Scott, who offers her love, security and all she and her new baby could ever wish for. But their dream is about to turn into nightmare...

GOLD MEDAL WINNER in the Global Book Awards psychological thriller category

FINALIST in the Page Turner Awards

Five Fatal Flaws

When psychotherapist Trudy's baby disappears one afternoon, the individual motives of four members of her post-trauma therapy group are gradually revealed. But when the police begin investigating baby Benny's disappearance, the seemingly unrelated death of a town councillor brings each member of the group under firm suspicion, along with Trudy herself. *Five Fatal Flaws* is a whodunnit psychological suspense with a #MeToo thread, for fans of Liane Moriarty and Lucy Foley.

Shortlisted for the Page Turner awards

Writing historical fiction as L.S.Mangos

The Secrets of Morgarten – a medieval mystery

A young nation in peril. A web of deception. A triangle of forbidden love.

The year is 1315. The fledgling nation of Switzerland – the Confederation Helvetica – is under threat from the Habsburgs. In France, the Knights Templar have been disbanded and declared heretics by the king. Magda, a beautiful weaver living near the alpine village of Morgarten, befriends Walter, a messenger and tracker who is the son of the legendary Wilhelm Tell. Walter and Magda's budding romance is threatened by the arrival of Sébastien, a French fugitive. What secrets is this foreigner hiding? Can Walter solve the mystery of a murder and a stolen religious artefact before a mighty battle with the Habsburgs ensues? And who will be the victors in their turbulent triangle of love?

FINALIST in the Page Turner Awards

BRONZE medal winner in the Global Book Awards medieval mystery category

Printed in Dunstable, United Kingdom

63587592R00198